THE DEVIL IN BELLMINSTER

ALSO BY DAVID HOLLAND

Murcheston: The Wolf's Tale

Croydon Libraries

You are welcome to borrow this book for up to 28 days.
If you do not return or renew it by the latest date stamped
below you will be asked to pay overdue charges. You may
renew books in person, by phoning 0208 726 6900 or via the
Council's website www.croydon.gov.uk

**CROYDON
COUNCIL**
www.croydon.gov.uk

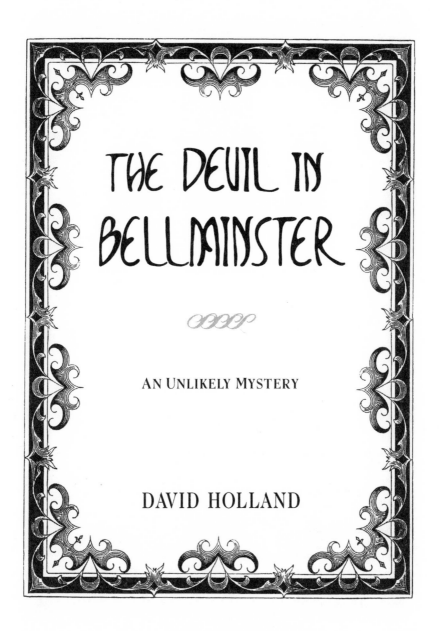

THE DEVIL IN BELLMINSTER

AN UNLIKELY MYSTERY

DAVID HOLLAND

THOMAS DUNNE BOOKS
ST. MARTIN'S MINOTAUR ✙ NEW YORK

THOMAS DUNNE BOOKS.
An imprint of St. Martin's Press.

www.minotaurbooks.com

Design and title typography by Lorelle Graffeo

Maps by Mark Stein Studios

ISBN 0-312-27998-1

First Edition: March 2002

10 9 8 7 6 5 4 3 2 1

For their faith, their devotion and, above all,
their perseverance,
I dedicate this novel to Bob Solinger
and in memory of Sam Hughes.
My wish for all writers is that they might know
the nurturing care of agents
half so supportive.

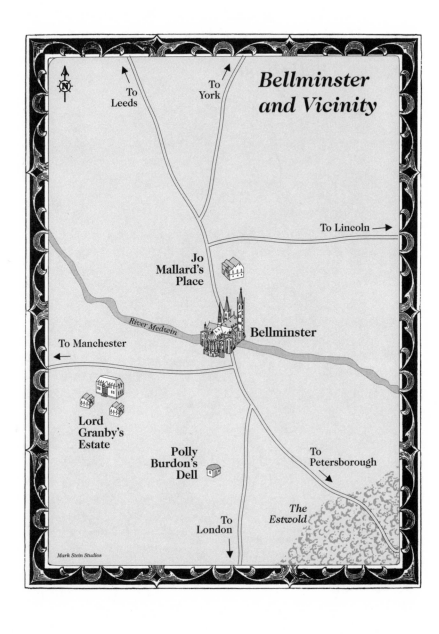

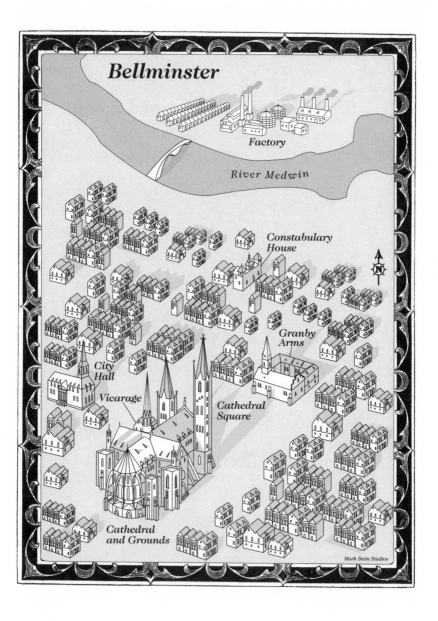

Bellminster

Factory

River Medwin

Constabulary House

Granby Arms

City Hall

Vicarage

Cathedral Square

Cathedral and Grounds

Mark Stein Studios

BOOK 1

CHAPTER THE FIRST
INCARNATE

Night in Bellminster, and the cold, hard sliver of an October moon cut like a dagger in the sky. Its pallid glow washed all beneath in a frosty rime, casting sufficient light about the streets and alleys to fashion shadows with, to darken the deep corners and guard the secret places of the town from curious eyes. Through the silent lanes, only the wind kept company with the moonlight, moaning about chimneys and around houses, pushing at windows and doors to be let in, rattling bolts and shaking panes. But no hand raised the latch to any dwelling. No face peered out a glass to see what might be crawling through Bellminster this night.

The wind seemed to rise up out of the slow waters of the Medwin Ford at the bottom of the town, to skip across the surface of the river, lapping at the shallow waves. On the far side of the bank the wind threw out an arm to embrace the brick walls of the millworks, where three black smokestacks thrust their dirty fingers upward, reaching greedily toward the distant moon, eager to escape the night's wild caress. The wind leapt upon them, brushing away their soot and ash in gray-black clouds over the sleeping houses of the town.

The wind sailed up the near bank to catch the dust as it fell and send it flying again, driving it into holes and cracks in the town's face, eating away the mortar that held the stones of Bellminster together. It set the dust a-dancing through the cobbled streets in dwarfish cyclones before coming at last to the very height of the town. Here, at the summit of the bank, this devilish progress settled into idleness. The moon itself was hidden behind the great towers of Bellminster Cathedral.

They rose out of the town, their roots reaching deep into the soil of Bellminster, stretching back in time to another age, and ages before even that. Along the cathedral walls, inside and out, an army of stone martyrs stood at attention, halting the wind, driving it back upon itself, ready to give their lives once more for the faith that had raised this monument. The wind was only gathering strength, however. A sudden blast blew up from the Medwin, roared through the town like a locomotive and shot up the sides of the cathedral, carrying dust and debris to blast the faces off the martyrs and clog the gargoyles' mouths, to scrape away at the lead roof and find secret passageways into the holy places, to rain soot and ash down upon the spirits of the dead. The cathedral stood, unmoved, impervious. Yet perhaps some flakes of stone were chipped away by the force of the storm, maybe a bit of the fine dust from the statues mingled with the leaves carried on the wind, and the weight of the cathedral was made lighter by a few grains of sand.

The wind raced on anew, over the roofs of Bellminster, out past the houses, across the fields and pastures to the edge of the Estwold, that shivering mass of trees whose branches sliced the wind and moonlight into a confusion of air and shadow. The moon and the wind and the forest, these are the denizens of the night. And still one more, a mere shadow amid the trees, a figure, blacker than the darkness, more implacable than the wind, huddled in the heart of the Estwold over his grisly work. Our eyes are too used to daylight to see what he fashions so carefully, though he sees clearly enough, and worries and frets over his creation, tugging at it, pushing at it, propping it here, bending it there, until he is satisfied with his handiwork at last. Stepping away, he drops slowly to his knees, clasps his hands together in supplication. His fingers make a sickening noise as blood seeps from between the joints, but no one is there to hear it save the spirit of the forest.

Soon he rises, pulls a cloak up over his shoulders and, taking a last, lingering look at his craftsmanship, he turns and walks away, back through the Estwold, out of the darkness and into the pale light of the splinter moon. He bows his head before the wind as he descends along the plain toward the houses of the city. His cloak whips behind him like a trail of smoke to mark his passing. Reaching the town, he moves furtively, aware that eyes might be watching, ears might hear his footsteps on the stones. From shadow to shadow he progresses, the darkness his road, the night itself his carriage. He slinks through the town until he reaches the vast doors of the cathedral. He pauses for a moment, lifts gray, almost-colorless eyes to the tympanum overhead, cold eyes, eyes that pierce the night. He stares up at the image of God triumphant, sending the few righteous men to paradise, the numberless sinners to damnation. He studies the tortures depicted there, the scathing whipcords wielded by devils of ungodly imagination, the rivers of torment in which infinite pain is multiplied by infinite remorse, the gnawing canker of sin set to fester for all eternity. He studies these scenes. Then he enters and leaves the door ajar behind him. Outside, the wind renews its assault upon Bellminster Cathedral, clawing at the walls, charging the now-open door, finding at last a way into the very heart of this sacred place.

CHAPTER THE SECOND
THE VICAR

eheaded?" a rough voice gasped.

"Yes, sir," came the officious answer. "De-capitated, to put it official-like."

The office of the mayor of Bellminster, in the Year of Our Lord one thousand eight hundred and thirty-three, was an office indeed, a dank, dark well into which a great many things fell down and, with the certainty of Newton's Law of Gravitation, almost nothing ever came out. It was, in fact, less an elected position than an actual room buried within the winding corridors of the old City Hall of Bellminster, occupied for a time by one man or another, attended by any number of assistants and vice mayors, an ill-lit, ill-furnished, close and cloistered chamber where the mayor was regularly hung in a corner, to be brought out on holidays and occasions of public display.

"And his head was done . . . done what with?" a third voice queried.

"Like this," the officious answerer replied, picking up a vase to demonstrate.

The office of the mayor was not a place to be comfortably crowded, which perhaps explains why it was occupied in the present instance by a variety of foul tempers. Besides the mayor and his usual pair of deputies, there were in the office Chief Constable Hopgood, with his agent Constable Wily; the rector Reverend Mortimer, leading spiritual officer of the town; the rector's curate Mr. March, a sort of clerical clerk; Mr. McWhirter, the owner of the millworks, with several lesser administrators of no further consequence; and Dr. Warrick of the Municipal Hospital. This catalogue of worthies allowed room for perhaps one more, if that person were under the usual size and did not require much air, but as no one was forthcoming to apply for the position, we shall leave it open.

The rest of the office was occupied by silence. All eyes were held in thrall by the vase nestled quaintly in Chief Constable Hopgood's arm.

"Am I to understand," McWhirter seethed after a time, "that this fellow was holding his head in his hands like a damn rugby football?"

The mayor looked at Chief Constable Hopgood, who looked at Constable Wily, who looked at his notebook. "The head, bein' separated from the body with a axe," the notebook read, "was situated with some care in the crook of a folded arm."

"Holding it in his arm," Hopgood emphasized with a nod of his grizzled, close-shaven head. "Like this."

"And why the bloody hell wasn't I informed of this yesterday when it was discovered?" stormed McWhirter, his broad sidewhiskers crackling with electrical tension.

"There were official procedures to be . . . to be followed," the mayor stammered, drumming his fingers upon his desk in an agitated manner. "The doctor had to be called in and . . . and . . . and the body had to be taken off without drawing attention. If the thing is to be kept quiet, we must proceed very . . . very carefully."

McWhirter steamed like one of his machines, his whiskers flaring. "You call this quiet? The whole damn town's abuzz with news of a murder! Rumors stinking about like flies in the air! Regular damn circus!"

The mayor's fingers ceased their tattoo, and he glanced angrily at one of his deputies. "Bick!"

"There's been no word from this office," Mr. Bick assured the mayor.

"Bates! Bates!" the great man barked at the other deputy.

"Silent as the tomb," Bates affirmed.

"Well, somebody's been talking," McWhirter bellowed, Bick and Bates notwithstanding. "Who found the bloody thing?"

All eyes searched about the office until they fell upon a dark corner. "I found him," Tuckworth confessed. Did we neglect to notice the vicar of Bellminster Cathedral at these proceedings? He was easy to miss, standing in the shadows at the back of the room, as easy to miss as the black armband he wore against the black of his coat.

"You found him?" said McWhirter. "And did you tell anyone?"

"No one," the vicar stated, pulling off his spectacles nervously and cleaning them with the neckerchief he had tied on against the unnatural chill of the day. His face, full and soft, was kind but not merry, sympathetic yet sad, the sort of face you would have thought was made to smile at the least provocation, though it very rarely did so. "I told no one but Hopgood here, and the rector, of course, and I suppose Lucy and Mrs. Cutler were with us in the parlor at the time, but no one else." Indeed, Tuckworth had been in desperate need of company ever since he discovered his sexton Will Shaperston, the cathedral's caretaker and official gravedigger, dead in the Estwold. Tuckworth's daughter and his housekeeper had been by his side, either one or both, almost constantly since then.

"No one else!" McWhirter fumed. "As if that weren't enough! Two women!"

"Gentlemen," the strong, young voice of Reverend Mortimer interposed, "it hardly matters how word of this atrocity has spread," and he cast a condoling look toward Tuckworth that struck the vicar as oddly pitying. Indeed, the young rector had always shown a strange paternalism toward the old vicar, perhaps because it was Mortimer's presence in Bellminster that was bringing about Tuckworth's retirement. Mortimer was severe and evangelical in his attitudes and, as the newly appointed rector of the once-great town, had decided to reside himself in Bellminster, to preach his own sermons and to collect his own tithes, and not pay a vicar to have it done for him. Still, for all the kindly intent there must have been behind such condescension, it irritated Tuckworth endlessly.

"Indeed, gentlemen," Mortimer proceeded, "the gossips have been let loose, and can't be snared again. In a town like Bellminster, any man's news is every man's news, after all. But the public welfare is our divine trust. What concerns us now is how these rumors are to be contained so that a general panic does not ensue."

"Try containing a fart while you're at it," scoffed the mill owner, ruffling his cheeks. "I say we find the villain who did this and make a great show of hanging him before another day passes! Draw and quarter the son-of-a-bitch while we're at it! That'll quiet the gossips!"

"Mr. McWhirter's right," agreed the mayor. ("Quite right," asserted Bick. "Undeniable," Bates allowed.) "Hopgood!" the mayor shouted. "What . . . what progress?"

"Progress, sir?"

"Progress! Progress, man! Are you on to the culprit?"

Hopgood put down the vase at last, shifted his feet about and turned to Constable Wily, who flipped through the stiff pages of his notebook.

"Body was found . . ."

"We know how the damn thing was found!" McWhirter blasted.

The constable made a wry face and went on. "The murder weapon bein' a axe what is property of the vicar, it appears what the victim took it into the Estwold to chop firewood. Some person as yet unknown wielded said axe and incapacitated victim with it, usin' for that purpose the blunt end, on which was found bits of bone and strands of hair. Unknown person then laid victim across a old wind-fallen oak and severed his head clean off his body."

"Just like that?" McWhirter inquired with a fleshy snap of his fingers.

"One swift stroke applied at back of the neck. No sign of struggle. Then said culprit arranged victim sittin' upright against the oak with his head tucked in the crook of his right arm, for what purpose we can't at the present time say." The notebook clapped shut again.

"Is that all? All?" the mayor asked dubiously.

"Afeared so, sir," Wily answered.

"Did you find nothing else to incriminate the man?" Mr. March, the curate, wondered aloud, looking befuddled.

"Naught save the man and the axe. And his head."

"You see," Hopgood explained, turning to the mayor, "we're really not equipped to conduct an investigation of this nature, sir. The town's grown so quick this past twelvemonth, and you've never given me charge to hire more officers. We're spread rather thin as it is, and we've no experience, as you see what I mean. That's why I must recommend once again that we send to London for assistance."

"The detective constabulary," Mr. March murmured, as the rest of the company glanced about at one another.

"Bow Street Runners?" sneered McWhirter, his whiskers quivering in derision. "And while we wait about for them to arrive, this foreign interloper gets away!"

"I should think," Tuckworth suggested from his corner, "that the murderer has already had the chance to escape, if that's what he wants to do."

"All the more reason to act decisively!" the mill owner thundered. "I tell you, we need more activity, not more blather! Find a likely candidate, Hopgood, and hang the fellow!"

"But we must be careful," insisted Tuckworth. "We wouldn't want to accuse the wrong person."

McWhirter snorted. "I don't see much danger of that. Foreigner in Bellminster can't go unnoticed. Shouldn't be more than a handful about. Round 'em up, lock 'em down and weed 'em out! That's my method!"

"Beggin' your pardon, sir," Wily interjected, opening his notebook, "but we've seen no evidence as might suggest this unknown person bein' a foreigner."

McWhirter blew his whiskers out in exasperation. "It's all over the business! Some sort of vendetta killing! A Neapolitan intrigue! The axe, the way the body was arranged, any fool could see the hand of an Italian in it! This sort of thing is on the rise, you know. Violence is in their blood. One of their secret criminal societies, I'll wager anything. The heat of the Mediterranean sun does it. Boils them from inside. The head in the arm likely a sign of retribution. Meant to impress others in the fraternity. Just read the *Policeman's Periodical Gazette.* Or the *Weekly Gazetteer.* It's all in there."

A hush cloaked the office. The mill owner's tastes in literature were not to be openly derided.

"I don't think a foreigner—" Mr. March began.

"Gentlemen," Reverend Mortimer interrupted, with a quick, withering glance at his curate, "I agree with Mr. McWhirter that a swift resolution to this ghastly business must be our chief concern. We all want to see justice done." (Bick nodded vigorously.) "But justice delayed is justice debased. The criminal, whoever he is, must be made to feel the force of righteousness brought to bear upon him. The pursuit must be unrelieved and highly visible to the public. We must not tire, we must not pause." (Bates whispered, "Never!") "We must let everyone witness the unflagging strength of our purpose. Only so may we retain the confidence of the populace. The devil walks among us, gentlemen, and we must roust him out, even at the peril of seeming intemperate." ("Not at all," from McWhirter.) "Even though we risk the appearance of rashness. So that we act with the support of divine guidance, we shall not be misled in this. For the devil grants no quarter, nor none shall have." (A silent, "Amen," from the congregation.)

There was a good deal more of this, but we will not tempt the reader's impatience. Enough to remark that all present were inspired by the rector's words, though brought no nearer a resolution as to what should be done. Did we say all present? All save one, perhaps. In his dark corner, Tuckworth could not keep his mind upon Mortimer's speech. His thoughts instead wandered back to the sight of his sexton sitting amid the rotting leaves of the Estwold, propped against a worm-eaten oak, cradling his head like a babe. Poor Will! A shudder raced up Tuckworth's spine and back down again into his vitals as he pictured the scene once more: the congealed gore spilling out from the headless torso, blackening everything in stiff blood; the head staring from the bend of the elbow with one white eye open and expressionless, the other closed in a horrid wink; the lips delicately parted, teeth glistening between, as if to bid farewell to a heartless world; the axe—Tuckworth's axe—splattered and stained, still embedded in the decaying wood where it had parted life from body; and worst and most frightful of all, the army of birds making their meal of the poor man's meat. Tuckworth could not agree with the belief that some foreign intrigue was afoot in this. What ties would his sexton have with secret societies and vendettas? What interest could there be in Italy that would result in poor Will Shaperston's death? Yet intrigue there was, not murder plain and simple. No act of passion this, but one of madness, the deed of a tortured soul suffering more profoundly than any of them in that room were prepared to comprehend. He caught his breath to think of it, to imagine the tainted mind that could have swung the axe and then arranged such bloody work into a mordant tableau. And why? This was the question that gnawed at him. Even more than who had done this dreadful deed, Tuckworth wondered over and again, Why has it been done, and done in this awful way? This was the greater mystery.

Meanwhile the debate continued, now as a series of various discussions in different parts of the small room. McWhirter was haranguing the mayor and his two deputies on the importance of order to a well-run community. Hopgood and Dr. Warrick were conferring over their notes about the murdered man, searching for some new tidbit of information they might offer for their reputations' sakes. And Reverend Mortimer had backed Mr. March against the door, motioning furtively at McWhirter and making some comment about parochial finances, when the curate leapt forward and gave out with a sharp yelp. Mr. March being a middle-sized, white-haired, sensible sort of fellow, this demonstration attracted some notice among the assembly. The poor fellow could only point to the doorknob, which had just prodded him rudely in the small of his back, before they all saw the door swing slowly open and an elderly man, tall but stooped, old-fashioned yet smartly dressed, sidled his way into the room.

"Forgive me, gentlemen," this new member of the party said.

"Lord . . . Lord Granby!" the mayor uttered, rising from his chair in surprise. "An honor, sir!"

"Now, don't trouble yourself, Winston. It's not a professional visit. Just a friendly 'how-de-do,' " His Lordship returned, smiling at the mayor. And yet there certainly was trouble made to accommodate the Earl of Granby Hall. Such a shuffling and rearranging of bodies ensued before Lord Granby could be settled comfortably behind the mayor's desk, that one of McWhirter's lesser administrators had to be removed altogether and was left standing in the outer hall.

"Well," Granby exclaimed after a stillness had fallen at last upon the office, "what a singular collection of important people." He screwed up his face and surveyed the group in front of him, nodding pleasantly to each man in his turn, although it was doubtful he knew more than two or three of them by name. One he did recognize, craning his neck forward into the shadows. "Is that you, Tuckworth?" he asked.

"Morning, Your Lordship," Tuckworth replied good-naturedly.

"Good fellow!" Granby called to him, waving his hand. Then he returned his gaze to the faces nearer to him. "All right," he proceeded, "I suppose I can dispense with the charade that this is an impromptu visit. I don't think we've all met here by accident."

A hearty laugh rippled across the room, leaving Granby flustered for a moment, unaware that he had said anything particularly witty. "So tell me," he continued, "what have you lot been up to about this sad affair?"

Reverend Mortimer stepped forward. "We had just been on the verge of concluding the direction Mr. Hopgood's investigation should take. We feel that not a moment can be lost."

"Quite right." Granby nodded, looking through the rector toward the vicar. "Sound thinking, Tuckworth. Giving these young rogues the benefit of your wisdom, eh? Age has its prerogative." The vicar could only smile warily at this and shake his head in useless denial. "Now let me tell you what I've been up to," His Lordship announced. "I've wired Bow Street and a man should be on his way this very afternoon."

The silence that followed was profound but only momentary, as Mortimer stepped in once again. "You have read our intentions admirably, Lord Granby. We were just commenting on the need for dispatch, and you appear as a ministering angel to show the way."

"No offense, Hopgood," said Granby, ignoring these kind remarks. "Just not your sort of thing. Keeping the peace is one job, eh? This is quite another. Miserable business," he murmured. "Sorry state of affairs the world is come to. Are we settled, then? I expect a Bow Street officer here by this evening. I'll manage expenses, naturally. No worries there. I've asked for their best man, but of course that counts for nothing. I'm sure they'll tell us anyone they send is their best man, and so he shall be, for our needs at least. You well, Tuckworth?" Granby inquired, turning his attention once more to the back of the room, a note of genuine concern in his voice. "Awful business, losing your sexton. And then you discovered the poor fellow, didn't you?"

"I'm well, Your Lordship," Tuckworth lied.

"Stout chap. Now, if we're agreed . . ." And with that, Lord Granby rose from behind the desk, putting an end to this meeting. For an instant, it appeared that McWhirter was on the verge of saying something, but a glance from Granby left the man's whiskers limp, silencing him as perhaps only the grave could. The mill owner understood the hierarchy of Bellminster, and if the mayor piped the tune and McWhirter paid the piper, it was the Earl of Granby Hall who hired out the ballroom where all of them danced.

As the crowd parted to allow Granby to leave, His Lordship motioned to the vicar. "Come along with me, Tuckworth," he said, beckoning. "I want a word with you."

It took Tuckworth some maneuvering to make his way from the corner, but he finally emerged, somewhat rumpled, and proceeded with Granby out the door and through the labyrinth of dark corridors to arrive finally into the sunlight. The two men walked along the street, followed at a respectful distance by His Lordship's coach. Tuckworth bundled himself tightly in his coat against the cold, while Granby unstooped his shoulders, almost growing young in the bracing chill.

Never had Tuckworth known such weather in October. Prickling, biting cold that numbed his flush cheeks, nipped his round nose, frosted his spectacles, left his fat fingertips insensitive to touch or pain. Clear, brilliant, tingling kind of weather! A hoary crust glazed thick over everything and puffs of vapor whispered on the air. No fitter breakfast for your soul than the sting of arctic breezes. No better cure for lethargy, no finer tribute to the life flowing through your veins than such weather.

Daylight in Bellminster, with the sun crawling into the expanse of an autumn sky. It was a dawning to lift the heart of any man, and even Tuckworth's spirits rose to the call of the light. Such days—when the cloudless heavens stretch overhead, not azure or cerulean, but blue, a deep and startling British blue; when the birds sing nearer to the ear as you walk, nature perched upon your shoulder, inviting you to join your voice to the song; when the air tastes delicious in your smarting lungs so that physical food seems mean and coarse, mere gruel to the manna feeding your soul with every breath—such days are rare and to be treasured, and Tuckworth, under his scarf, with his shivering fingers, paid ungrudging homage to the cold day. All nature seemed to spring forth into sharper life at this final bright pageant before the gloom of winter. Yet, not all. The shadows of the night shrank and faded, twisted about to avoid the day's approach, but they did not disappear, not altogether. Some tatters of shade clung to the dirt at the foot of the houses, crouched within the corners and holes of the town, for there is always some bit of the night that remains, even on the brightest morning.

"So tell me," His Lordship began, "what were those fools carrying on about before I got there?"

Tuckworth faltered for an instant in his reply. "It was a most productive discussion," he managed.

"Productive of nonsense." Granby chuckled, but then turned gravely serious. "This really is a terrible business, Tuckworth. We're not London, you know. Murder, riot, bloodshed. Those chaps back there don't understand what this will do to the people," and he scanned the crowded streets about him. "They don't understand and they don't care."

"I'm sure they feel this as deeply as anyone, Your Lordship," Tuckworth tried to reassure Granby.

The older man only shook his head and looked out over the jostling throng. "They care about keeping order, not about the people whose lives this will touch. Fear is a dreadful disease, Tuckworth. It infects a community like a fever. Drives them to a kind of madness. Do you remember that cholera epidemic some . . . oh, at least twenty years past? Horrible time. Neighbor shutting out neighbor. The whole countryside wary and suspicious." The two men walked along for a time in silence.

Yet, to look at Bellminster this fine morning, who could imagine a time so dark in its long history? The streets were crowded, the sunshine warring for and winning the people's spirits against the cold. Shopkeepers rushed about, setting up their wares in enticing displays to trap the unwary traveler, polishing their windows until they sparkled with the promise of what lay within. Bakers seemed to blow the yeasty scent of their loaves across the town with the force of the blacksmiths' bellows, and the blacksmiths glowed and poured sweat as if they had just stepped out of the bakers' ovens. The butchers hoisted great marbled joints and sides of beef and mutton about and hung geese and ducks from hooks in their ceilings, that their shops might look like temples of sacrifice paying tribute to men's bellies. The grocers' shelves were aflame with color, brilliant red apples and plump green pears, bright yellow oranges and chestnuts a rich and musty brown, so that the autumn trees would have been shamed to peek their leafy heads in for a look at such splendor. And what are we to make of the dressmakers and the tailors! What fabrics and gowns, waistcoats and dapper jackets! Miles of stuff to wrap the town withal and keep it warm against the frost! Carts and wagons of every description rumbled down the streets, carrying a far greater wealth of goods than it seemed possible the stores could hold. But if you had for a moment suggested that these conveyances must all turn about and take their loads elsewhere for want of room, you would have been run out of Bellminster as the thought passed your lips. Everything looked that much brighter for the sunshine and sounded that much crisper for the cold morning air, that Bellminster appeared to be dancing a country jig, the people all flying about to a music that none of them heard, but felt to their core.

Every man and woman had a polite nod for earl and vicar. Every greeting held a smile and every smile a merry wink. But as they passed, this pair caused another kind of stir among the people. In their wake clusters of humanity gathered, with pointing fingers and knowing looks, hushed voices that whispered, "Vicar is the one as found it." "Looks that pale and horrified still, he does." "As who wouldn't, I ask ye?" A murmuring undertone of gossip crept and crawled behind the pair like a hungry mongrel. The two old gentlemen walked along, oblivious to the interest they occasioned, only quiet in each other's company.

One pair of colorless eyes, one cold pair of eyes amid all the crowd followed them, perhaps more closely than the rest, more silently to be sure. Cloaked in the waning shadow of a dark corner, biding his hour, a figure watched, and waited, and prayed in the darkness.

At last, Granby restored his good humor by force of will. "It occurs to me you'll be retiring soon, Tuckworth," he commented, somewhat too casually.

"At the end of the year, Your Lordship."

"The end of the year. Think of that. And how long have you been vicar here?"

"I couldn't say, really. I don't keep track of such things."

"Oh, don't you?" Lord Granby remarked with a twinkling eye. "Well, I do keep track of such things. It will be thirty-three years. That's rather a long time, don't you think?"

"Yes, Your Lordship," Tuckworth acknowledged, smiling in spite of himself. "It is rather a long time."

Granby nodded. "And what will you do with yourself once your time is your own?"

"Do with myself? I hadn't considered."

"Hadn't you? Well, it's about time you did consider. You'll be wanting a new place in the world. No wasting away for you, my fellow." Tuckworth coughed uneasily. Unlike the rest of mankind, you and I, who find moments of fascination in discussing the least detail of our lives, the vicar took little joy in offering himself as a topic of conversation. "For one thing," Granby pursued, "you'll want a new residence."

"Leave the vicarage?" It hadn't occurred to Tuckworth that he might be asked to relinquish his home with his position, and yet what was to become of a vicarage when there was no longer need for a vicar, when the rector's presence eliminated the post? "I'd assumed . . ." he began, though stopping short at expressing his desire. "But if the rector wants it . . ."

"The rector doesn't want it."

"Doesn't want it?"

"No. Too small for his tastes," and Lord Granby coughed at the unintended slight to the vicar's home. "Mortimer says he wants to make an impression in the community, to make his presence felt, or some such idea. Seems a trifle evangelical to me, a bit enthusiastic, you know, but that's how he sees it. He'll stay on where he is while we build him a new residence. Something fashionable, eh? The rectory. Still, that leaves us with a vicarage and no use at all for a vicar." Tuckworth glanced at Granby. It was one of His Lordship's less attractive qualities that he enjoyed toying with the sentiments of those about him, like a cat with a cricket, an idle exercise of power that could catch you off your guard and afford needless worry. One look at Granby's jolly face and Tuckworth saw that there was more to come. He stopped, therefore, and confronted His Lordship with a severe countenance.

"All right," Granby confessed, laughing, "I'll out with it. The cathedral is coming alive again, Tuckworth. The restoration is reviving the place, generating interest from all quarters. It seems the world had forgotten about our little country church, but now there's all this rage about Gothic architecture. So I've decided to revive the position of dean of the cathedral. Someone must look after it, you know, devote himself heart and soul to all that stonework. Keep up appearances." Granby grinned brightly down upon his companion.

"I suspect after all these years you'll have the devil's own time remembering the new name of your residence. But as you're dean, we must call it the deanery from now on."

Tuckworth was transformed to stone where he stood. The dean of Bellminster Cathedral! It was most certainly the one position he might have coveted in all the world. Dean of Bellminster! To give up his duties as vicar, this had been his secret desire for some time, to lay aside his clerical responsibilities, abandon his flock. And why? With others he offered his advancing years as a likely excuse, or the rector's residency, or merely his own inclination. But when he was alone, perfectly alone, only then could he call up his secret desire, the true reason for leaving his vocation. He could lead the parish no longer, on this point he was adamant, though only with himself. Yet to be responsible, not for the people, but for the cathedral. Mightn't he manage that? Wouldn't his conscience allow him to find even that much happiness? It was a profound temptation that challenged his innermost resolve.

"What's this?" Granby clucked, staring at Tuckworth, matching the vicar's furrowed brow with his own stern appeal. "Hesitancy? Reluctance?"

"Forgive me, Lord Granby," Tuckworth spoke at last. "I'm honored. Of course I am. But this is very sudden, and I'll need time to consider."

"Stuff and nonsense! You're the new dean and that's that. Besides," His lordship whispered, "as dean you won't have to answer to the rector. That's something, isn't it? We'll make it official at year's end." Granby put a hand on Tuckworth's shoulder and the two moved on down the street. "Now, don't go spoiling my fun with your infernal hemming and hawing. That's the trouble with you, Tuckworth. You think too much. Always asking needless questions. Always this pausing to consider. There's such a thing as being too logical, you know."

Yes, Tuckworth thought as they moved slowly along, one can be too thoughtful. One can be plagued by questions, by doubts, by demons of one's own invention. But once those demons had been invoked, how were they to be dispelled? Could Faust unwork his will?

Can the genie be rebottled? Or must the tragedy play itself out to its inevitable conclusion once the curtain has been raised? Tuckworth thought as he walked, and in thinking he found no peace.

Before long, Lord Granby tired of exercise and called up the coach, and he and Tuckworth rode along to the cathedral, Granby intent on seeing how the restoration was getting on, Tuckworth desirous of nothing more than to escape into the solitude of his study, to think.

CHAPTER THE THIRD
THE CATHEDRAL

*B*ut what distressing scene awaited the vicar and the earl as they proceeded toward Bellminster Cathedral? Surely not Mrs. Cutler, the vicar's housekeeper, tall, thin spike of a woman in widow's weeds, for she was behind the vicarage out of view from the street, beating the dust from the carpets with a frightening alacrity, keeping up a perpetual discourse with an invisible auditor. "She just sittin' there lookin' pretty as you please, ungh! Only to be a-stared at by that painter, ungh! And her a woman as has a position to uphold, ungh! I don't call it paintin', what he's up to. Any fool might see it in his eyes, ungh! But not her! No, thank you, miss, ungh! She'll just go on sittin' there as it suits her to be a-stared at. Vanity is what it is! Ungh! Guile and vanity!" Pity the poor rug to feel the heat of Mrs. Cutler's wrath!

The object of her scorn, and the vexing sight waiting to greet Tuckworth on his return, was at that moment sitting in front of the vicarage, staring wanly into the emptiness of a cloudless sky.

"Lucy," a voice, a youthful voice, a man's voice, scolded from behind a large blank canvas balanced on an artist's easel, "you must look at me. And try a smile."

"I can't smile, Raphael. Not today," Lucy insisted. "It's too hard. I keep thinking about poor Will." And she bit her lower lip to stifle a something in her throat. "I don't see why I have to sit for you now. It's cruel to ask me to smile today."

"I'm sorry, Lucia," the man answered, sounding sincerely re-morseful, though whether for the dead sexton or his pretty subject was uncertain. "I would spare you, but the light is so pure today. We can't let this chance slip by." And his hand made a sweeping pass over the canvas with a bit of charcoal, leaving a graceful line in its wake.

So Lucy smiled. Her lips parted dutifully, her dimples appeared in the rosy smoothness of her cheek as ordered, her teeth shone in bright contrast to the ebon ringlets of her hair, and yet her eyes re-fused that sparkle, that luster emanating from her soul, last remnant of the girl about to transform into a woman. Raphael looked at her, thoughtfully, deeply, with the intense concentration of the artist, but with something else as well, an admiration that might have escaped all notice had Mrs. Cutler not been so wise. His long, light hair passed across his face, stirred by the frigid breeze. His open collar, a scandal to the more delicate sensibilities of Bellminster society, flapped noiselessly at his tanned throat. A careless scarf swayed upon his breast. Raphael's strong, clear eyes captured the light streaming from Lucy, allowing it to pass effortlessly through his arm onto the canvas. The charcoal danced here and there, sometimes hovering over the stark white before it, circling uncertainly in mid-air, suddenly darting forward, trailing a sharp line across the blank-ness to be softened by the gentle stroke of the artist's fingertips. Lucy's image gradually swirled out of the void, as though freed from life into art, that other reality that understands what the eye cannot see, that reveals more than it knows. Raphael sketched with the ex-citement that all beginnings hold for the artist, when for a brief time perfection is possible. And yet, even now, perfection eluded him. Her eyes. He could not draw what was not there, and her eyes held no joy today. With a sigh he stepped back from the canvas and looked at his subject, studied her mood, peered past her charming features into her heart. His own eyes briefly reflected the sadness he found within, turned it upon himself, saw his own hopeless longing in the mirror of her soul. Then, with a spark and a flash, he rushed at the image again, his hand a whirlwind, his mind afire with inspiration.

The coach pulled up before the vicarage, and Tuckworth descended with Lord Granby. "Lucy!" he called, with the least hint of reproach.

"I'm sorry, Father," she cried, rising from her pose and running to him, throwing her arms about him.

"It's my fault, Vicar," Raphael confessed, coming up behind her. "I insisted that we begin today. The light—"

"Raphael," Tuckworth said hotly, "this is not the time. Will's not even buried yet."

"Well, what have we here?" Wandering past the others, Lord Granby had stopped to look at the canvas. "Is that our Lucy?"

Lucy dropped a quick curtsy. "It's merely a study, Your Lordship. For a painting of Ophelia. Isn't that right, Raphael?"

"Ophelia?" Granby repeated. "Well, you're a dashed sight prettier than any Ophelia." He turned his eyes back to the sketch. "Fine piece of work this."

"Thank you, Lord Granby." Raphael beamed, pulling himself up and stepping forward.

"Only you've got her with her eyes closed. She looks about to cry."

Raphael seemed visibly to shrink. "It's meant to convey humility."

"Ah, well," His Lordship opined.

"This is Raphael Amaldi, Lord Granby," Tuckworth offered, studying the sketch himself and feeling suddenly sympathetic toward the young artist. "He's been painting studies of our cathedral for over a year now."

"Amaldi?" Granby repeated. "Italian?"

"My grandfather came to this country, sir, from Florence," the painter replied proudly, with a formal bow.

"Raphael is a graduate of the Royal Academy, Your Lordship," Lucy interjected. "His paintings are attracting a great deal of notice."

"Are they?" Granby asked enthusiastically. "Then you must let me buy one off you."

Raphael puffed up once more. "It would be a privilege, Lord Granby! If you'd care to stop by my studio at your convenience . . ."

"Oh, there's no need for that, young man. Just pick out something nice and send it along with the bill. Something with lots of trees." Raphael shriveled away almost to nothing.

Tuckworth felt a twinge at the young man's suffering. In spite of his brusqueness, he liked Raphael and wanted to help him. "Lord Granby and I were about to inspect the restorations. Why don't you children come along?" he offered.

And so they made a party of it, the two young people and the two old. Together they climbed the twelve steps (one for each Apostle, Raphael informed His Lordship), passed through the tall doors under the celebrated tympanum (famous throughout Christendom, the artist pointed out) and entered the length of the great nave.

Behind, they left the unremitting light of the world. In its place they discovered the glorified brilliance of a higher realm. The dazzle of sunshine without was remade into something greater, something richer, rays of sacred design staining the sun, touching the spirit of the place with an angelic caress, blanketing the interior of the cathedral in celestial illumination. Light, filtering down through swirls and eddies of rippled glass, created washes of color about the floor and walls, greens and blues and reds like varicolored fish glimmering in the depths of a spectral pool. The vast arcade stretched out before them, each stone support rising into this miraculous light, not thick and heavy, but mere wisps of stonework, delicate, almost impossibly thin, gathered together here and there in more substantial though no less graceful piers. These lithe columns drew the eye upward through the realm of light, colored windows transforming the sturdy walls into a dream of architecture, some ephemeral fantasy that could never stand on its own, but must be upheld by a higher hand. Up the eye climbed, past the arcade to the somber heights of the triforium, lofty corridor encircling the nave, surrounding the faithful above with elegant tracery and, standing at stiff attention, an army of saints and martyrs, protectors of the cathedral. Above this, higher and higher, the eye moved to an even more celestial realm, the clerestory, with more windows, more light, more color. Up there, at the very limits of space, the birds lived next to God, flying about oblivious to the meaning of all around them, singing their simple hymns to a more natural creed than any sung below. They darted and soared through rays of magnificence, angelic sprites from the world without. Above them, the sweeping vault overspread their sphere with shade and shadow. Such was Bellminster Cathedral, such the seat of faith, the home of timeless wonder. The four visitors looked up as children from ages long dead had looked up, and each found there something different, something personal stirring and thrilling their four hearts.

They moved forward, four separate souls drawn together and embraced by the visible grace of a power unspoken and unspeakable, the luminous radiance of the air calling up a reverence from deep within, not the false solemnity men exhibit in moments of studied piety, but a genuine sense of awe filling each of them as they advanced slowly down the center aisle. Even the wooden scaffolding for the laborers appeared to burn with a heavenly fire, though the noisy work of restoration continued unabated, the sharp report of chisel and hammer breaking the sacred stillness of the place, the narrow scaffold slowly wending its way, week after week, down the length of the nave from the rose window to the apse.

"You lot down there! Look out!" a voice cried from above as they stepped beneath the framework of crossing beams. A load of rotten timbers was being lowered by workers at the massive windlass high overhead, and the four visitants moved aside to let it descend.

"Quite a deal of activity," Granby observed, staring up at the men scurrying about like profane cherubim.

"Yes, Your Lordship," Tuckworth acknowledged, embarrassed that Granby should see the cathedral like this, a grand dowager without her makeup on. He glanced uncomfortably at his feet and saw something that startled him. A patch of dark had stained the floor of the nave. The vicar knelt down and scratched at the mark.

"What's that you've found there?" Lord Granby asked.

"It appears to be blood," Tuckworth replied, rising and looking up. "It almost looks to be a handprint. One of the workers must have cut himself."

"Well," commented His Lordship, following the vicar's upward glance, "it's dangerous work, hanging about up there all day. Be grateful no one's died."

An awkward silence followed this inapt remark. The day seemed already too full of death and the talk of death. "Come this way," Tuckworth tried after a moment's pause, ushering his guests along, away from the laborers, out of the shadow of the scaffold. Yet before they had traveled a few steps, a great clattering of timber erupted from some unseen corner of the cathedral, followed by a voluble curse that echoed and reechoed amid the cavernous space above and about them, so that each member of the party glanced off in a different direction for the cause of this blasphemous outburst.

"It's over there," Tuckworth said, with the easy assurance of one who has lived his life amid the stone tracery of those walls, "where the carpenters are working, by the St. George window." Instantly, a clamor of voices rose from out of that hidden corner to confirm Tuckworth in his observation. "I'd best look into this," he went on. "Raphael, why don't you take Lord Granby around and show him some of the work? Mr. Amaldi is a great student of the Gothic, Your Lordship. He'll make an admirable guide, far better than I." Granby accepted the recommendation, and so the older gentleman and the younger walked off into the mysteries of the cathedral, while Lucy excused herself to return to the vicarage.

Tuckworth wove his way about the piers and columns, following a path that only he could sense, until the carpenter's workshop revealed itself, a dusty, dry corner of an ancient chapel recessed into the wall of the cathedral, with St. George's dragon flaming in the sunlight to one side of the altar, and the Knight of the Cross glowering dimly from the other. Within, a pile of long timbers lay strewn about the floor like matchsticks, and a lively debate seemed to be going on among the huddled workmen.

"Now, lads," Tuckworth announced himself, "what's all the row?" The carpenters parted, and Mr. March emerged from the fray.

"Vicar," the curate breathed heavily, obviously caught up in whatever disturbance had occurred. "I'm gratified to see you."

"March," Tuckworth answered in surprise, "what are you doing here? You've not taken to carpentry, I hope?" This weak attempt at humor met no welcome, however. Clearly, something was up. "What is it, March?"

"It's these laborers, Vicar. They insist on disturbing the sanctity of this holy place."

Tuckworth looked about at the scattered timbers. "I admit they've made a deal of ruckus, but I'm sure it was an accident."

"Warn't no accident," a burly fellow insisted, stepping out from the mass of sweat-stained laborers. "Least, warn't no accident on my part. Chap there sneaks up on a feller, damned if he ain't like to jump out'n his skin and knock over the whole scaffold to splinters. Damme if he ain't."

"That's the disturbance I speak of, Vicar," Mr. March stated, an accusing finger thrust forward at the offender. "It's bad enough to hear their language on the streets, but within the walls of the cathedral itself . . . !"

"Let's calm ourselves, please, gentlemen," the vicar begged, but the curate was not to be calmed with a word.

"Look to your salvation!" he preached rather loudly at the carpenters, his finger wagging all the while. "Look to your souls!"

The burly man snorted defiantly. "Feller might look to a clout o' the head if he sneak up on me again," he muttered.

"We'll none of that," Tuckworth commanded, marching right up to the burly man until his nose almost touched the fellow's grizzled chin. "Now, I'm willing to make allowances, but I'll not stand for threats. You clean up this place and set about your business, or I'll have a word with the architect."

The carpenters dispersed, not without a few grumbling remarks that just escaped being heard, and Tuckworth pulled Mr. March away.

"You know, March," he offered as they stepped back out into the gallery, "these men are really too involved in their labors to recall this place. Poor St. George's chapel is just another workshop to them."

Mr. March stopped. "A *workshop*?" he repeated, the word sounding distasteful on his tongue. "This is God's house, Vicar, and no man's workshop."

"It's a house that needs repairs, March, and a fellow can't keep his mind on his hammer and on heaven at the same time. He'll lose a finger doing that."

"Better your finger than your soul, Vicar."

Tuckworth sighed. He'd had enough of wrangling for one icy morning. The curate must have felt his exasperation, for the man looked suddenly confused and crestfallen. "I know you think I'm obdurate, Mr. Tuckworth," he said, his voice almost a whisper.

"Oh, come now," Tuckworth demurred, though unable to deny the truth of the statement. He liked Mr. March, had grown strangely fond of him over the past year. He would have felt kindly toward anyone forced to live in the rector's shadow. Still, he knew the man to be an odd mixture, at once reserved and anxious, quiet yet filled with an evangelical zeal.

"Yes, obdurate," Mr. March continued. "I know it to be so. And your good example has made me consider whether I am not mistaken in my methods." The curate shook his head. "But I haven't your manner with people, nor the rector's grand eloquence."

"Well, we must all just do our best in our own ways, mustn't we?" offered Tuckworth, not entirely comfortable with such a penitential attitude and eager to end this part of the discussion. "Now, what can I help you with? I don't suppose Mortimer sent you here to preach to the carpenters."

"Yes, he did. That is, I was to speak to them of thrift. Some of the bills for timber are altogether exorbitant."

"Well, then," Tuckworth went on, "that's a matter for the foreman. Come, I'll point him out to you."

It was several minutes still before Tuckworth could manage his escape from the curate's business. Yet they were blessed minutes, for they were minutes spent with his mind on something other than murder. No sooner had he left Mr. March with the foreman, however, and turned to leave the cathedral, than his eye fell upon a corner of the nave by the south transept where a little wooden chair sat empty and alone. Will had used to rest there, all day sometimes, not uttering a sound, only sitting in the shadows and watching the light. The vicar walked over, sat down in the chair and looked about him. It was an ideal location from which to appreciate the grandeur of Bellminster Cathedral. All the music of the light played out before him, and his heart could not help but sing with it, if for only an instant. Then he dropped his gaze, and his eyes caught something glinting in a dark niche at his feet. He reached down and picked it up. It was one of Will's bottles, and this one still half full. A gentle smile danced fleetingly across Tuckworth's lips. He put the bottle back and rose, determined that the chair would stay where it was as his own act of restoration.

Tuckworth returned to the vicarage, that homely little cottage constructed more than a century past against the very shadow of Bellminster Cathedral, like a domestic postscript scrawled upon the massive walls, the little chimney dwarfed by the steeple piercing the sky more than two hundred feet above. Once at home, he found Lucy waiting for him. She took his arm the instant he was through the door and led him into the parlor, settling him in his well-worn easy chair. Then, sitting herself upon the arm, she laid his head gently against her shoulder. Mrs. Cutler looked in from the kitchen. "A nice pot of tea, your worship?" she asked tenderly.

"No, thank you, Mrs. Cutler. Nothing," Tuckworth answered. There was a sudden flurry of black feathers from a window niche, and a great raven flapped clumsily with a malformed wing across the room to perch itself on Tuckworth's knee. He laid a lazy hand upon its head and scratched gently. Mrs. Cutler glared with lethal intent at the bird before withdrawing into her kitchen.

Left alone again, father and daughter sat in comfortable silence for a time. They felt no need to talk, communicating as they did through other means less harsh, more direct, as one soul speaks to another. After a time, Mrs. Cutler reappeared with a tray and a tea service. "Nice pot of tea for you," she announced, as though they had been waiting expectantly for her. She poured and then left them alone once more.

"The mayor's office," Lucy began. "It was miserable as all that?"

"Worse," Tuckworth answered. "Bloodthirsty ranting about vendettas and retribution. Barely a word about poor Will. He's just 'the victim' now."

"Jack, too?" she pursued.

"Oh, Mortimer did very well. He managed to enforce a degree of solemnity on things. Kept the wealthy mob from getting out of hand, at any rate. You would have been proud of him, really." Perhaps Tuckworth obscured his own feelings a bit with these remarks, but he was nonetheless convinced of the essential truth of what he said.

Lucy scowled. "I'm surprised. He's usually so quick to kowtow before that set and toady to that awful McWhirter."

"These are different times, Lucy, and the parish tithes don't come in as regularly as they should. Mr. McWhirter's contributions to the cathedral are greatly welcome."

"Oh, Father, you never ran off to any man's open purse strings like some sort of real estate broker. Jack's degrading himself."

"Lucy," her father scolded, "if you must refer to the rector by his Christian name, I wish you wouldn't be so familiar with it. He is my superior, after all. And he's a widower. That gives a man a certain station."

The girl laughed, and the sound disarmed Tuckworth's anger at once. "But he insists I think of him as a friend. He told me so. So I call him Jack to keep him at his word."

Now it was Tuckworth's turn to scowl. He didn't approve of this friendship. "You call him Jack to annoy him. Call him Jonathan, if you must. Your mother never used my Christian name after more than thirty years of marriage, and I'm only a vicar. She always called me by my surname."

The mention of Tuckworth's wife cast a shade over father and child. Her death five years before had left a hole in the fabric of their lives, a hole they had mended as best they could, though the stitches showed. They rested together, just a moment more. Then

Tuckworth rose and, taking the raven onto one hand and giving Lucy a pat with the other, he retired to his study. Lucy watched him as he disappeared behind the heavy door, heard the solid click of the latch, felt his absence from her life. Her light spirits disappeared like a vapor on the breeze. She sighed and bowed her head. But she did not weep.

CHAPTER THE FOURTH
THE INVESTIGATION

ight faded into darkness, and Bellminster Cathedral reigned over the night like the Ancient of Days. No point in the town lay nearer to heaven than its exalted spire. No cellar sank deeper into the earth than its damp crypt. Nowhere could day be made more lustrous, or shadows more impenetrable. Mystery was gathered in its stone walls. Architects, long-moldering and forgotten, had possessed the plans for its many passages, its hidden staircases, its inner streets and twisting alleys, but those plans were moldering, too, and no one living knew all the secrets of this labyrinth, nor what dread Minotaur might house in its heart. Bellminster Cathedral was as dark and awful, as light and airy as the faith over which it presided, and no one could grasp its entirety.

Yet who knew it better than Tuckworth? The world was asleep as the vicar peeked through his private entrance, through his study into the back of a small side chapel, and looked about. The cathedral held its own beauty at night that few ever witnessed. The great rose window transfigured each weak, watery moonbeam, muting and magnifying it with an otherworldly aura, a suffusion of color. Here and there a sacred candle flickered to add some ounce of illumination to the weight of darkness, like a beauty mark on a powdered cheek. Tuckworth smiled an appreciative smile, closed the door behind him, and began a slow circuit about the nave.

This hour was his own in the cathedral, a private time when

night hung her heavy drapery about Bellminster and he could enjoy the serenity of being alone. Sleep was wasted effort for him, and his solitude seemed sweeter here, in a space where two thousand men and women might gather easily, two thousand murmuring voices hushed beneath the weight of stone and light, two thousand minds left numb and empty by the daily travails of life, coming to this place, bringing their emptiness with them. Tuckworth sighed, and his breath almost stirred the colored light hanging like gauze in the air. It was all so different here, by himself, with no one else to see him, no one to watch as he allowed freedom to his secret thoughts. For this was always his fear, that in the harsh severity of day, some motion, some stray look or inadvertent gesture might give him away. He lived in perpetual anxiety that his soul should be discovered, his heart exposed, left open for the jackdaws of society to feed upon.

Now, as Tuckworth passed through this cathedral that was more home to him even than the bed he had slept in and the table he had supped at for more than thirty years, as he traveled in perfect solitude those stone paths so worn by ages of unwavering faith, his secret rose from the dark pit of his heart to inhabit every corner of his consciousness. Here he was safe to ponder it, to acknowledge it, to make it real. No one could find him out in this place. No man stood by to peer into his eyes and unleash the truth. No, not even God could penetrate his heart.

He had lost his faith. This was his secret pain, the wound that would not close, the suffering he must not share. That which had sustained, not just his own spirit, but the spiritual life of an entire community had dried up inside him. He looked out into the vaulted darkness, past the shimmering hues of light, into the black overhead and saw nothing. No heavens opened up to his inner vision. The glories of Bellminster Cathedral reflected no greater glory of a life beyond. The light, so beautiful to him, so stirring to his eye and to his mind, stirred no like transcendence in his soul to carry him out of this mundane world. In the place where his faith had once been there was only an ache, the yearning of a man abandoned by his own resolve, left out in the cold from walls that had comforted him, sheltered him all his life. His was not the violent atheism of the young rebel, strident and angry, daring God to show His face in the world, but the sorrowing emptiness of the mature man who knows what he has lost, who struggles to find feelings no longer alive. Tuckworth would have prayed for the rebirth of his religion, but who was there to answer such a prayer?

There was only his love for this place, last relic of a dead creed. It had seemed that the more his soul had withered within him, that much more had he relied upon the cathedral's magnificence to move him. This grandeur was real. No power of belief could alter a single stone or move one ray of light from its course. The saints who lined its walls without and above were too weighty to fly off to heaven on angels' wings. Others might walk here blindly, unaware of the strength of beauty so near at hand as they cast their gaze beyond the stained windows, above the soaring spire and massive towers into a chilling void. But he knew the power of this realm, something solid, something true in itself, raised from the dust of the earth by generations of nameless men, laying stone upon stone, a faith struggling through three lifetimes of labor to erect a new Babel. And yet, such faith had not acted in vain, for it had made this.

He envied the flock their blind certainty in a divine hand. To return again to that state of devotion, he thought, when all questions were stilled, when no answers were needed, it would be peace indeed. A narcotic peace, perhaps, the peace of sleep, but peace at all was a thing he longed for. What did his questions bring him, after all? Not answers, certainly, for the more he searched for some truth to hold on to, the less sure any answers seemed. Restlessness, humiliation, perpetual yearning, these were the only answers he received from life. Tuckworth cursed his faithless soul and wished it to hell. As like to wish he were a child again. Or wish himself into slumber. There was no turning away from his unbelief. For a time, he had doubted and managed to live with his doubt. All doubt was gone now. He suffered, not from a crisis of faith, but from a certainty of chaos.

He could not continue with this hypocrisy, a charlatan to those he loved most in the world. When Reverend Mortimer had first been named rector, Tuckworth asked to be relieved of his office. It only seemed right that the new man select his own vicar to run the parish for him. Mortimer had surprised everyone, however, by announcing that he would live in Bellminster himself, would eliminate the office of vicar and collect his own tithes. Of course, such a transition could not be effected at once, and the young rector had insisted that Tuckworth stay on for one year, time enough to accommodate the parish to this new authority. So Tuckworth's clerical duties had slowly dropped off over the months winding down. Mortimer held Sunday services now, and preached to the congregation, and tended to their souls, and performed all the rites of the church in Tuckworth's absence while the vicar continued to hide his secret from everyone it might hurt. And with the setting by of each task, he had felt a burden lift from his heart.

Tuckworth paused to rest in a side pew, burying his head in his hands. Now this offer had arrived from Granby to upset his plans. Dean of Bellminster Cathedral. Was it possible? Could he deny his qualms and embrace this new position? For what was the dean? A glorified housekeeper, a handyman to watch over this vast house. No holy office. No rite or ritual. No phantom God to appear to call upon. Most of all, no faith placed in him for his own faithlessness to betray. Might he not be allowed to worship here at the last altar his life had left him? Dean of Bellminster?

Colorless eyes glared down, piercing the moonlight as it enveloped Tuckworth, observing the vicar. A figure knelt as though in midair among the timbers of the scaffold, a shadow within shadows, a darkness that gathered the night about itself. Like stone it stayed, unswayed, unswerving, its cold eyes turned from above to that other figure below. The eyes narrowed, watched the vicar, head bowed, sitting as if in prayer. The shadow breathed a silent invocation, and watched.

A noise overhead interrupted Tuckworth's reveries, and he jumped in startled surprise, staring up into the scaffolding. A web of crisscrossing shadows stretched over him into nothingness. "Is someone there?" he called too loudly, and his words echoed about the vault. Nothing stirred overhead, though he squinted to penetrate the darkness. What had he heard? A breath? A footfall? The wind? He couldn't be certain. He only felt that something was up there.

Silly fears to plague an old man's dreams, Tuckworth thought, and continued his slow circuit of the cathedral. Yet as he paced, he could not escape the sensation that his movements were being followed. The phantom of a sound, an errant breeze, a wandering shade, these are more frightening, perhaps, than a palpable threat, for they cannot be dispelled. Something was there, he felt, marking him from the shadows, hiding in some recess, a dark corner, an obscure niche. Tuckworth glanced nervously to left and right as he passed, and everywhere he saw eyes peering at him, judging him, trying to find their way to his secret self. He shivered, doubtless from the cold of the late October night seeping through the walls of the cathedral, and hurried back to the vicarage.

The next morning, a Sunday, brought no relief from the vicar's worries. A rap on the door, a hasty introduction, a long wagon ride and Tuckworth found himself trembling with cold in the one spot he least cared to visit in the world, back in the Estwold looking on as Detective Inspector Myles of Bow Street, London, stirred about the desiccated leaves of autumn with the end of a stick.

The inspector had come calling upon the vicarage, Chief Constable Hopgood in tow, almost with the dawn and had addressed himself to Tuckworth with a quick, professional air. Myles was a small man in a long coat, but he appeared more compacted than diminutive, as though a great deal of energy were wrapped up in a convenient parcel. His head he kept always lowered, following some trail that only he could discern. His movements were abrupt, active, his body held ever in preparedness, and he looked like nothing so much as a terrier on the scent. A wisp of dark hair barely covered a strong brow, and thin lips pursed tightly in reflection behind the expanse of a great bushy mustache as he paced about the scene where the sexton had been discovered. Myles stopped suddenly, bent down and picked up something sparkling from the forest floor.

"Can you tell me what this is, then?" he asked Hopgood, who was standing off to one side.

"Glass?" the chief constable hazarded. Myles gave a suffering wince and then held the shard out to the vicar.

Tuckworth approached and examined the brown splinter in the inspector's fingers. "I'm afraid it's Will's bottle."

"Was your sexton a drinking man?"

"Yes," Tuckworth admitted. "He was a good worker, but he drank, and sometimes he drank to excess."

Myles nodded his head thoughtfully, and Tuckworth wished they might leave now. It was scarcely two days since he had found Will, and already he felt so deeply sunk in this affair that he would never be able to drag himself from its grip. Yet there was some small part of him, that curious, questioning part that could never be quiet, that wondered what the inspector was thinking, what did it all mean, the singular murder of an insignificant man, the mangled body, this grotesque display like an awful signpost that none of them could read. This business might actually have been suited to Tuckworth's nature, the dry, methodical field of investigation, the game of seek and find. Question and answer, question and answer, all in an effort to derive meaning from the meaningless. It might have proven congenial to the vicar's temper had he not been occupied with thoughts of a warm fire and a large breakfast.

Myles motioned to Tuckworth without looking at him. "I'll be asking you to sit against the log in the same attitude as the victim."

Tuckworth gazed uncomfortably at Hopgood. "Is that absolutely necessary?" he wondered aloud.

"It would be a great help to me," the inspector replied, tapping his brow, "to form an image in my mind."

Tuckworth hesitated for a moment, to make sure no one else was about. When they had first arrived, the three men chased away a gang of boys sporting about the place, and in fact the entire town seemed to be wallowing in macabre fascination with the murder. News of London's involvement had spread like floodwaters the day before, and many an aged citizen walked more proudly through the streets of Bellminster today because of it. "Our murder," they were calling the affair. "Our murder." Looking about, and satisfied that they were alone, Tuckworth sat down with his back against the log.

Myles stepped up to the oak and peered along its surface. "Excuse me, Vicar, but the axe fell farther down this way. The mark is quite visible."

"Yes," Tuckworth acknowledged.

"Had the fellow been positioned that far along when you saw him?"

"No, he was about where you're standing."

"Could you please bring yourself down here, then?" the inspector requested, and reaching down, he picked up something from under the leaves. "And perhaps you could hold this stone in your arms? It's small, but it might suggest the man's head."

Tuckworth stood up. "No, Inspector, I'm afraid I couldn't do that."

Myles looked into Tuckworth's eyes for the first time since they had arrived, and his brow furrowed in profound scrutiny. "I'm sorry, Vicar," he apologized. "I forgot how troublesome these things can be to men not used to them. I've seen enough of this sort of business to be fairly easy with it myself."

"You can't mean this is a regular occurrence in London?" gasped Tuckworth.

"Not regular, no. But it's not unknown, either." Myles took one last, rapid survey of the scene before turning back toward the road. "I'll be needing a look at the victim now."

Tuckworth followed the two policemen. He might have objected to being a party to any more of this investigation. He might have pleaded his squeamish nature or his missed breakfast or the sanctity of his position. And he had surely seen enough of Will in his waking dreams to last him the rest of his days. Yet he was curious, too. It seemed such a puzzle, and he delighted in puzzles. The thought made him vaguely uneasy, of course, but he didn't reflect upon it for long. There was too much of interest going on about him, occupying his mind. The three men climbed into the wagon that had carried them into the Estwold, Tuckworth squeezing awkwardly into the back and Hopgood taking the reins as they started into Bellminster, to the Municipal Hospital.

As they moved slowly down the road, the chief constable

quizzed his more worldly colleague. "Did you find anything telling back there?"

"Just that bit of glass."

Hopgood nodded. "Likely the poor chap was drunk when it happened," he surmised.

"Wasn't it a scandal for you, Vicar, having a drunkard for a sexton?" Myles asked offhandedly.

Tuckworth leaned forward. "We'd had to speak with him about it, yes, and there was even talk of letting him go."

"You say 'we.' "

"The rector and I. We'd talked with Will often over the past year, told him he had to give it up, and he promised countless times that he would."

"But he never did. And you never sacked him."

"No," Tuckworth confessed. "I suppose I should have, but the poor fellow had nowhere else to turn in this world. And he worked that hard, I couldn't bring myself to do it."

Myles was silent for a time. Question and answer, the vicar thought. What did the inspector suspect? How did he understand the bizarre details? What importance did he place on the broken glass, the severed head? Question and answer, question and answer.

"Had the sexton any regular drinking partners? Anyone that he'd meet to share a dram with?"

"No one to my particular knowledge. Certainly not since he'd come to work at the cathedral."

"And how long was that?"

"Perhaps three years."

"And before? Any acquaintances he might have called on for a drop?"

"None I ever heard him mention. He kept much to himself."

"I see it," Hopgood mused aloud. "Two men drinking in the woods. An argument. One grabs t'other's axe. Murder."

A cloud passed over the clear sky, and the air turned sharply colder. Tuckworth bundled himself tightly. "Of course," he commented, "if this has to do with drink, I'd imagine there'd be the signs of a drunken brawl. Yet all we have is the broken bottle."

"He sneaked up on him, of course!" Hopgood exclaimed, slapping his thigh. "While the sexton is resting from his work, the murderer creeps up, takes the axe from where it's been tossed aside, knocks him senseless first, then finishes the job."

"But Will hadn't started working yet," Tuckworth observed. "There was no firewood lying about. And how could anyone sneak up through those dry leaves? It doesn't seem likely, unless Will was already drunk and insensible. But then, how did the bottle get smashed? Why would the murderer throw it to the ground? It all seems rather strange."

Myles gave Tuckworth a meaningful glance before responding. "Yes, it does seem rather strange." That look startled Tuckworth, so filled as it was with calculation, and for an instant he wondered whether the inspector might not suspect him of the crime. He said nothing more until they reached their destination.

They were met by Dr. Warrick, a man neither old nor young. He had come to Bellminster as the first step in a brilliant career and had failed to take another step since. As the population grew, the doctor had floundered in the tide of progress that engulfed the town. He never noticed his dreams of a lucrative practice floating away, or the ideals of his greener days rusting beneath the waves of human suffering that daily drifted past like so much flotsam upon the seas. He had never acknowledged that his superior training as a physician gradually succumbed to the manual labors of a mere surgeon. He was too busy. Dr. Warrick's chief occupation at the Municipal Hospital was attempting to heal as many people as he could with as few resources as possible. He greeted his guests, therefore, with an air of abstraction as he hurried them along to view the body.

"We've been fortunate in the weather, you know," he informed them as they wound through a crowded hallway darkened with the sick and ailing.

"The weather?" Myles repeated.

"This cold spell has frozen some of the smaller ponds about, so we've had plenty of ice. For preserving the remains, you understand. You'll find the body a trifle bloated, the extremities slightly distended, but the head is remarkably fine." Tuckworth felt his stomach upend at this report. He breathed deeply and forced himself onward.

The party descended into a black well of an operating theater with only a sputtering oil lamp overhead to offer any hope of illumination. At the center of this darkened chamber was a table covered over with a soiled cloth, a puddle of water forming on the floor from underneath, the incessant drip, drip sounding oddly incongruous. With no warning Dr. Warrick stepped up and threw back the sheet, revealing the cropped torso of Will Shaperston lying amid chunks of ice. The encrusted axe lay beside him like a faithful dog. Tuckworth turned away with a sudden, heaving gasp and steadied himself against the wall, but no one gave him any notice.

From the sounds behind him, Tuckworth assumed that the three men were circling about, examining this specimen with the cold patience of their craft. "This wound appears clean," he heard Myles observe. "Your axe has been sharpened lately, Vicar."

Tuckworth inhaled deeply. "Will must have done it," he strained to reply.

"And you handed him the axe yourself, before he went off to chop firewood?"

The vicar tried a guttural, "Yes," but only moaned. Question and answer, he thought, question and answer. Nothing must stop the game.

The inspector murmured quietly to himself, making a detailed study of the body, mental notes to be sifted through later, then asked, "Where's the head?"

A clattering followed, the sound of a bucket being lifted onto the table and something wet and dripping pulled out from it. Tuckworth shut his eyes tight and flared his nostrils as he breathed in strong, sharp pants.

"This wound to the back of the skull, from the blunt end of the axe," he heard Myles query the doctor. "Would you say it was sufficient to have killed the victim outright?"

"I'd say there's little doubt of it," Dr. Warrick answered. "Look here, you can see a bit of the cerebrum peeking out, that gray tissue there."

Tuckworth felt his nausea rise violently, then subside as his mind grasped the significance of this. "But that means Will was already dead when the axe-blade fell," he said, without turning about, "so the beheading served some purpose other than murder."

Myles grunted his agreement.

The inspection soon ended, and Tuckworth felt a hand take him firmly by the elbow and lead him out. "You know," Myles commented as they walked back through the hospital, "you needn't have accompanied us."

"Quite all right," Tuckworth replied, his stomach more at ease now that the corpse was behind them. "I thought you might have further questions for me."

Myles gave him another narrow, calculating gaze and then turned to thank the doctor for his trouble.

"Excuse me," Dr. Warrick said by way of farewell, "but that's a good sixpence worth of ice melting away down there."

Myles stared blankly at Hopgood, who coughed and said, "Deliver your bill to the constabulary, Doctor, and we'll see you reimbursed." Dr. Warrick looked as if he could see his sixpence sailing over the horizon, lost forever, and he turned dejectedly away.

Back outside, Tuckworth ventured to ask Myles if he was finished with Will. "With your examination, I mean, of the body."

"Why do you ask?" the inspector returned.

Without understanding why, Tuckworth felt himself accused of something. "The man should be buried, you know," he answered defiantly.

Myles considered. "Of course he should. Yes, I'm finished with him."

"Where to now?" Hopgood asked, rubbing his hands together in the midmorning chill, clearly enjoying this investigation.

"I believe we can return the vicar home and thank him for his trouble," Myles replied.

"Home?" exclaimed Tuckworth, unnaturally disappointed at this news. "Am I excused?"

One calm, unfeeling stare from Myles, and Tuckworth saw that they would none of them be excused, not until this business was truly finished. "I'll be calling again, I'm sure, but for now we're done." The three men climbed once again into the wagon and set off.

They were forced to postpone their return to the vicarage, however. Before they had traveled fifty yards, a young boy came running up, flagging them to a halt with his arms.

"Constable!" he wheezed, though looking at Myles. "Constable, sir! They've gone and found another murder!"

CHAPTER THE FIFTH
THE INVESTIGATION

(CONTINUED)

R aphael stood marveling at Lucy's hair. Before, in the city, it had appeared black, black as a moonless midnight, a black you could fall into forever. He was going to use that black, to make the entire painting revolve around Ophelia's darkling locks, with flowers laced throughout like stars in the sky. But here, in the fields outside Bellminster, under the same sun, with the same pure light suffusing the air, her hair had altered. It was streaked now with a glowing russet, a radiant crimson that glimmered amid the black across her pale white brow. Where had they come from, these bolts of deep red? How was a man to paint such hair, inconstant as a flame? He approached her, under the spreading branches of a fiery oak tree, and taking a few locks in his fingers, he pulled them gently from their place and let the breeze play with them. Lucy glanced up at him with eyes made watery by the wind and smiled, and in that moment Raphael's heart was irretrievably lost.

"You must think me an awful fidget," Lucy said, looking down at the bright bouquet of fall flowers she held in her lap.

"Ophelia was a fidgety sort. I don't think it matters," Raphael answered blandly. He was trying to keep his emotions at a distance, to maintain his artist's dispassionate air. Yet the more he looked at her, the more he studied her, the less he saw of Ophelia in her. What was Ophelia, after all, compared to Lucy? Raphael returned to his easel, peered intently into the canvas, squinted this way and that trying to retain the vision which had guided him, finally gave up and, tossing his pastels aside, dropped down to the grass.

"Are we finished?" Lucy called to him.

"I certainly am."

She rose and came over to where he sat pulling up blades of grass in frustration. "Am I being that difficult?"

"Oh, God, it's not you, Lucia!" he assured her. "You're perfect! You're more than perfect!" She blushed, and the color in her cheek made his fingers ache to paint it. "It's not you. It's me. Every time I try to find Ophelia in you, I end up with Lucy."

"That must be a great disappointment," and she laughed that gay laugh of hers, that taunting, tempting, devilish laugh. He rolled away from her and stretched out on the green, while she looked at the sketch. "I must say, I don't look very mad, for an Ophelia."

Raphael said nothing, yet this was the very point where his frustration stung the sharpest. He had hoped to use Lucy's abundant joy to define his Ophelia, to make of her madness an excess of life, with flowers all about her, in her hair and on her arms and her dress, cascading over her like water, a girl too filled with exuberant spirit to live long amid the artifice of Elsinore. Yet wasn't his entire practice an artifice, trying to change Lucy's joy into something else? Wasn't that why it all seemed so impossible now? Yesterday he had sketched simply Lucy, to learn her face, her form, and every line was a triumph. Today he had tried to make Ophelia and failed.

Lucy strolled off a little way across the field, looking out over the town spread below them. "It doesn't seem possible, does it?" she said. "Just a few days ago everything was the way it always had been, so simple and certain. And then it all turned dreadfully different somehow."

Raphael stood and began to pack his tools away. "Nothing is certain, Lucia," he answered. "Nothing stays the same."

"But everything is already feeling the same way again, that's what I mean. Here we are, under the sun, with the breeze in the trees, being pleasant and merry, and poor Will is dead." She turned, and her eyes spoke to Raphael of some fear within her, some anxiety she couldn't name. His heart rose in his chest, to go to her, to comfort her.

"Lucy," he replied softly, moving toward her, "you weren't meant to grieve, not any more than the sun can grieve or the breeze."

"But it's heartless of me. I know it."

"No, not heartless. Your heart is so true you can't even imagine the sort of false mourning that other people find natural. Believe me, Lucia"—and he took her hands in his—"you feel more genuine grief over Will than all the rest of them, only you can't mimic their dumbshow. Your heart won't let you."

"You talk more like a poet than a painter," she teased.

They stood, the two of them, motionless for an instant, Raphael frozen by the words he could not say, his mind stilled by the deep concern in her eyes.

Lucy turned away. "Why did you come to Bellminster, Raphael?" she asked far more easily than she should.

"I came to paint the cathedral."

"You've made twenty paintings of the cathedral," Lucy laughed. "Why do you stay?"

"You know why I stay."

A faint call came to them on the wind, a voice hallooing in the distance. They turned and saw a figure in black across the field on the road standing by a pony cart. It was Reverend Mortimer, waving his arms to attract their attention. Lucy waved back. Raphael returned to packing his tools.

"Jack wants something," Lucy said.

"Then why doesn't he walk over here and tell us what it is?"

"He seems rather excited. I'd better go see what he's up to," and Lucy lifted her skirt and tripped through the knee-high grass, as light as a thought. Raphael followed her for an instant, saw the strand of hair wave behind her as she ran. A cloud passed in front of the sun, and the chill of the air sank deep within him.

"Lucy!" Mortimer called when she had come close enough for him to converse with. "Whatever are you doing this far from town alone with that person?"

"Why do you ask, Jack?" She laughed wickedly. "What is it you suppose we were doing?"

He gave her a look of shocked propriety, the kind of look he had used from the pulpit that morning to thrill the congregation. "You are frivolous, dear Lucy," he scolded, but she only smiled the brighter at this reprimand, and not even his austere demeanor could stand against her spirits. Mortimer relented with a sigh. "Come along. I've come to fetch you home," and he offered a hand to lift her into the pony cart. She glanced back at Raphael slinging his easel and pack upon his back. There was clearly not room for all three of them in the cart. "I'm certain Mr. Amaldi can find his way to town," Mortimer told her.

Lucy stepped up into the cart and spun about, as she sat down, to watch Raphael watching her. She raised a hand in farewell, but he only turned and walked off through the field, alone.

"Strange fellow," Mortimer commented as he settled into the cart and gave the reins a shake.

"Not so strange at all," Lucy replied, as much because she believed it as because she enjoyed goading Mortimer. She knew he detested Raphael. "He's really very charming. Unique in his ways, perhaps, but honest, too. He can't abide any falsehood or pretense."

"I sincerely hope that is true," the rector muttered with great clerical dignity. "Still, it won't do for you to go out with him like this in the future. I, for one, would never have allowed my late wife to be alone in the country with such a . . . a gentleman."

Lucy bridled. "I don't see how that concerns you, Jack. I am not your wife."

"Your welfare concerns me, notwithstanding," he responded, turning softer to her, a little less formal. "Your safety is, one might say, of paramount importance to me, Lucy."

She smiled. She didn't want to smile, but she smiled nonetheless. Lucy enjoyed the attentions she received from the rector, though she never encouraged them. It had become obvious that he saw her as something more than the vicar's child, and she was flattered, of course she was. Besides, being courted twice in one morning by two such different lovers was delightful. Still, she was silent, letting his comment hang there in the air until it floated away on the breeze.

"What brings you out so far from town, Jack?" she asked finally.

"Mrs. Cutler told me I might find you here. I came with the express intention of returning you to the vicarage."

"Why trouble yourself? I might have walked back with Raphael easily. It's a delicious day."

The rector shifted in his seat, straightened his back, bent his head slightly in the same attitude he affected when his sermon had come to the telling point and he wanted the congregation to make note of it. "There has been another tragedy, my child," he intoned.

Lucy raised a hand to her lips. "Dear God, no!" she cried. All of her light spirits fled at once, leaving an empty place in her heart for reproach to fill. "Who is it?"

"No one of particular consequence," Mortimer replied. "Josiah Mallard. Found dead out on the roadside."

Lucy turned her face away. No one of particular consequence. It was true, in a way. Jo Mallard was a repulsive man, cruel and brutish, a drunkard and a philanderer. Still, it was hard to hear that said of any man. No one of particular consequence. "Does Father know?" she asked.

"Yes, he's in company with the detective inspector from London. Rather awful business for the Sabbath. I'm rather surprised your father is taking part. I passed them on their way to view the body. My first thought was of you, naturally." And Mortimer smirked in the near approximation of a winning smile.

"Thank you, Jack, but you needn't have worried for my safety," she told him. "I was with Raphael, after all."

Mortimer said nothing at this, but only inclined his head sharply and cast an admonishing gaze at Lucy. It was clear, though he was silent on the matter, that this was precisely why he had been concerned for Lucy's safety. She didn't see this look, however. Her eyes were taking in the fields as they passed, the sunlight and the swaying grasses, the birds and the red-gold trees. It had all seemed lovely moments before, lovely enough to make her forget about ugly things. But that was a vain desire, she thought. Vain and stupid and sinful, and she closed her eyes and prayed quietly for forgiveness.

At that moment, Lucy's father was approaching the body of Josiah Mallard. Tuckworth was not the only person with this design. On their way out of town, the four men (for they had compelled Dr. Warrick to join their party) had been accompanied by an army of the curious. Half of Bellminster seemed to be on the road, and a carnival air stirred the crowd as they traveled to view the dead man. Neighbor greeted neighbor gaily. Children cavorted like a savage tribe, screaming and bawling at one another, eager to see "the cor'se." The idle and the industrious alike were joined in their desire to witness this extraordinary sight, and many a home and street corner were emptied by news of a second murder. One shrewd fellow, a baker, had filled a sack with buns and meat pies and was selling them to the hungry throng as he strolled. Through the midst of the crowd, the wagon carrying Tuckworth and Myles, Hopgood and Warrick, moved like Cleopatra's barge, given the right of passage at every byway and crossing, deferred to with the humility due the masters of the ceremony. And as they passed in state, all eyes followed them, every hand pointed them out, all tongues wagged with report of a thousand clues and a hundred suspects. The constabulary-house of Bellminster might have burst with murderers if even half these suspicions proved true.

Yet Tuckworth remained oblivious to it all. This news, this second murder, had produced an odd effect in him, a sense of excited anticipation. Arriving on the spot, he leapt down from the wagon with an unaccustomed agility and followed Myles and Warrick, with Hopgood bringing up the rear. Three hundred prying souls and more had gathered along a stone wall that separated the road from a fallow field, and the officials had to force a way through to the body. They could hear two voices, the pleading tones of Officer Wily and the whining of Mr. March as they attempted to preserve order.

"You must give way!"

"Keep back, please, until the chief constable arrives! Please!"

But their words made a poor dike against the swelling waters of curiosity.

The body of Jo Mallard lay just within the field, buried under a pile of stones that left a gaping hole in the wall. He was lying on his back, and Mr. March had already uncovered the head and chest, tossing the stones about like corks so that they littered the area around the body. Tuckworth undid his neckerchief and bundled it in front of his nose and mouth. It was repellently clear that Mallard had been dead for some days. His arms, crossed delicately upon his breast, were bare and swollen almost to bursting. His face was distorted into a mass of red and black pulp. The only sign that might identify him was the absence of the ring finger upon his left hand, a mark the man had always offered as proof to whores that he was never meant for marriage. Tuckworth studied the misshapen figure at his feet with a strange fascination, sickened, it's true, yet equally engrossed.

Myles knelt beside the body and the crowd closed in above him. He glanced at Hopgood, and the chief constable tried to push these spectators away, managing only a bit of breathing space. "Dr. Warrick, if you please." The detective motioned, making room on the ground.

Warrick studied the body closely, prodding and poking, looking underneath to see the work of worms already well advanced, releasing the noxious gases trapped within. A few of the assembly backed away at this, the limits of their interest defined by such a demonstration of decay, but there were other, hardier souls to take their places. "I'd say he's been dead almost a week now," Warrick proclaimed.

Wily bent down to display his notebook to the others. "Farmer Redman says as he noticed the hole in his fence four or five days ago, and only got 'round to mending it this day. That's when the body were discovered."

"So this is the first murder," Tuckworth mumbled through his neckerchief.

Myles looked up at him. "Yes, it would appear so."

"Do you notice," Dr. Warrick continued, "the massive damage to his tissues? I'd say this fellow wasn't buried so much as pummeled with these stones."

"Are you saying he was beaten to death?"

"Repeatedly beaten, yes. Whoever did this laid him out here, took the stones from this wall and threw them down upon his prone body. Rather forcibly."

Warrick and Myles rolled stones aside to uncover more of the body, raised the moldy clothing between their fingers, examined the rotten flesh beneath, engaged in an intricate discourse with the lifeless thing before them. Question and answer, question and answer. It occurred to Tuckworth that even the dead could play this game. The vicar kept a lively eye upon the entire proceedings, his stomach strangely cold and empty now, his mind heedless of the press of humanity crowding him in on all sides. Myles reached out and twisted the head left and right, to find the telling blow, the death blow, causing a revolting army of creatures to come scurrying out from underneath.

"Look there," Tuckworth announced, pointing to a spot under the body. A stone, smaller than the rest and brighter, lay buried like a pillow beneath Mallard's skull. Myles pushed the corpse to one side and pried this stone up with his nails. Brushing it off, he stood and held it above the shadow of the encroaching mob so that the sunlight glinted off of it. "It's whitewashed," Tuckworth exclaimed. "You see? It's bloodstained there, but on the other side you can still see it's been whitewashed."

"And what do you suppose that means?" Myles asked.

All eyes turned to Tuckworth now, and he realized for the first time that he was at the center of a great show. "It's only," he almost whispered to the inspector, "that this wall isn't whitewashed, so it would appear that stone came from somewhere else. From Mallard's cottage, most likely. It's just around that turn in the road ahead."

"What's 'at?" someone shouted from the back of the crowd, and a dozen voices repeated Tuckworth's comments.

"So he was assaulted there and then carried here to be finished off," Myles muttered, completing Tuckworth's thought.

"Or assaulted here by someone lying in wait, someone who had been to the cottage first," Tuckworth added.

"Very well, Vicar," Myles said, standing, "what say we go have a look at this man's cottage?" The two moved off through the crowd, leaving the others to complete a cursory examination and then load the body into the wagon. "And do try to get this mob dispersed," the inspector begged Hopgood. The spectators were not to be denied, however, and only stepped back a few paces at the chief constable's insistence, while a score and more were already running off down the road to Mallard's cottage, to the second act of this drama.

As they strode down the lane, Myles gave Tuckworth another of those piercing glances, studying him, observing. Tuckworth could not help noticing this interest, and finally he stopped and confronted Myles.

"Is there something you wish to ask me?" he demanded.

Myles stood silently for a moment. "No, nothing in particular." A moment more, and they continued on their way.

A shadow crept up beside the men, a slight, brittle figure wrapped in a shawl. "It's a fierce judgment on the man," a voice croaked at them. As they neither one acknowledged this remark, the figure repeated it, plucking with bony fingers at Tuckworth's sleeve. "I say, God's passed a fierce judgment on the wicked old screw!"

"Yes, yes, Pol, it's a terrible fate for any man," Tuckworth answered wearily without stopping.

"There's many as would have liked to see that one in his grave," the crone went on, certain now of her audience. "Many as would have liked it, but only one as has done it, eh?" And she cackled to herself.

Without slowing his step, Myles darted a look at this woman. She was a wizened old hag, dried and decrepit, with more whiskers than teeth, more teeth than hair, and a sharp nose that seemed always to be sniffling the air. "Do you know anything of this business, grandmother?" he asked casually.

She sidled up to the inspector now. "What I might know ain't but mere gossip, is it, Vicar?" she crowed. "Poor Pol ain't naught but a mean old gossip. But even a gossip's got eyes, ain't she? And a tongue what might be loosed."

"Now, Polly Burdon," Tuckworth advised the old woman sternly, "we'll have none of your stories here. The inspector has serious matters to attend to with no time for your tales. Run along with you."

Polly pulled herself up short in spirited indignation, a weird sort of pride filling her scant frame. "Tales, is it!" she screamed. "No time for Poor Pol! Well, let him look into his 'serious matters' hisself, then! And when he runs up against it, let him seek out Poor Pol, and then we'll see who's got time for gossip!" And with that, she turned and huffed away.

"You must excuse her," Tuckworth explained. "Poor woman's turned spiteful and vile in her loneliness."

"Is there any reason she might not have information about this affair?" Myles asked.

Tuckworth considered. "No, except that she's always spreading wicked stories about. The boy who cried wolf, you know."

Myles only nodded thoughtfully and continued on his way.

The crowd had gathered about Jo Mallard's cottage by the time they arrived, peering in at the door and peeking through the windows. The place was remarkable-looking, small and run-down, the thatch moldy and drooping, the shutters all but fallen off, panes of glass cracked here and there or boarded over entirely, and yet it was clean and cozy for all that, with late fall flowers already blooming in unpainted window boxes and laundry blowing on a line in the back. Myles paused for a moment to notice a path leading from the road to the door, lined on either side with whitewashed stones. Tuckworth followed his glance and saw that one of these was missing.

The two men proceeded up to the cottage, where a party of onlookers crowded the doorway. As they came up, Myles stopped and heaved a weary sigh, staring down at his feet for the briefest instant. Suddenly he exploded in a ferocious burst of energy, reached out with both hands and grasped two men by their collars, throwing them back into the dust. Not satisfied, he turned and kicked them where they lay, until both scrambled up and ran off.

"Would someone get these bloody people out of here?" he shouted, and the crowd immediately melted away from him, like ice giving way before a roaring flame. He waited a moment, and Tuckworth gaped at him in amazement. The inspector had seemed so cold and emotionless, a machine for asking questions, with no hint of feeling about him. And now this attack, like an eruption with no warning. Myles composed himself quickly, regained his calm, even temper, and without looking at anyone, passed into the cottage.

Inside was darkness, the light of the sun obliterated by the wall of faces pressed against the windows. There was little the sunlight might have shone upon: a bare room with a few sticks of worn furniture, the refuse of other homes, other families; a hard dirt floor kept level and dry, but cold, too, and comfortless; rough, open cupboards, just so many unplaned boards nailed artlessly to the walls; neat, threadbare curtains, pieced together from scraps of fabric; and at a small, uneven table, two figures, a woman—a girl, really—slight and pale, huddled with a hulking man. She seemed to be soothing him, cradling his massive head in her gaunt arms, running scrawny fingers through his dark tousle of hair.

Myles said nothing at first, but took the time to examine them. Perhaps the girl had been beautiful once. Her hair appeared dry and sandy, no longer gold but straw. Her cheeks were sallow and drawn, her lips thin and colorless. The only life in her shone from black, watery eyes and a sweet voice that murmured comforts to the man. He was a huge fellow, little more than a shadowy mass crouched at her side like an enormous dog, possessed of a clenched face with a misshapen nose, slits for eyes and fat, cracked lips through which a thick tongue protruded. He was older than the woman, yet he whimpered next to her like a whipped child. Tuckworth stepped through the door behind Myles and the pair sprang to life where they sat.

"Vicar, what's goin' on?" the girl pleaded frantically. "What's all these people here? They says Jo's done for! They says he's murdered! Murdered! Is it so, Vicar? Please, God help me, tell me the truth on't!" The man simply released a stream of tears, his emotions suddenly unleashed by the girl's outburst.

Tuckworth sat down beside them and took their hands in his own. "Yes, Mary," he told her, "Josiah is dead." He put it just that simply, his manner straightforward and blunt, and she appeared released by the news, as if something inside her could relax now at this confirmation.

"Dear God," she stated flatly, "what's to become of us?"

"You needn't fear. You'll be cared for," he assured her, but the words felt barren to him, uncertain, more like a wish than a promise.

"Excuse me," Myles interrupted, stepping forward.

Tuckworth gave the inspector a pained look. Now was not the time, he thought, but he knew it was useless to object. Question and answer, always question and answer. The game would not be denied. "Mary," he said, turning back to the girl, "this man wants to speak with you. We need to discover who did this terrible thing."

"But I don't know," she insisted. "Jo ain't been home a week or more. He gone off and he ain't been back!"

"Where's Jo?" the man muttered beside her, apparently ignorant of what had occurred.

"Mrs. Mallard—" Myles began.

"Black," the girl interjected. Myles paused and looked at Tuckworth for an explanation.

"Her name is Mary Black. This is her brother, Adam," Tuckworth replied. "They've lived here with Mallard for some years now."

"As no one would take in a poor girl with a simpleton for a brother," she explained. "Jo's done good by us. He's provided and we're content, ain't we, Adam?"

The man only smiled a weak smile, looking anxiously from his sister to the vicar and back again.

Myles seemed unmoved by this pathetic tale, and the game began. When had Mallard disappeared? Perhaps a week before, maybe more. He was always going off, vanishing for days at a time, with no word that he was alive or dead. Had he any enemies, anyone who might want to do him an injury? Enemies enough. Mallard was not a well-liked man. The crowd at the pub, nasty little alehouse that it was, was always getting him into some scrape or other, some business for Mallard to soil his knuckles with. But would anyone want to kill him? The girl couldn't say. She didn't know. Mallard kept such things apart from them, from the cottage, and never spoke of what he did in the world, or how he got his money. Money? Did Mallard keep a lot of money about? He used to, at times, but things had been hard these past months, for almost a year, now. Things had been frightful hard.

Question and answer, question and answer. The last time she had seen him, what was his temper like? Just as always. Close, dark, but not mean. He hadn't hit her or nothing, not with his fist least-ways, only his open hand. He just didn't come home one night is all. And what of her brother? No sense asking him nothing. Does he come and go as he pleases, too? He stays about the cottage mostly. Or sometimes to the town and such. Myles nodded his head. Like a wall rising from the dust, one brick at a time, deliberately, method-ically, the game went on. Question and answer, question and answer.

"Did you wish Mallard dead?"

The girl was silent and Tuckworth pressed her hand firmly, giv-ing Myles an angry glare.

"Did you wish him dead?"

Mary stammered. "He was all we had, you understand. He might've been rough with us at times, not but I'm sure we deserved it. Poor girl and her simpleton brother. He'd tell us we was useless flesh on the face of the earth, and without him we'd be charity cases or worse. Sent to the workhouse and split up for good. Adam needs me. We's all we has, and he needs me." Her voice died away.

Tuckworth felt helpless there, kneeling next to the girl and her brother, and his helplessness galled him. He glanced about at the faces in the windows, staring in at them, watching them like gawkers peering in at a traveling menagerie. His heart burned for these two cursed souls sent adrift from the one mean harbor they had ever found. For Mary was right. The only home for them now was the workhouse—abject, filthy, loathsome place, where families were de-stroyed under the grindstone of a merciless charity. But first they must be subjected to this scrutiny, these onlookers pressing their fat noses against the glass to see what depths misery can reach. And

Tuckworth among them, one of them, with nothing to offer but empty words of idle consolation. He pressed their hands harder still and tried to smile. Adam looked up at the vicar and smiled back.

"Vicar," the man asked, "where's Jo?"

Tuckworth stared into Adam's questioning eyes that could only just understand what was happening around him. "Jo's gone away again, Adam," he said. "He's gone for a long time now, and you and Mary must try to get on without him. But you can do that, can't you, brave lad? Help your sister on and stick by her? You can do that, I know."

A sadness slowly descended upon this man-child, a deep worry as the words filtered through the cloud always about him and settled vaguely into his mind. But he said nothing. He only stayed quiet, sulking, looking occasionally at his sister.

The inspector ended his interrogation abruptly and stepped back outside into the light. Tuckworth rose to follow, but Mary gripped his arm, looked pleadingly into his eyes. He patted her lean, wasted hand. "It will be all right," he reassured her, his voice steady and sure. "We'll see what the parish can do for you. You'll not be abandoned, my girl." Yet she was wise enough to know that the parish had little comfort for a woman whose life was a sin, and she kept a fierce, clawing grasp of Tuckworth's arm. He looked down at her, into the dark, sunken eyes that shone upon him with a desperate light, eyes begging silently, begging for comfort, for hope, a mere word that she might hear and believe in, believe that this would all come out right, that her life was not now a ruin and a wreck. Her eyes tried vainly to draw upon Tuckworth's faith, that it might lift her from despair. But his soul was empty. All he possessed was an aching desire to give her what she wanted, a longing to shed the light of peace upon the darkness engulfing Mary Black. Her eyes shone on him and showed him his own despair. He gently pried himself away and left.

The crowd was beginning to thin now, and Tuckworth found Myles waiting for him, looking at the whitewashed stones that led from the lane to the cottage door. The two men proceeded back down the road in quiet contemplation, the straggling throng keeping pace beside them, murmuring, exchanging their own views on these remarkable proceedings like an audience streaming out of the theater.

When they arrived back at the wagon, Tuckworth turned aside. "I'll leave you here," he told Myles. "It's been a long morning, and I'd prefer the walk. Besides, there's no room in back of the wagon for me, not with Mallard lying there."

One last time, the inspector looked at Tuckworth in that prying way he had, but the vicar no longer cared. He turned his back on it all—the interrogations and surmises; the probing and prodding for evidence, for signs; the mechanics of investigation, slow, inexorable, nurturing suspicion and mistrust—ignoring the pain occasioned by it all. He had joined in the sport with the enthusiasm of an amateur. Even the death of Will Shaperston, his own sexton, had left him more puzzled than sad, like it was all part of some parlor game. Question and answer, question and answer. He had allowed himself to become a part of it, this dry inquisition, and the realization disgusted him. Not until he had looked into that girl's eyes had he seen that these were lives they were dissecting, and the answers they sought could bring no relief for the hurt that had already been inflicted. He turned from it all now, walked off the road and across the field, making his own lonely way back to Bellminster.

From within the swarm of figures streaming away behind him, from the crowd he had just left, a pair of eyes, cold eyes, colorless eyes, followed Tuckworth into the distance.

CHAPTER THE SIXTH
THE INVESTIGATION
(CONCLUDED)

No!" the vicar barked in disbelief, sending the raven flapping noisily to the top of a nearby bookcase. He sat bolt upright in his easy chair, and across the room Lucy leapt to her feet while Mrs. Cutler wrung her hands in her apron. "It's not possible!"

Raphael looked from Lucy back to her father, shaking with anger and indignation. "Forgive me, sir, it is possible. I saw him with my own eyes, dragged in chains into the constabulary-house."

"Father, how could they, how could anyone think such a ridiculous thing?" Lucy pleaded.

Tuckworth sat back again, shocked, stunned into a stupor. "I don't know, my dear," was his only answer. Adam Black. He repeated it again in his mind, to see if it felt more real, more plausible: They have arrested Adam Black for murder.

"Oh, the poor child!" Mrs. Cutler exclaimed to no one in particular, and left the room.

Raphael stepped farther into the parlor of the vicarage and sat on the edge of a convenient chair. "You were with the inspector most of the morning, sir," he observed. "Was there anything, anything at all, that might have led him to this? Did Adam say or do the least thing?"

"Of course not," Tuckworth burst out impatiently. "The poor man can hardly grasp what's happened. He only sat there the whole time, whimpering in his sister's arms."

Mrs. Cutler came back with a shawl around her stiff, straight figure, tying a bonnet about her neck. "The poor dear won't know what to do with herself," she muttered. "Not a soul to turn to in the whole world."

"Where are you off to, ma'am?" Tuckworth demanded, annoyed and angry at all this turmoil.

"I'm off to get poor Mary and bring her back here, that's where I'm off to," she shot back at him. "Child oughtn't to be alone on a night such as this."

"I'm afraid you won't have much luck," Raphael informed her. "She's in with her brother."

"Don't tell me they've arrested her, too?" the vicar shouted.

"No, only she refuses to leave Adam's side, so they've put her in the cell with him."

"Oh!" screamed Mrs. Cutler, and she was gone in a rush, banging the door as she left.

The others remained behind in silence. Now that the first blow of this news had subsided, all they had was the grim fact of it before them. Lucy sat back down, looking wretchedly concerned. Raphael fumed, staring at the floor between his feet, anger boiling within him. The vicar sat as still and cold as marble, feeling very old and very weak. The only movement in the room came from the raven, hopping about nervously at the top of its bookcase.

At that moment, the world appeared a black and ugly place to Tuckworth. Ever since leaving the inspector and marching off through the fields that morning, he had felt downcast and irritated, his mind beset by mean thoughts and base meditations. What kind of world was this, he wondered, where men and women make an amusement out of the suffering of the hopeless? He knew the excitement in the town since the murders had begun. He had seen the merry faces of the crowd, rapt and hungry, eager to hear every awful detail of this dreadful business. What compelled such ferocious curiosity? What pleasure did they derive in witnessing such pain, so much anguish? Were they comforted to think that it was someone else who suffered, someone else whose life was destroyed? Were their lives so bereft of meaning that another's agony made their own suffering seem more tolerable? Tuckworth considered all of this, and for the first time in his memory he despised the people of Bellminster.

He despised himself most of all. For wasn't he one of them? Hadn't he joined in the game, been carried along in the ferment and commotion? And that very morning, hadn't he felt more alive than he had in years, thrilled to be at the center of it all? He had held an honored place beside the inspector from London, tossing out suspicions and suppositions like darts, anxious to hit the mark before Myles did, eager to find answers sooner than the rest of them.

Where had it all led in the end? Adam Black was to hang, another life sacrificed to the entertainment of the mob. And he, Tuckworth, had helped to make it happen. He felt sick at himself, at the world.

"So what are we to do?" Raphael asked.

"Do?" Tuckworth responded wearily. "What can we do?"

"Father, we must try to do something for the poor man," Lucy insisted. "He can't be expected to do for himself."

"Lucy, we can't meddle in this. It's beyond us now."

"Beyond us," she repeated in dismay. "When is compassion beyond us? When is righting an outrageous wrong beyond us?"

"Do we know that Adam didn't do it?" Tuckworth asked fiercely, looking from one to the other of the young, hopeful faces before him. "Can we be certain, I mean completely certain, that this arrest is a mistake?" The two youthful brows clouded with doubt, and Tuckworth felt a dull ache in his heart to see it. Yet he continued. "Adam is like a child, and have you never seen a child lash out in rage? As often as the poor man was abused by that fiend, and as often as he saw his sister beaten at his hands, mightn't he have finally had enough? Couldn't he have done it?" Tuckworth sounded cold and logical, and his words almost succeeded in convincing himself.

"But they've arrested him for the murder of Will Shaperston, too," said Raphael.

Now it was Tuckworth's brow that clouded over in uncertainty. "Are you sure of that?" he asked.

"They're accusing him of both murders," Raphael said again.

The vicar sat forward in his chair. "But what reason on earth would Adam have to murder Will?"

"They haven't said. They feel convinced that he killed Mallard, so they assume he must have killed the sexton."

That's insanity, Tuckworth thought. He sat so still now, sunk deep in reflection, that the raven fluttered down from its perch and dropped awkwardly onto his knee. He stretched out an idle hand and scratched its head. "Where is he now, the inspector?" Tuckworth asked at last.

"He must still be at the constabulary-house. I only just left there to bring you the news."

Tuckworth took the bird on his hand and placed it gently atop the bookcase once more. Then, without looking for his topcoat or neckerchief, he charged out into the looming dusk. Raphael came along beside him. "Stay with Lucy," Tuckworth commanded. "I won't be long."

Lucy trotted up behind, pulling on a hooded cape. "I'll not be left back," she insisted, in the same severe tone her father used. "Besides, Mrs. Cutler's right. Poor Mary needs our charity as much as her brother does. Perhaps more."

Tuckworth glowered uselessly at the two, then turned and marched ahead to the Bellminster constabulary-house. It was a house indeed, an old pile of flats afforded new life by the sudden and awkward growth of the town, hastily purchased with municipal funds and renamed for the scant force of officers that occupied it. A place where families once lived, it was now walled up with bricks and bars. Within, some few rooms were set aside for violent criminals, with sturdy locks and tiny doors, but most of the inmates wandered about the yard throughout the day, retiring at night to whichever dismal corner suited them. It was a casual sort of prison, designed primarily to house the drunken and the disruptive, the vagrant and the base villain, and Myles was at first outraged at its easy system. He had insisted that the suspect be locked in one of the dark cells, secure against any attempt on his behalf. But Mary's resolution to remain at her brother's side, coupled with Adam's continued docility in the face of his arrest, finally determined a compromise. The pair was given a suite of rooms for their own use, with barred windows and a sturdy door behind which they were locked and bolted, a guard standing by at all hours.

Detective Inspector Myles, on the other hand, was established in large, bright, comfortable apartments at the front of the building. Lamps burned from every wall and corner of these rooms, a flood of light from which no shadow might escape. Myles liked an office where everything was clean, everything laid out and open to view. It was to this suite of rooms that Tuckworth was directed when he arrived. Raphael, in the heat of his indignation, had wanted to accompany the vicar, but Tuckworth insisted he stay by Lucy while she sought out Mrs. Cutler, as much for his daughter's sake as that he might speak to the inspector alone.

Myles greeted Tuckworth with an extended hand and a satisfied smile. "Your local gazette has issued a special edition," he announced, indicating a single-leaf flyer lying upon the desk, bold capital letters blaring across the top, MURDERER IN CUSTODY! REIGN OF FEAR ENDS! JUSTICE TRIUMPHANT!

"Yes," Tuckworth acknowledged, blinking painfully in the light. "You've made rather quick work of things, Inspector. I wonder it hasn't been too quick."

"How do you mean?" Myles asked, sitting down now behind the neat, orderly desk and motioning Tuckworth to take a seat. The vicar remained standing, however.

"I just heard the news myself, and was wondering what you had discovered after I left to lead you to suspect Adam Black."

The inspector chuckled. "I'd have thought the matter was obvious, Vicar. Mallard the abusive type. Sister in constant dread for herself. Imbecile brother finally takes matters into his own hands. Not that I don't sympathize with the fellow, of course. Only that's not my job. Sympathy falls more in your line, doesn't it? Making an arrest, that's what I'm paid to do." This last was spoken almost defiantly. Myles clearly understood the nature of this visit.

"Yes, it makes perfect sense for the murder of Josiah Mallard," Tuckworth continued politely, almost pleasantly. "There is at least a cause there, if no clear evidence."

"Need I remind you of the whitewashed stone? It came from Mallard's cottage, a handy weapon for a simple mind."

"It certainly appears incriminating. But how were you able to connect Adam with Will Shaperston? I'm sure that took a remarkable feat of detection."

Myles coughed. "As to that, we became privy to information that implicates the fellow beyond question."

"Might I ask what this evidence is? I'm only curious, you realize, but Will's death does concern me directly."

Myles hesitated for an instant, then brought himself up stiffly, as though he were accepting a challenge. "An eyewitness."

"A witness?" Tuckworth blurted, and the inspector grinned at his evident surprise. "You mean someone saw the murder?"

"Not the murder, no. But the victim and Black were seen in company on the day of the murder, walking out in the direction of the woods."

"Who saw them?"

"That's privileged, I'm sorry," Myles announced formally. "I can't say, but doubtless you'll be present for the trial. It should come up in two days' time. You'll see her give her own testimony then."

"Her?" and Tuckworth leapt at once to the answer. "Polly Burdon?" Myles rearranged a stack of papers on his desk. "It's Pol, isn't it?"

The inspector looked sharply at Tuckworth, rising slowly, prepared to end this discussion. "I'm not at liberty to say, Vicar."

"Good God, Myles, don't you realize what sort of creature you're dealing with?" Tuckworth had known Polly Burdon to be a notorious gossip, but he had never suspected that she was so depraved as to implicate an innocent man in murder. The two men stood for a moment, confronting each other, sizing up each other, two minds well matched, two wills equally set to their conflicting ends, the inspector's certainty a wall held fast against the assault of Tuckworth's outrage. Yet before the vicar could say anything further, the door to the inspector's office burst open and McWhirter stormed in with a cloud of petty administrators about him.

"Brilliant goddamn work, Inspector!" he bellowed before seeing Tuckworth. "Sorry, Vicar. Brilliant work! Soon as I heard, I had to come up myself and commend you. Myself, sir! McWhirter. Owner of the mill. I must confess, I'll be the first to admit it, I was skeptical of bringing Bow Street up here. Loss of time and opportunity. Needless delay. But you're a man I respect, sir! No dawdling for you, sir! No shilly-shallying! No buggering about! Brilliant damn work!" And the petty administrators echoed this acclaim wholeheartedly, shunting Tuckworth aside in their flurry of praise, leaving him to fume in a corner.

"My thanks, Mr. McWhirter," Myles said and, looking over at Tuckworth, he added, "Funny you should enter at this moment. The vicar was just reprimanding me on my haste."

"What!" A host of withering looks were cast upon Tuckworth, who stood his ground silently against them. "Well, the clerical nature, eh, Vicar?" McWhirter trumpeted, willing to be magnanimous in victory. "All forgiveness and sacrifice. Turning the other cheek. Can't abide to see the wickedness in his fellow man."

"On the contrary, McWhirter," the vicar shot back, "sometimes I think I'm too aware of the wickedness about me. Good evening, gentlemen," and he squeezed out the door.

Tuckworth went off at once in search of the others. He had no trouble locating them. As the first murderer ever to be detained in the constabulary-house, Adam Black was awarded a kind of celebrity, and every inmate and officer about the place knew where to find his cell. When Tuckworth arrived, Mrs. Cutler, Lucy and Raphael were all arguing at the door with an officious-looking constable.

"If you can't let me in, at least allow the ladies to enter!" Raphael was insisting. "Certainly you can't suspect either of them!"

"I knows my orders, and I'll stick to 'em," the fellow pronounced crisply, with a military lift to his chin and a puff of his chest.

"What's going on here?" Tuckworth asked, still smarting after his interview with Myles.

"Father!" Lucy exclaimed, pointing an accusing finger at the guard. "This man won't let us in, and we can't offer comfort through an oak door."

Tuckworth looked the man over. He was young, a petty official of the constabulary, undoubtedly occupying the lowest rung of authority on the force. He was only fulfilling his duty, and it would have been a simple matter to sympathize with the poor lad. But Tuckworth was no longer in a mood for sympathy.

He stepped up to the guard, his nose mere inches from the fellow's face. "Do you know who I am?" he demanded.

"Yes, Vicar," the guard answered, startled.

"Then you open that blasted door and let me in there! Those people need the consolation of religion, and by God, I'm going to give it to them!"

The guard fumbled for his keys, dropping them twice before managing to get the door open. The whole party stepped forward to go in. "Excuse me, Vicar," the fellow pleaded, "but I'd appreciate it if only you was to go in there. I has my orders," and he grinned sheepishly.

Tuckworth gave him a hard look, but then softened and motioned for Mrs. Cutler to go in ahead of him. "Lucy, you and Raphael wait here. We won't be long." Lucy wanted to object, but one look from her father and she held her tongue. The guard, appearing satisfied with this arrangement, renewed his officious posture.

The room was hardly less bare than the cottage Tuckworth had been in earlier that day, though not so mean. The chairs were hard but sturdy, the wallpaper stained though bright and cheery, and on a nearby table the leftover scraps of a prodigious meal spoke of a fuller cupboard than Adam and Mary had known for many months. The pair sat side by side in a window seat overlooking the prison yard, and the last faint light of the setting sun managed to stream through the dirty glass and light their pale faces warmly.

"Can I go out tomorrow then, Mary?" Adam was asking, looking down into the yard.

"No, Adam," she said, her voice sounding calm and easy. "I'm afraid not tomorrow, either. But that's all right. We'll have games what we can play here, won't we? And fun of our own making is fun twice over, ain't it?" She looked at the vicar and Mrs. Cutler as they entered, her eyes brimming with fear.

Adam glanced over as well, and his face lit up. "Hello, Vicar!" he greeted happily.

"Hello, Adam." Tuckworth smiled. "How are you?"

"See, Vicar," the man announced, sweeping his hand across the room. "It's our new home, Mary says. Ain't it nice? Only"—and a shadow darkened his face—"only, we can't go outside yet. But that's all right, ain't it?"

"Yes, it's grand, Adam. A lovely home." And Tuckworth cringed within to think that he had played a role in this miserable affair. "Adam, why don't you show Mrs. Cutler the other rooms, while I speak with Mary for a bit?"

"That's right, love," said Mrs. Cutler, stepping over and taking Adam's large, meaty fingers in her own. "Let's have a look about, shall we? And you can show me all the fine ways you'll pass the time here, and the games you'll be playing."

They moved off to another room, and Tuckworth sat in the window seat next to Mary.

"He don't understand, and that's a blessing," Mary whispered. She appeared even paler and more frail than she had that morning, and Tuckworth's heart bled at the child's suffering. He patted her delicate hand and tried to comfort her.

"Mary," he murmured softly, but before he could utter the least soothing word to her, she grasped him about the neck and wetted his collar with silent tears.

"Help us, Vicar," she sobbed softly. "Please God, we got nobody else, and I ain't up to this alone. If you won't help us, Adam's done, and there ain't nothing for it but to let him . . . to let him . . ." but she couldn't finish the thought. She choked with grief at the mere imagining of it.

"Mary," Tuckworth said at last, putting his arms about her and whispering in her ear. It was clear the girl didn't want Adam to know of her sorrow. "Mary, you must be brave, child, and answer a few questions for me. Just a very few."

"But I've already answered all their questions," she cried. "They come back after you left, and they asked all them same questions over again, all sorts of different ways. And then they clapped the irons on Adam, and the poor dear was that frighted!" Her words died out in sobs once more.

The same game, question and answer, and yet it must be played. "And you told them nothing new? Nothing you forgot to mention while I was there?"

"I don't think so," she muttered. "It's hard on me, Vicar. You've got to know how hard it is to remember it all right now."

"And what did you tell them?"

"Only the truth, so help me God!"

"Yes, of course you did. And what might that truth be?"

The girl pulled herself up and dried her eyes. "They asked me what I knowed about Jo's running off that last time. And I told them he never made nothing of his comings and goings. He only just vanished, that's all. We expected him at supper and he never showed. But we kept a place for him every day at table, as he liked us to be ready should he come back. It's the same as I told that inspector when you was there!"

"I see. You're doing splendidly," Tuckworth assured her with a smile, though within he was struggling, frantic to form these simple facts into an accusation of murder. What might the authorities have learned that he had missed? What questions was he neglecting to ask? What answers did he lack? Tuckworth looked down into the yard, at the shades gathering now below, the night rising out of its hole to take charge of the world, and a chill passed through him. "Mary, did the inspector ask you again about Mallard's acquaintances at the alehouse? Did he inquire after any other enemies Jo might have had?"

Mary thought for a moment. "No, sir. Not that I could have told about them. Jo was close about such things. The inspector only asked me about Adam, and where he'd been over the past days. But he'd been with me the whole time, just stepping out to play a bit in the garden."

"Mary," Tuckworth continued, "did you know Will Shaperston?"

"The sexton? Only as to point him out in the street. Never to speak to."

"Did Mallard ever know him?"

"Not to mention."

"Excellent, child. You've done bravely, as I knew you would. I have one last question, and it might seem an odd one. Is there any reason you can think of that Polly Burdon might owe you a grudge? Anything at all?"

"Polly Burdon?" Mary looked puzzled. "Old Pol the witch? I ain't never shared two words with her. Nor has Adam, that I knows on."

Tuckworth nodded. "That's fine. Now, do you think you'll be all right here? Is there anything you two want, anything at all?"

"Only help us, Vicar," she implored once more, her voice sounding more desperate now, a note of wild energy creeping upon her. "Help us, please. Adam needs me, that's certain enough, but I need him, too. More than anyone might think, I need him." And she pressed her damp cheek against Tuckworth's shoulder again and sobbed.

"I'll do what I can," he tried to comfort her. But what could he do? he thought. Realistically, what was there that might be done for Adam Black? Even his own doubts had not been stifled by this interview. Wasn't it too probable that Adam had killed Mallard in a fit of passion? Wasn't that the assumption around which Myles was building his case, constructing it out of scraps of hearsay and supposition, not so much discovering the truth as prying it out of the available evidence by force? And what did it matter if Tuckworth was convinced of Adam's innocence? What could he do? Myles appeared quite content with his solution. No other possibilities seemed to interest him. No other suspect appeared half so inviting. And the inspector had the formidable resources of the constabulary to call upon. Against this, what could Tuckworth do?

They left, and, as Tuckworth and Mrs. Cutler, Lucy and Raphael went back out into the black of approaching midnight, such doubts and fears assailed the vicar as left him empty within. They were all turning to him, yet what had he to offer? Tuckworth walked apart, alone, with only his dark mood to keep him company.

Unable to contain his curiosity, Raphael came up at last beside the vicar and asked, "Did you learn anything, sir?"

"No." Tuckworth shook his head. The night looked bleak to Tuckworth, and he kept his head hung low before him, scanning the dust at his feet, the refuse of the town blowing through the deserted streets. Through his mind, a single thought rattled about like a scrap caught on the breeze, tossed absently from one side to the other, thrown here and there so that some vague light might shine a bit of understanding upon it. "What has Polly Burdon got to do with this?" he muttered, more to himself than for Raphael's benefit.

"That's simple enough," Raphael replied.

"What?" Tuckworth pulled up and looked at his young companion. "What have you heard?"

"I was talking to the guard while you were inside. Old Pol got two pounds for her evidence, and she'll get two more for her testimony. That's more than the woman will see in six months."

"Four pounds!" Tuckworth exclaimed. "They bought their case from her!" And he felt the final flicker of their last hope die away inside him. He stood there, in the street, unable for a moment to proceed, feeling utterly beaten. What could he do against such men, Myles and McWhirter and the rest, men who could purchase away a human life for four pounds? What could he do? What could they expect him to do?

CHAPTER THE SEVENTH
TOPHET

uckworth locked himself in his study. Not locked, precisely, for they had no need of locks and bolts in the vicarage. Yet the women knew this was his sanctuary. Not even Mrs. Cutler with her dust rag might enter this inviolable cell without the vicar's leave. He ensconced himself there, in the one place on earth his own, where he might escape it all, the frets and worries, the gossip and the whispering. But he could not escape those pleading eyes. Alone he sat, yet Mary Black sat with him, beside him, at his elbow as he surveyed the chess table.

An interesting problem, to capture the queen. What might he be willing to lose in order to remove her from the game, with all her strength and mobility? His mind scanned the possibilities, looked briefly into myriad futures, sacrificed a pawn one time, a bishop the next, arranged his men in phantom order, moves leading to moves, prodding her along, forcing her to go this way and that, trying to impel her into an inescapable trap. With the prescience of an experienced gamesman, he peered three, four, five moves ahead. But he did not raise a hand to the board. What could he do? What could any of them expect him to do?

Lucy and Raphael, they were young, at an age when wanting to do good is all, when life is still a storybook filled with happy endings. His child, whom he had protected from so much that was hurtful in life, whom he had sheltered and shielded from doubt, she couldn't understand. He saw it when she looked at him, her belief that he could save Adam Black from the gallows, the strength she placed in him to answer her faith. Even Raphael, trained as he was to the supreme control of his art, even he confused hope with certainty, believed that good must triumph at last, that life somehow was ordered so. They, who had never learned life's pain, the dreadful agony of doubt, for whom GOOD was writ large in golden letters by a holy hand, how were they to understand? How might they know the awful price exacted from this "doing good"?

He abandoned the chessboard, sat back in his chair and let his vision drift across the ceiling, a blank expanse offering the comfort of emptiness to his troubled mind. They had no right to beg so much of him, he thought pettishly. He might do what he could to comfort Mary Black, to ease her suffering. He might even squeeze a drop of charity from the parish, he might do that, give her the freedom of her life again. But for Adam? There was nothing he could do. Inspector Myles had established his suspect, arranged his pieces in order, was advancing with the inexorable weight of justice behind him, blind and deaf. No other solution interested the Bow Street man, no alternatives were to be pursued, no bothersome doubts would be entertained. Only build the case, brick on brick, stone upon stone. Tuckworth recalled McWhirter's words of just the day before. "Find a likely candidate and hang the fellow!" That prophetic command must prove true enough in the end.

Tuckworth glanced down at the floor below the door that led into the cathedral. A flash of something had caught his eye, a movement of something white. He rose and, opening the door, looked about in the little side chapel. It was empty. He stepped out into the aisle, stared about the nave. Nothing, not even the sound of footsteps to disturb that holy place. Turning back, he found upon the hard floor a piece of paper folded into an envelope. Tuckworth picked it up and returned to his study.

He turned the paper over. Upon its front, in large letters scrawled by a nervous hand, he read: *TUCKWORTH*. The note was sealed on the back, a blob of red wax with no mark upon it. He reached for a letter opener and gently pried the seal away. Unfolding the paper, he read in the same anxious handwriting: *THE INNOCENT AND RIGHTEOUS SLAY THOU NOT.* What is this? Tuckworth thought. Scripture? Below the printed line was an address. The vicar did not know the place, but he knew the street, as disreputable a district as Bellminster had seen spring up this twelve-month past. The rough patina of new red brick couldn't disguise the filth that bred there, as it were overnight. Low, dirty and diseased, inhabited by the sort of creatures that cling to the underbelly of society, it was a region to be avoided at the height of noon, and most especially after dark.

Tuckworth looked left and right, half expecting to see the author of this cryptic note standing in the study with him, materializing out of the shadows. A chill passed through him. The day had been long already. It appeared that it was not over yet.

He stuffed the paper into his pocket and left the study. Lucy and Raphael were still in the parlor, and he could hear Mrs. Cutler rattling about the kitchen. Reaching for his overcoat, for the night promised a killing frost, he turned to the others.

"Raphael, stay by Lucy until my return. I have an errand to run."

"Is it something I can help you with, sir?" Raphael asked excitedly.

In truth, Tuckworth would have welcomed his company. But whoever had dropped that note outside his door was not far away, and this thought left a sickening qualm in the pit of his heart for the safety of his child. "No, I'll not be gone long. You wait here." Then, considering for a moment, he stepped to the writing table and scrawled the address quickly on a piece of paper, folding it and sealing it with wax. "This is where I'll be. If I'm not back by midnight, I want you to take this to Inspector Myles."

"Father!" Lucy gasped.

"It's just a precaution, my dear," he tried vainly to reassure her. "A simple precaution." So, with a halfhearted smile and a gentle kiss atop Lucy's head, Tuckworth stepped out into the night.

Night in Bellminster once more, darkness seeping out of its hiding places to swallow the town in twilight. Clouds coursed across the moon, wispy harpies obscuring her pale glow for a time, devouring her light with avaricious hunger, then sliding past and allowing her beams to escape again to earth. The dust and soot of the mill whipped up the bank from the Medwin Ford, but Tuckworth, pulling his collar tight about him, defied this incessant blow, trod in the face of the wind, descended into the bottom of the town. The streets were not yet empty, not entirely. Occasionally a shaded figure would hurry past, clutching at a coat with one hand, pressing a hat down upon a shadowy head with the other. The sound of footsteps, solitary, echoing, only heightened the strangeness of the scene, as though the vicar were treading the boards of a stage after the audience had gone home and the lights had been extinguished, leaving behind that pervasive sort of loneliness that seems to creep into our peopled world from another place, a separate reality not ours, though like enough.

After a time, Tuckworth left behind the familiar buildings of the old Bellminster and made his way through the new town, the brick town. Gradually, the streets he wandered were less deserted, though no less strange. From time to time he passed the garish glare of a pub, drunken revelry spreading out from the doors like a pool in his path, and he would be forced to weave through stumbling bodies clinging to one another for support, or to step over wasted figures who had no one to raise them up from the filth of the gutter. Tuckworth found himself staying to the shadows, avoiding the company of the streets, moving with furtive, secret steps. The darkness became a comfort to him in this alien place.

As he neared the mill, the grit spewing from its three grasping smokestacks pervaded the air, darkened the moon, stung his eyes and sank into his skin. He had wandered these awful streets before in daylight, to bring solace to such dregs of life as were forced to live beside this behemoth of industry, in the shadow of its relentless toil, amid the mud and squalor. Yet never after sunset. Here, now, by the uncertain glow of the waning moon, humanity seemed out of place. What pubs he passed offered drink but no company, no songs to split the desperate stillness of the dark, no camaraderie with which to face the bleakness of another night, another far-off day.

Rotting offal covered the lanes and mixed its steaming odor with the tainted smells of piss and beer, and worse. Even the moon, veiled behind a sudden bank of clouds, hid her slender face from such depravity as gathered here. The lone inhabitants kept to themselves, separate, aloof. The only companionship in this forsaken hell lurked in the darkness, accompanied by the rustle of soiled petticoats, the vulgar whispers of painted lips. Here, in the bottom of the town, even comfort was but a commodity, bartered for and sold.

Tuckworth pulled the paper from his pocket and huddled himself in the faint light of a nearby window. He looked again at the address, assured himself that he was where he meant to be. It would not do to lose himself now.

A harsh voice, raspy with tobacco and gin, breathed by his ear. "How'dja like a patch o' cunny, love?" and a hand groped at him from behind.

He jumped and spun about, his heart bursting, his lungs gasping at the stale, fetid air. "I . . . no, I only. . . ." A shape stepped out of the shadows into the pale light. She was dressed in the cast-off elegance of another time, her skirt soiled beyond color, her bodice straining to encase the ample flesh that peeked through in rents and tears, her bosom hoisted in grotesque display. He could not see her face, kept hidden under a shapeless hat. "I—I'm looking . . ." he stammered, and held out the address in trembling hands.

With a gurgling cough, the whore stepped closer to him, and Tuckworth's nostrils flared at the sweaty stench of her. "Can't read, love," she cooed terribly.

"Number forty-one," he managed. "Totham's Boardinghouse, top floor, back."

She stopped and made an annoyed, snorting sound. With a jerk of her head she indicated a pile of brick across the street. Then, certain that they had no further business together, she vanished back into the darkness.

He crossed over and stood for a time in front of the building, no boardinghouse except by name, just a mean block of flats. It was new. All these buildings were new. And yet it already showed signs of neglect: rubbish heaped against walls; drooping shutters with rusting hinges and missing slats; flecks of paint sanded away by the wind. Of the numbers that once had been drawn upon the lintel above the door, only a chipped, haggard "1" was left.

Tuckworth entered into a lightless hallway. A staircase thrust almost straight up into the blackness. Somewhere a man was singing the remnants of a tune. An airless reek permeated the building, and Tuckworth dug out a handkerchief and clutched it to his nose. He climbed into the night, his eyes adjusting quickly to this nether-world, this realm of grays and deeper grays. He huffed breathlessly as he made his way past one floor to the next, and the next. The smell got stronger as he rose, more fetid, more stifling, until finally, at the top of the stairway, on the fourth floor, it seemed almost to brush past him in the air.

He stepped down the short hall to the last door. There was no way to be certain that this was the address, save one. Tuckworth knocked and waited. Nothing happened. He knocked again, rapped sharply on the thin wood. The man below kept singing, but no other sound broke the spell of the place. Tuckworth took one deep breath, almost retching on the rotten stink, and tried the knob. The door opened easily, almost readily, as though it had been waiting for someone to open it. Tuckworth stuck in his head and whispered, "Hello?"

It was a single room. Through a small casement window with broken glass, the moon shot rays of milky light. Against a wall stood a chest of drawers with a mirror tilted back and overwrought finery strewn across the top. From a line strung across the opposite wall, mildewed rags hung limply toward the floor. In front of Tuckworth rested a bed. Upon the bed lay a figure, naked, bound to the corners of the posts and gagged. Desiccated, gaunt, wasted, it had once been human. Its skin was now darkened, like tanned leather. A gaping slit in its throat lay open to the night air. Black bile ran in congealed streaks down the side of the sheet on which she lay. Blood caked and crusted about her, frozen upon the mutilated breastbone. On a table by the bed, two black lumps, hard, shriveled flesh, sat with a stiletto blade placed between them.

Tuckworth convulsed, reached to hide his eyes from this unholy vision, turned and stumbled back to the stairs, dropping to his knees, heaving. His spectacles fell from his face, and he did not see them sail down, down, into the blackness below.

BOOK II

CHAPTER THE EIGHTH
"WHAT IS TRUTH?"

hat was she?"

"Some whore."

The words throbbed in Tuckworth's memory as he sat, forgotten amid the plodding ritual of the investigation. Acolytes of the law shuffled about, collecting evidence, studying the victim, examining the most minute articles of her wardrobe and her dressing table, formulating theories and suspicions. Tuckworth sat, and he remembered. It was only a chance exchange, the passing comments of two minor officers overheard as they strode by him in the stifling darkness of the landing, yet the words resounded in his thoughts like a melody one cannot release. "Some whore." Tuckworth remembered, and as he remembered his chin dropped slowly to his breast.

He threw his head back with a jolt. How could he doze at such a time, in such a place? He must keep himself alert. There was work for him yet to do. He rubbed his eyes and was surprised once more to find that his spectacles were not there. They had been shattered where they fell below, after that first wild convulsion. He tried to rouse himself, but he could not breathe, had not drawn a healthy breath since he had stumbled down the stairs hours before, rushing headlong into the street, shocked by the slap of the night's cold hand. Running, running from that thing in the garret. Even in his anguish he had known he must control the urge to cry out, to wake the town, warning them of the danger that lurked so near. He must not cause a panic. She had kept there, undisturbed for days, perhaps weeks, and she would stay there alone for a time still, until he could bring assistance.

He had fled down the street madly, hoping for a cab, though none dared wander into that district after dark. So he trod on, a wraith in the fleeting moonlight. The night shadows swarmed about him as he moved through the town. Fear gripped at him from every black alley along the way. From around corners and down dark and dreary lanes, evil reached out to him with the chilling odor of mortality. How long? he wondered as he raced ahead, and his thoughts stumbled and reeled against the blunt terror of the night. How long has this horror been beside me? How many days have I lived not knowing a fiend is out here, preying on the world? How many nights have I slept in uneasy slumber, unaware that the nightmare lay at hand, not in fantasy but in the town, in the streets of Bellminster? How long? Tuckworth ran. He ran as though the dogs of hell were snapping at his heels.

He had reached at last the constabulary-house and returned with Myles and a squad of officers.

"What was she?"

"Some whore."

A nameless woman. Myles had been unable to discover even that much about her. The sort of tawdry creature whose identity changed nightly, almost hourly. Agnes, Sue, Nancy, Helen—she had been known by all of these names, and as many more, so that finally she was known only by what she was: some whore. And yet now her life was fixed to Tuckworth's, like a parasitic vine that buries its roots deep into the heart of the oak, clinging even in death, inescapable, grasping, demanding his life in exchange for her mystery. What was she? Why had he been led to her, forced to discover her? What was her connection to Mallard, to Will? And why was he trapped within this affair at all, this grotesque gallery of slayings? Who was drawing him into this madness? The questions lay open like an ulcer inside him.

He had already spoken to Myles, told everything that had led him to this place, showed the note, described how it had materialized. The inspector seemed irked, almost angry at this new murder, and displayed little more than a cursory interest in the investigation. Yet Tuckworth had asked to wait. He wanted to speak to Myles privately when his official duties were concluded. For surely this discovery altered their situation. The woman had been dead at least a month. He heard Dr. Warrick affirm as much. She had been tied to the bed, her throat cut and her body mutilated, then left to rot for weeks in that pathetic hovel where even the stench of decay might be ignored. Surely this exonerated Adam Black. Though the man might have had cause enough to murder Mallard, and though Myles might manufacture a case against him for Will Shaperston's death, surely they could not believe the sorry fellow had a hand in this wretched business.

A disturbance roused the vicar from his reverie. A commotion below reached up to him through the dark and the fetid air.

"None but official members of the constabulary," Tuckworth heard an officer stating. The constables had been hard put to chase away the curious gathering in the street, and by now a formidable crowd was assembled. "Move along with you before you end up back at the constabulary-house yourself."

"I must get through to see the vicar!" an angry voice replied. "I have an important message I must deliver to him!"

It was Raphael. He would have waited until midnight, then opened the note Tuckworth had scrawled, read the address, and hurried after. Rash fellow, the vicar thought. Still, he was glad to have him there now.

"Excuse me." Tuckworth turned to Constable Wily standing nearby. "Could you hurry below and ask them to let that fellow pass, please?"

"Sorry, Vicar," Wily answered. "We've all been placed under strictest orders. Naught in, naught out, till inspector says different."

"Yes, but if you might stretch your orders somewhat, I would be obliged to you."

"Not without sufficient reason, Vicar. Afeared I couldn't."

Tuckworth looked at the constable, pleading. "I could use the company, Wily."

Constable Wily considered for a moment with a look that tried to be cold, then leaned over the railing. "Parkins! Pass that fellow through!"

Raphael bounded up the staircase, almost running past the vicar in his excitement. "Sir, are you well?" he asked breathlessly.

"I'm fine, Raphael. But how are you? And Lucy?"

"She's worried, of course she is, sir," he panted. "When we read your note, I'm afraid she became agitated. She insisted I run after you while she went off to the constabulary-house."

"She must be there now," Tuckworth considered. "That's as well. She'll be safe, and she'll know as much as she needs to about this matter."

Raphael looked about for the first time, and his eyes turned toward the room down the hall. A mass of figures at the door kept him from seeing within. "Is she in there still?" he asked in a morbid hush.

"Do you know of this already?"

Raphael nodded. "Out in the street they're saying she was dismembered entirely, left in bits about the room."

"Oh, dear God!" Tuckworth exclaimed. "No, it's not as bad as that, though bad enough." Just then the figures about the door stepped back, and two men along with Dr. Warrick proceeded down the hall, carrying between them a long, stiff pallet draped with a sheet bound by cords. Tuckworth rose as it passed, reaching again for the phantom spectacles as he turned his face away, certain of what lay beneath the sheet, trying to forget the image of that woman on the bed. Raphael stared intently at the white form, however, studying it with a dispassionate eye that labored to delve its secrets.

"Wait here," Tuckworth told him after it had gone. "I want a private word with the inspector," and the vicar moved off down the hallway, toward the room.

Myles was conferring with Hopgood, issuing some terse orders to the officers milling about, looking miserable in the midst of the hubbub and confusion of a half dozen men laboring in a room so close and airless. "Excuse me, Inspector," Tuckworth hemmed, squeezing through to stand beside Myles, "might I have a moment?"

Myles turned toward him wearily. "I thought you'd left, Vicar," he replied, clearly wishing that Tuckworth had.

"I wanted to ask you about Adam Black," Tuckworth began.

"I'm not at liberty to discuss the prisoner at this time."

"Yes, but I wouldn't want him to be overlooked in all of this," continued Tuckworth with a sweeping glance at the bustle of work going on about them. "His release—"

"It's for a jury to decide that, at the trial," Myles cut in.

Tuckworth stood silent for a moment, trying to understand what these words meant. He could not believe, not at once, that Adam remained a suspect in this, and his mind tried vainly to place some other meaning to the inspector's pronouncement. "But you're not proceeding on the assumption that Adam Black murdered this woman?" he asked finally.

Myles glared at Tuckworth and something within him, something base and crude that threatened violence, crept up from beneath the depths of the man's professional demeanor. "I'll not discuss this matter with you. Not now."

"We will discuss it now," Tuckworth answered warmly, abashed at such stupidity. "That poor fellow has no one to look after his interests but me, and I'll not abandon him just because it inconveniences you."

"Not now!" Myles shouted, his ire boiling over, his voice taking on the clipped accents of the London streets. "Look here, old sod! I've had about enough of your interference! I don't take kindly to it, not during my investigations, not from any quarter, least of all not from some nosy bleeding priest!" Tuckworth could see the anger he had witnessed before shake Myles again, like the tremors accompanying an eruption, and he felt his own temper leap to the occasion, unwilling to yield. Yet reason told him this would only hurt his cause, to antagonize the one person he must appeal to. Myles was frustrated, watching his case fall to pieces about him, and he must not be pushed too hard, not yet. Tuckworth stilled his mind, therefore, breathed evenly, and steadied the impetuous beating of his heart.

"My curiosity is doubtless a great annoyance to you, Inspector," he managed at last, calmly, soothingly. "But you must believe that my interest here is more than the meddlesome needling of some amateur."

"Your interest is getting in the way of official police procedure."

"Damn your procedure!" It was Raphael. The inspector's shouting had drawn him into the room, and now he rushed to the vicar's side. "Your police procedure has muddled this business from beginning to end!"

"Somebody get these two out of here!" Myles roared, and Tuckworth tried to back his young protector out of the room. But Raphael would not be silenced now.

"You've managed to arrest the only innocent man involved in all of this! And now you're ignoring the one man who can help you!"

"Raphael, that's enough!" Tuckworth pleaded, but too late. Myles pounced upon the two, pushing them through the door until they stumbled and sprawled at his feet. Raphael was up again in an instant, eyes defiant, fists clenched, muscles tense and quivering. His anger seared the air about them. His legs bent, and his whole weight seemed ready to rush upon Myles, who stood, crouched and deadly, in the doorway.

A cry from Tuckworth ended the confrontation as quickly as it had flared. "My knee!" he groaned. Raphael stooped to his aid at once.

"Can you rise, sir?"

"Yes, just give me your arm." And together the two men came up from the ground. When they turned back to Myles, he was standing stiff and impassive, his anger once more buried.

"I'm sorry," the inspector muttered, almost embarrassed, and then turned and disappeared into the room. The officers in the hallway stood about nervously, looking on while Tuckworth and Raphael limped back down the stairs, the one resting his weight upon the other's shoulder.

When they reached the street the weight miraculously disappeared. "Well, that was quite the adventure," the vicar chuckled as they passed through the crowd, flexing his knee to get the stiffness out.

"Are you healthy, sir?" Raphael asked, concerned.

"I'm not so frail as all that, my boy. I'm well. But you might control your temper better next time," and he cast an admonishing eye upon his companion. "That man is not to be provoked, not needlessly. He'd have throttled you as freely as shake your hand." Tuckworth glanced over his shoulder at the light wavering in the upper-story window. "He's dangerous, Raphael."

"Dangerous how, sir?"

Tuckworth did not answer. He only thought to himself that there was a great deal of anger in Myles, a world-weary resentment kept ever in check, like a bullterrier on a taut leash, held back though always snarling. "You needn't fear him, I think," he said. "Only don't provoke him. Not needlessly."

The two walked along in silence for a moment. "What do we do now, sir?" Raphael asked.

"Now we collect Lucy, if she's still at the constabulary-house. Then home to bed. I feel like I haven't slept in a fortnight."

"And then?"

"Then I'll pay another visit to our friend the inspector. Alone." Raphael looked away guiltily, and Tuckworth placed an arm about his shoulders. The vicar felt oddly cheered, in spite of his aching fatigue. "Don't fret too much, lad. Your little set-to might actually have done us some good."

"How's that?"

Tuckworth sighed, able to breathe at last in the cold air. "No more questions tonight, Raphael. Why don't you run ahead and find us a cab?" And the young man trotted off into the darkness, leaving Tuckworth to rub his tired eyes, to clear his head, and to nurture the faint ember of hope that glowed finally in his heart.

The next morning found the vicar once more (and far earlier than he might have wished) in the neat, well-lit office of Inspector Myles. The inspector rose deferentially as Tuckworth entered and offered him a chair.

"I apologize for my rashness of last night, Reverend Tuckworth," Myles began formally. "Should you wish to file a complaint against me with the department, I'll not challenge it."

"What's this?" Tuckworth exclaimed, feeling confident, supremely confident. "I suppose two intelligent men can have a difference of opinion without having to file complaints afterwards. It's I who should ask your pardon for the behavior of my friend Mr. Amaldi. Youth, you know," and he smiled easily across the clean desktop.

This magnanimity seemed to make Myles even more self-conscious, and he fumbled with some papers for a moment, spreading them haphazardly before him. "I believe you wished to ask me about the prisoner Black," he mumbled. "I'll try to answer you as fully as I may. But understand, nothing I tell you is to leave this room."

Tuckworth nodded agreeably, considering within himself that forgiveness has its uses beyond the good of one's conscience. "So," the vicar began, "what's this you were telling me about Adam Black going to trial over this murder? Surely that theory is played out. The real murderer slipped that note under my door last night."

"Someone slipped a note under your door," Myles replied in his officious manner, tidying his desk once more and folding his hands before him. "I can't say who. I doubt the murderer would be so bold as to advertise his handiwork. More likely it was someone who found the whore, some low character from the neighborhood with his own purpose for keeping out of this."

"Even more reason to delay these proceedings against Adam. How can the trial go on with so many questions unanswered?"

"And what questions might those be, then?"

Tuckworth paused for a moment. He had thought the matter self-evident. "Why, the question of cause, for one. Why would Adam do it?"

"I couldn't say."

"When would he have had the opportunity? How could he, a poor simpleton with the mind of a child, devise such a thing as we saw last night?"

"Again, I couldn't say."

"But the murder of this woman—"

"—is not at issue here, Vicar," and Myles's voice carried a sharp note of finality to it. "We've two murders already for which Black has been arrested and charged. It's for those crimes that he'll stand in the dock. The murder of this whore is a separate concern, and as it's still under investigation, I'm afraid I can't tell you anything more about it."

Tuckworth hesitated. He knew that the inspector would be reluctant to admit his mistake, would fight against any kind of retraction. But he had been so sure that this new murder must prove Adam's salvation. It was a perverse hope, but it was real nonetheless. He had rehearsed this conversation in his mind, prepared for every objection, every logical excuse not to release the man, and in the end he had hung all his expectations on the certainty that Adam could not have done this awful thing, in a place he could never have been, to a woman he could never have known. Myles must see that. Yet now Tuckworth felt betrayed by his certainty; and the hope, which he had tended and trimmed into a modest flame, flickered. "I don't understand. Are you saying you believe there's a second murderer?"

"I believe nothing. Belief isn't my business. I'm in the job of ending this, Vicar. I do it by producing likely suspects. I give them up to the magistrate and then wash my hands of them."

"But finding out the truth behind this horror, uncovering what really happened, isn't that what we've been working to accomplish?"

"Truth?" Myles spat out. "What's that? I'll show you a dozen truths that explain what's been happening here, each one contradicting the other eleven. The only one that's real is the one that puts a man at the end of a rope. You'll forgive me. I'm not a religious man. Truth is something people come to you for, not me. You tell them things that feel certain and sure. You give them faith. But now their lives are threatened. Their safety is shattered so your truth can't rebuild it and their faith's no good to them. So now they come to me."

"And you give them a sacrifice?"

"Fine. A sacrifice. That suits me as well as anything."

Tuckworth shifted in his chair. He had never imagined the conversation would proceed in this manner, and he felt the hope within him dying, extinguished with a puff of air. He tried to rouse his anger, but his heart was too beaten down, his spirit too buffeted and bruised. He was so tired.

"Vicar," Myles continued, sounding almost sympathetic, "the people of this town want to sleep soundly again. They want to think the murders are over. I give them a suspect, one that fits the available facts. Perhaps another suspect will do as well, perhaps not. That's more than I know. What I do know is that the case against Adam Black is good enough for a hanging."

"But the man is innocent," Tuckworth stated.

"Did no innocent man ever hang before now?" Myles answered chillingly. "Twelve men will form their own opinions on Black's innocence. That's the chance he has. But a hanging will put an end to these murders, that I promise you."

"How? How in heaven's name will an innocent man's death accomplish that?"

"By giving the guilty man a reason to stop."

Tuckworth sat frozen for an instant, horrified at the steely pragmatism of this cruelly modern man. "So the killer gets away and it all ends there? Is that it?"

Myles nodded. "If Black is not the man—and I don't say he is or he isn't—but if he is not, then his death will still finish this. Believe me, no man will continue to risk his own neck when he's offered the chance to get off scot-free. So either way, your town will sleep peacefully again."

Tuckworth lowered his eyes to the floor, lost in the recognition that he was mistaken, fatally mistaken, about the investigation, about Myles, about everything. He had played his hand, almost every card, and only now did he realize that he failed to understand the game, or the ruthless nature of his opponent. "And what of justice?" he asked feebly.

"It keeps company with truth. There's no romance in what I do, Vicar. It's a cold, brutal profession, no holy calling like yours."

Tuckworth rose abruptly. "Forgive me for wasting your time, Inspector."

"One thing more, Vicar," Myles said, standing. "I want you to know that your assistance in this has been noted and acknowledged. You've been entered in the report, officially recognized for your co-operation and insight." The inspector tried a friendly smile, though it seemed oddly out of place on his lips. "You have a detective's gift for intuition, you know. You'd make a welcome addition to the force, if you weren't such a religious man."

The words pricked Tuckworth like a red-hot needle. If this is the force, he considered, the devil can have it. He stepped back outside, into the diffused light of a cold morning. Clouds gathered across the sky in great flocks, toying with the sunlight, scattering it here and there upon the wind, like the hope that always seemed to be dying in Tuckworth's breast, never wholly dead. He looked up into the sky. There were two more avenues still to explore, two appeals that might do some small good. The one seemed improbable, it's true, and the other frankly impossible, but they must be at-tempted. Every effort must be made. Yet a dread cowered deep within Tuckworth, the fear that accompanies a man's last rattling gasp. He filled his lungs with the sharp, chill air and set his steps toward Granby Hall.

Before he could venture very far, however, he was waylaid by an importunate voice. He turned and saw the rector pacing slowly down the street toward him.

"Mr. Tuckworth," Mortimer said by way of greeting.

"Mortimer." Tuckworth nodded in reply. "Oh, hello, March. I didn't see you there."

The curate stepped out from behind the rector, bobbed a quick hello, then stepped back again.

"They said at the vicarage that I might find you here," Mortimer began, the formalities having been dealt with. "I see you have just come from the constabulary-house. I trust all is well with you. No need on your part for the civil authorities?"

"No," Tuckworth answered.

"I see. Then you were ministering to the unfortunate prisoner?"

"No, actually. I was going over some matters with Inspector Myles."

"Really?" the rector answered in feigned surprise. "Does the inspector require religious guidance, Mr. Tuckworth?"

Tuckworth sighed. There was no avoiding this, then. "I have been attempting to assist him in his investigation," he admitted.

Mortimer looked knowingly at the vicar, and a cold smile creased his lips. "Yes, I had thought as much. There is a deal of talk about your . . . shall we call it your contribution to the constabulary?"

"I'm only doing what I can to put a stop to this business," Tuckworth said wearily, trapped into defending himself.

"Yes, I'm told you were at it all day yesterday. The Sabbath was made for other labors I think, Reverend Tuckworth. Besides the business is already at an end, as I understand it. The man Black has been apprehended."

"If you must know, Mortimer, I'm not entirely convinced of Black's guilt in this."

Mortimer coughed. "You will pardon me if I ask, but is it really within your sphere to be satisfied as to the man's guilt?"

Tuckworth could feel his temper fraying in the middle, like a rope pulled too taut to hold. "I only wish to get to the truth," he announced.

"Yes, of course. But our realm is spiritual truth, Vicar. These sublunary matters, these earthly affairs, don't properly concern us." The rector was being indulgent, and this paternal manner from one so comparatively young irked the vicar. "Oughtn't we to turn our attentions to this higher plane," Mortimer continued, "and leave such worldly investigations to those better suited to deal with them? Your efforts are causing a great deal of talk, and—honestly, now—they can do very little good at this late stage."

"Yes. Well, then I suppose I can't do any harm in continuing my efforts, either. Good day, Rector."

Yet Mortimer was a master at having the last word. "I will bid you a good day, Vicar," he said, with a menace that, in him, seemed almost petulant, "with this one admonition. Keep to your own sphere, Mr. Tuckworth. Serve the greater truth, sir, and not the lesser." And with that, the rector spun about and sailed off.

Mr. March was left behind, for only a fleeting instant, yet in that instant he looked imploringly into the vicar's eyes with a confused appeal, and Tuckworth felt his anger melt momentarily inside him. "The fellow can't have done it, Vicar," the curate murmured. "Help him."

"Of course, March. I'll do whatever I can," Tuckworth assured him.

"March!" the rector called irritably, and Mr. March scurried away, back to Mortimer's shadow.

It was already early in the afternoon by the time Tuckworth appeared along the shaded drive and approached the medieval splendor of the ancestral home of the Earls of Granby. A great deal of activity was in progress about the estate, for, inspired by the cathedral (and by McWhirter's expansive mansion), His Lordship had begun his own project of restoration. A new wing was going up, a mass of Gothic pretension to dwarf the stone simplicity of the original hall, and an army of laborers set about the place like ants, scurrying and hurrying under the astute direction of no one in particular. It took Tuckworth some time to locate Lord Granby amid all the noise, and more time still to extricate him from the excitement of construction and get him into the garden, where His Lordship could devote his entire attention to the vicar's appeal. Unfortunately, it took less time than that for Tuckworth to receive his answer.

"Afraid I can't help you, Tuckworth," Granby told him as they walked along through the neatly manicured hedges and elaborate topiary. "It's not for me to interfere in this. I set it all rolling, you understand. Myles is here at my express invitation, with my banknotes in his pocket. I've paid for his assistance, and if I were to step into it at this point and intercede for Adam Black . . . well, it wouldn't look right, now, would it? Might send the wrong message."

"The wrong message?" questioned Tuckworth.

"It's politics, old fellow," Granby explained. "Filthy politics. We're expecting elections soon, and, just between us, that McWhirter chap is going to put forward his own man for Parliament. Try to take the borough right away from us. I'll tell you, confidentially, now, I don't like that man. Too forward. Too much of this modern air about him. All business, business, business. No thought for the people."

"Do the people include Adam Black?" Tuckworth muttered, sounding more bitter than he had intended.

Granby stopped and glared down upon the vicar. "None of that," he scolded, and Tuckworth cursed himself. "Now, I'm sorry for the fellow. I truly am. But this is politics, Tuckworth, and it's a mean, scurrilous business. Besides," His Lordship went on, returning to his stroll and his easy manner, "we can't really be certain that the fellow didn't do it, can we? Oughtn't we to leave that up to a jury? I think twelve good men can uncover the truth as well as you or I can, eh?"

Once again that word: truth. It had haunted Tuckworth his entire long walk out to Granby Hall, and it stayed with him as he began the whole long way back again. "What is truth?" He kept hearing Myles's voice in his head, asking that question over and over, like the ghost of Pontius Pilate, interrogating him, daring him to an answer. But not even the Gospels offered an answer to that question.

So he must come at last to his final hope, if hope it could be called. Tuckworth turned his steps away from the grandeur of Granby Hall and set his path across the fields, to a spot on the very outskirts of Bellminster, so distant that some refused to include it within the limits of the town at all, and glad they were to deny it a place. Only desperate fools walked out to Polly Burdon's cottage, it was said, for who but the foolhardy would want dealings with a witch?

CHAPTER THE NINTH
THE DAY OF CALAMITY

The autumn wind shook Tuckworth's overcoat as he descended through the failing sunlight into the dell. This wooded declivity amid the fields and pastures, little more than a pit caused by an errant pool that welled and bubbled at its heart, hid Polly Burdon from the rest of the curious world. The only sign of habitation one might detect from the lonely cow path skirting the place was a trail of smoke leading up to mingle with the clouds, a wispy vapor that seemed to point down toward a cottage, though it might just as easily have been a chance trick of the wandering mists that gathered regularly among the trees at dawn and twilight. For all its reclusive aspect, the road to Polly Burdon's den was not an untraveled one. Often enough some young girl might be seen disappearing into that misty valley, some poor, sweet creature who required the conjurings of Old Pol to restore her good name before it was proved forever false. And as every farmer about Bellminster knew, a dry milk cow was a certain sign that Polly was angered with you and must be appeased. Any person with a grudge to practice against a neighbor, any desperate mother with a sick child whom the doctors had failed, any lovelorn spinster eager for the crushing heat of a rapt embrace might make such use of Pol's lore as a few shillings would purchase. As Tuckworth walked the darkening path to her door, he jingled the odd coins in his pocket, thinking to himself what might be done to move the old woman from her unwarranted vengeance against Adam

Black. But no plan formed itself to his aid. His mind was too tired, too wearied by the day's disappointments, and he felt within himself that his mission was a hopeless one.

He strode to the cottage door nonetheless. The trees of the dell grew right up to its walls, seeming to stand about as guardians of the place. Smoke tumbled from the mossy chimney to drift with the thin vapors creeping up from the pool, its still waters black and unhealthy beyond the garden gate. Within, Tuckworth could hear the murmurings of Polly Burdon, her voice screeching a melody of some kind, or an incantation.

Before he could reach the door, she called out to him. "Come in, come in. You've been keeping your own time gettin' here this day."

Transparent trick, he thought as he pushed open the creaking door, to convince the impressionable traveler that Polly knew already of his coming. "Good day, Polly," he said as he stepped over the threshold.

"Good e'en, Vicar," she corrected him, without looking up and with no hint of surprise in her attitude. She was hunched over a precariously large fire, tending to a kettle that simmered and danced above the flames. The cottage was mean and dark, a foul-smelling, dank, dismal cloister that suited its occupant well, with dried herbs bound and hanging from the rafters like so many bats suspended in their daylight slumbers, pots and jars of every shape massing along the walls like the faithful assembled within some ancient temple, a smattering of furniture that seemed to have been hewn from the sticks that fell about the place, and a thick grease covering all, the renderings of a fire that never went out. In a corner, a mottled gray cat chewed unconcernedly at the entrails of a rat.

Polly turned from the fire, though she remained hunched and bent, and pointed a withered hand toward a hard chair. "Sit, Vicar, and let me take the tea off the hob."

Tuckworth recoiled at the idea of tasting anything from the woman's larder, but he silenced these qualms as he sat down and smiled when she handed him a drop of weak tea in a cracked cup. "I've come, Polly," he began, "to ask you a favor."

"A favor, is it?" she cackled as she sat opposite him, a harsh, breathless sort of laugh. "Ain't I come up in the world, to have Vicar askin' favors o' poor Pol."

"It's about Adam Black."

"I knows what it's about." She nodded, making the whiskers of her chin bob obscenely in the air. "You been busyin' all about town for that poor man, ain't you, Vicar? Shame to see a feller go to bad like that, but the gallows gets them as it deserves." She made a clucking noise, a pitying sort of sound, then reached into a deep pocket of her frock and pulled out a black stump of root. Taking a bite off of it and replacing the rest, she sat chewing for a time, then made the clucking noise once more, muttering, "Bad business. Bad business."

"Polly," Tuckworth started anew, "you know the poor man is innocent."

"Is that what I knows?" she answered sharply, her eyes black and malevolent for an instant. Then she grinned. "I must say, it's a great sufferance t' have a nice ol' chap like yoursel' tell me as much as I knows. It saves the wear on me poor nut," and she tapped a dry finger against her forehead.

Tuckworth took a deep breath to calm his frayed temper, and the sickly sweet aroma of the tea tickled the back of his throat. "Tell me, Polly," he tried again, "what is it you saw that day? When you say Adam and Will Shaperston went wandering out together toward the Estwold, what exactly happened?"

"Ain't no good tryin' that, neither," she crowed. "I'm under magistrate's orders not to say a word on't."

Tuckworth knew he would get nowhere with the old crone. There had always been tension between the two, not that they ever had dealings. Yet, as often as not, the same troubled souls who came to Tuckworth for the healing balm of grace would later find themselves in Pol's cottage searching for a more worldly intervention. They were competitors on the market for men's souls, his faith against her superstition, and Tuckworth had forgotten some time ago where the difference lay between them. He shook his head. "What is it, Polly?" he asked. "What have you against Adam Black?

Or is it Mary you're trying to hurt? For my very life, I can't comprehend what your interest is in this."

"Nor I yours ol' Vic'." She cackled maliciously, rising and stepping toward the fire to tend her boiling pot. She threw in a handful of leaves and herbs, sending an acrid, pungent odor to assault Tuckworth's senses. "This ain't no business o' your'n, Vicar, not at all. Must be tirin' to them bones, walkin' every step of the county to find . . . now, what is it you're seekin' after? Or don't you rightly know yoursel'?" Polly spat into the flames, and a hissing puff of steam went sailing to the rafters.

There it was. Tuckworth glanced about the cluttered shelves and shadowy corners of the place as though they were the appointments of his own mind. What was he after? The release of a man for murder? But what was that to him? Why did he bother himself so much? He had tried. Every effort that could reasonably be made he had tried. If he failed, what of it? Would the loss of Adam Black make the world any bleaker than it already was? Or if he miraculously succeeded, would the man's salvation touch the ache in his heart and ease his secret suffering? Polly was right. He didn't know what he was searching for, not really, not in himself. He sat, turned to stone in his chair, while Polly rattled about her pots and jars.

"Sorry thing, Vic'," she muttered sympathetically, in tones that almost soothed his weary soul. "Poor ol' feller runnin' about. Do better just to leave it be. Like that pot over the fire. Get itsel' done whether he meddles in't or no."

"I've got to meddle, Pol," he admitted quietly. "I can't leave off, not though I wished to. Those people are counting on me."

"I knows how 'tis," she cooed. "Folks place their faith in the ol' man, just as they come to poor Pol to cure their ills. And my little bit of potions does some good, 'cause I b'lieves they does some good, and I makes others b'lieve it. But what's Vicar place his faith on, that's what I wonder. I gots my herbs and roots for them as needs conjurin', but what's Vicar b'lieve in that might truly help folk?"

Tuckworth awoke from his trance and stared at the woman with her back to him, bustling about her mixtures as though he were gone from the place. What was she intimating? What was Polly guessing at? Was she only taunting him with his failure? Or could she perhaps see into the heart of a man, as the gossips of Bellminster whispered? He suddenly felt exposed before her, this wizened old hag, unable to hide his deepest secrets from her knowing eye, and he was frightened. He must leave, get away from her weird influence before it was too late. Why had he even come here at all? What did he want from Polly Burdon? Tuckworth rose and spilled the tea down his trouser leg. He pulled out a handkerchief and began dabbing at the stain, while Polly stood aside and chuckled. The sound of her mocking laughter returned Tuckworth to himself. This was not about him, he recalled. He was there to help Adam Black, and she was blurring his thoughts, confusing his intentions. She toyed with him like the cat with its meat. But he saw at last what her true interest was. In a flash, he could suddenly read her purpose, and the realization stirred his anger to life.

"Four pounds!"

"What's that?" Polly asked, turning about, her voice no longer soothing but gruff and harsh.

"That's all you believe in. Four pounds. You never saw Adam and Will together. It's all a lie to extract your blood money, paid in installments for the delivery of Adam Black to the hangman."

Polly stiffened and her eyes narrowed to murderous slits. "That's my lookout, ol' Vicar," she spat. "I seen what I seen, but it's a fool that gives what might just as well be sold."

"What of eight pounds, then?" Tuckworth offered.

"Eh?"

"Adam's soul is worth only four pounds to the inspector. What if I offer eight to redeem it?"

Polly hesitated. It was clear she had not expected such a bargain, and she weighed it seriously, very seriously. In the end, however, she rejected his offer. "I'd look the pretty fool, wouldn't I?" she muttered meanly. "No, me word's not for sale to you, Vic'. Like a young girl's maidenhead, eh? Only to be purchased once, or what's the value on't?" And Polly cackled at her rude jest.

This was senseless. Yet a quick inspiration showed the vicar another way that he might reach the old woman. "Well, it was worth the trip to make the offer," he mused, shaking his head and turning toward the door. "I'm sorry to find you so resolute, Polly Burdon. Adam Black never crossed you, so far as I am aware, and I don't know why you would do such a thing to him. Still, I suppose it's something the two of you will work out between you in time."

"Eh?" Polly croaked. "What're you goin' on about?"

"Nothing, Pol. Only, I'm sure you have your reasons for sending an innocent man to a place where he can find no rest. His spirit will be deeply put out with you."

The woman sank into a fitful study. "That idiot ain't got enough spirit in him to fill me thimble," she growled.

"I'm sure you're right, Polly. There's naught to fear. No harm can come back to haunt you over this filthy business, that's certain. Good e'en to you, Pol." And Tuckworth left, feeling that, at the very least, he had given the old witch something to consider in the darkness of her solitude.

The stars had already started to glimmer along the deep blue of the horizon as he came out of the dell and back into the world. Before he had traveled a mile, night settled in over the country, and it was very late when he finally approached the houses of Bellminster. Along the road, Tuckworth had passed no one, and with only his thoughts to accompany him on the way, it was a very long and lonely journey indeed. Pleased as he might be at shaking Polly Burdon in her confidence, that victory was short-lived. In truth, his wanderings had produced nothing that even smelled like hope. He looked up to find the stars, but clouds obscured the heavens from his sight. Adam Black was that many hours closer to the gallows than he had been this morning, Tuckworth knew, and there was nothing he could think to do for the man. Every card had been played, every trick lost. His hand was now empty, as empty as the night that surrounded him. Despair was not unknown to him. He lived with it, buried in his soul, deep in his heart, every hour of the day. Yet what he felt now was bleaker and more irrevocable than anything he had felt for himself. Why should he suffer so for Adam Black? What was there in this that touched him? Why did he feel that it was his own life he was fighting for, his own soul being sent to the grave? He received no answer but the stabbing pain of failure.

When Tuckworth walked through the door of the vicarage at last, Lucy rushed to him, folding him in a hard embrace.

"Where in heaven's name have you been?" she asked, half scolding, her voice mixed with relief and the remains of apprehension.

"I've just been about the county on Adam's behalf," he answered, startled at this intensity of feeling elicited by his return. "Have I done something wrong?"

"No, of course not, dear," she replied, relaxed now and managing an embarrassed smile. "It's only, with these terrible killings, I fear every minute you're away."

Tuckworth took her face gently in his icy hands. "Lucy, we can't allow ourselves to be ruled by fear," he advised lovingly.

Mrs. Cutler burst through the pantry door. "Well, you can be ruled by a decent sense of the time! Now take off that overcoat and you can eat the cold leavings of a Christian meal."

Her idea of "cold leavings" might as easily be described as a small banquet, and Tuckworth gladly settled behind a juicy roast, a lamb pasty, trout, cabbage and potatoes, brown bread, cheese and ale. The stomach has its own memory, and while he was eating the only true meal he had enjoyed since breakfast, all worries left him. Having exercised his appetite sufficiently and retired to the parlor, however, Tuckworth could feel the cares and concerns of the day mass together to fall back upon him, and he sat in his easy chair looking as uneasy as one conceivably might in such homely surroundings.

Lucy had seen him like this countless times, head bowed, brow creased and furrowed, eyes looking vaguely out at the nothing before him, and her heart ached to witness his suffering. What caused it, this brooding temper, this black mood that had sunk into their home, quietly, stealthily, a miasma of despair that even Mrs. Cutler had commented upon? These awful murders, the town's macabre amusement at this horror, even her father's fruitless efforts to rescue poor Adam from his fate—these had only pressed upon the hurt in his soul. Yet something else there was, at the heart of his pain, something she had noticed for many and many a month now, but could never approach. He would not let her.

How Lucy longed to rest a soothing hand upon that brow, to raise that head up to her hopeful gaze, to lend her light to his life and dispel the darkness that had gathered there. As soon as she tried to comfort him, however, he would smile a wan, mirthless smile, stay but a moment for form's sake, and then retire to the seclusion of his study, little knowing that he thus confined her to a seclusion no less painful than his own. More painful, rather, for it was a hurt not hers to heal, only to suffer. It was pain doubled by longing, trebled by futility and frustration, a vain hope to be the answer to a question unasked, and in her less guarded moments Lucy could feel her anger swell toward her father, that he should be so silent, so willful, not trusting that her heart was large enough to encompass his as well. As the anger rose, it would subside, leaving behind the flotsam of her confused emotions. Rare creature, little did she know herself how much her heart could hold.

She breathed a long, slow breath to hold back the tears she would never let fall. Lucy approached her father, and he, lost once more in his cloudy solitude, did not mark her nearness. She sat on the floor at his feet and curled up her legs, laying her head in his lap, inviting his hand to smooth her dark hair as he had done when she was a child. His thoughtless fingers laced themselves among her locks, idly stroking, delicately caressing her with a tenderness he had felt but not shown for too long a time. She closed her eyes and was a little girl again, and he the father, the protector, the keeper of her joy.

"Father," she whispered, lest her breath disturb the air between them, "I'm frightened."

"Don't, my dear," he reassured her, "don't fret. This thing won't hurt you, I swear it."

"No, not for that, dear heart, but for you. I'm afraid of this melancholy that descends on you. I'm afraid we'll never be happy, truly happy, again."

He reached down and lifted her head up, that he might look into her eyes. "Am I that bad, Lucy?" he asked.

She dared not admit, but could not deny, that he had indeed become a morose, sorrowing man, close and secretive, a shadow of what he had been. "Tell me, please, what's troubling you?" she implored. "Whatever it is, only tell me and I know I can help."

"It's just this business with Adam," he answered, not very convincingly. "I've failed that boy. I've failed him miserably."

"No, that's not it. This is something else, something that started long before. For months you've kept your distance from me, from your work and everyone who needs you. Why?"

Tuckworth looked off and was silent for a time. Finally he patted her head and said, "I'm just growing old, pet. Old and tired and sad. I suppose melancholy is a natural enough reaction to having outlived one's lifetime."

"Don't say it, dear!" commanded Lucy. "You're as vital as ever you were, if only you'd dare to be. Look at all you've done today. What other man would try half so much? That's why the people of this parish look to you. Every day they tell me how you are missed. And whatever keeps you from them, I can help you overcome it! Father, give me the chance to prove I can be of help to you!"

"But I'm leaving all that behind, Lucy. I'm retiring, and people will have to learn to get on without me."

"You're retiring from your position, not from life!"

Tuckworth hung his head. "I'm sorry, child. I don't mean to burden you. But you must believe, I am becoming an old man, that's all. And if that thought causes me some sorrow now, I'm certain to get over it. In time, my pet, in time." Then, with another pat of her head, Tuckworth rose and went into his study, leaving Lucy behind once more. Some minutes later she rose, too, and climbed the lonely stairs to her room.

Alone, Tuckworth leaned against the shut door of the study, cursing his weakness. Why did he cause so much suffering? What malignance within him forced this pain upon those nearest to his heart? What would it take to stop this nameless contagion? A word?

And what word was that? To tell Lucy, who had shaped her soul under the gentle force of his guidance, who had learned charity and mercy from the daily pulpit of his life, to confess to her that he no longer believed? What might it do to her and to her religion? He had once been so proud of her deep devotion to God, had watched the child at prayer, the young girl studying her scripture and acting upon it, making its lessons a part of her natural love for all things. Could he be responsible for shaking that faith? Or would his revelation only lead to revulsion? If her faith was preserved, could her love for him survive? And if he lost that, if the light of admiration was to die in her eyes, the love a father clings to slip through his fingers, how could he live?

Tuckworth dropped into a nearby chair, his elbows on his knees, his head gripped in his hands. Questions, a sea of questions rushed over him like waves against the shore, one after the other, dragging him down. Yet no answers came to him, to lift him up. Only the same silence, the same emptiness as always, the nothing that now pervaded his world.

Hours of darkness stretched over Bellminster. The clouds continued to gather, making a dark deeper than night. Tuckworth stirred at last, and took himself out into the cathedral, not to heal his pain, but to forget his soul's sickness. There was no starlight to stream through the windows this night, and the candles of the altar glowed like an island of pale luminescence in a sea of chaos. Still, Tuckworth knew every step of his way, every footfall and flagstone, the rutted paths that had become worn by generations of devotion. He proceeded about the nave, his slow tread falling lightly as he went, yet with a relentless pace, as if he were pursuing some phantom ahead of him, unseen in the darkness. Suddenly he bumped against something, and it seemed that the void had congealed to stop his way. His hands reached out and grasped the rough edge of a wooden post. The scaffold, of course, he thought, and he paused to rest in a pew.

A sound drifted down to him, so soft it seemed the silence itself had been given a voice. "Forgive me."

"What was that?" Tuckworth whispered back, for only whispers sounded proper in this place, at this hour.

"Forgive me!" A voice overhead, amid the scaffolding.

"I'm sorry, but you must come down from there," Tuckworth insisted anxiously. "You might fall, you know." But there was no answer this time. "Hello?" he tried once more. "Are you there?"

"Forgive me!"

"Of course, of course you'll be forgiven! Only come down here and let's talk about it!"

"No!" the voice hissed down at him. Then, more calmly, "God's voice beckons to me here."

Tuckworth winced. An enthusiast, he thought ruefully. He had met with such believers before, keepers of a feverish, almost feral faith that demanded the most remarkable absurdities to express itself. Usually it meant some poor old grandmother spending days in the cathedral at a time, forgoing food and drink, keeping on her knees until they bled, praying herself into sickness. "As far as hearing God, I should think His voice would carry down here," Tuckworth offered, growing uneasy, but he got no reply. "What is your sin?"

"I have been called," the voice stated flatly.

"Well, there's no sin in that."

"I doubt my calling!"

This was too near his own condition for Tuckworth's comfort, and he pitied the poor man above, seeking absolution from a failed confessor. "Doubt isn't exactly a sin, you know," he tried comforting the man.

"It's the mark of sin! The door to damnation!"

"Very well," Tuckworth acknowledged, acceding to the man's guilt, "suppose you have sinned. There's little I can do to help you while you stay up there. Come down and we'll talk." Tuckworth was frantic now at this precarious situation, some zealous disciple groping about, stories above the stone floor, ready to lose his footing in the thick shadows overhead. Besides, there was something unsettling in the man's fervid appeal, a note to his voice that almost frightened him.

"Forgive me," was all the answer he received, however.

So, Tuckworth considered, if the man requires a confession,

then it must be carried out like this. "Tell me," he asked, "what is it God has called you to do?"

"Kill."

The word came softly down to Tuckworth's ear, but it rang through the vastness of the cathedral like the tolling of a bell. He sat, how long he could not say, his heart keeping uncertain time in the dark.

"And whom does God ask you to kill?"

"The unrepentant."

Tuckworth gripped the pew in front of him and noticed that his palms were moist. With some part of his mind that refused to accept this, that rejected the fearful implications of the man's confession, he reached into his pocket and took out a handkerchief, wiping the perspiration from the cool, smooth surface of the wood.

"Who are the unrepentant?" he asked at last.

"Agnes."

"Agnes?"

"Mallard."

"You killed Josiah Mallard? And Will Shaperston?"

"Sinners all, unrepentant of their sin!"

The vast world rushed in upon Tuckworth, smothering him so that he could not move, could not even gasp. The weight of stone about him felt as though it would crush his body and burst his heart. His mind struggled to release itself from this paralysis of panic. And in his brain the words screamed silently, *It's him!* He was up there, looking down. His hands gripped the rough wood overhead, hands bloody with the murders of three souls upon them. His thoughts were working toward diabolical ends Tuckworth could not fathom, his eyes seeing where Tuckworth was blind, his ears hearing where Tuckworth was deaf. The vicar stood and reeled, dizzy with fear and confusion. He reached out and grasped the scaffold to steady his trembling. What must he do? How could he escape? The flames about the altar flickered miles away from him now, and he stood alone in the darkness. Yet a thrill deep within, some separate part of himself that embraced this moment in all its terror, slowly began to control his fear, to still his pounding blood. Here was Adam's salvation, he thought. Somehow, this must prove the way. He turned his eyes upward toward the vault and tried to pierce its black curtain, squinting, raising his hand to the spectacles that were not there.

"Have you come to kill me?" he asked, his voice quavering only slightly.

"No."

"Then you must come down and let me help you."

"No."

"But an innocent man is paying for your crimes. Surely you can't allow this. God cannot want you to allow this."

No answer came at once, and when at last the voice replied, Tuckworth had to strain to catch the words.

"You must save him."

"We must be God's agents together, you and I, to rescue Adam Black."

"No!" the voice spat into the darkness. "*You* must be his salvation!"

"But I've tried," Tuckworth confessed. "I've tried and it's no use, not without your help."

"They have profaned God's plan!" the voice above ranted, filled with anger and indignation. "They seek His will in a shattered vessel!"

"What? Do you mean Adam?"

"*I* am the will of God. *I* am His rod of chastisement."

"Y-yes, yes," Tuckworth stammered. "Of course you are, but—"

"They lay God's divine acts at the feet of a child. They have failed to heed the message."

Tuckworth was floundering now, drowning in this rising tide of madness. How could he induce the man to give himself over to authority? "They believe you'll stop killing if they hang Adam," he tried.

Again there was a long and chilling silence before the voice answered. "The day of their calamity is at hand."

No use, Tuckworth realized. The man was too single-minded, too filled with a passion of faith turned around upon itself. There must be another way. This moment couldn't be lost, for Adam's sake. This man must be made to return, to come back when Tuckworth could bring another, anyone who might corroborate this impossible scene. "Will you write me a note?" he ventured.

"A note?"

"Yes, you've done it before. Last night, that note you slipped under my door. Give me another. A note that might prove Adam's innocence. Something I can take to the authorities." The voice was silent. "We can meet again like this tomorrow, and you can give it to me then. Surely that's not too much, just a note to save a man's life. And we can talk some more, about your message."

A pause, and then, "Tomorrow." And a stillness like a curtain dropped over the cathedral.

Tuckworth stood for an instant, looking up. Nothing stirred. No sound descended to reveal the movements of his fiendish companion. It all seemed suddenly unreal, as though the entire conversation had occurred in some other place, some separate time. Tuckworth started slowly back to the vicarage, but as he moved, the fear he had kept suppressed gripped him at last, and he found himself hurrying, running through the darkness, stumbling until he reached the safety of his study, bolting the door behind him.

He sat there the rest of the night, staring at the locked door, waiting for the dawn.

CHAPTER THE TENTH
CONJURINGS

"Vicar is a ol' fool," Polly Burdon complained as she puttered about her cottage, disturbing the dust and the cobwebs. She moved pots about on the shelves, trying to find one in particular, an old earthenware jar with arcane scrawls scratched on its painted surface, a very rare receptacle for a very priceless herb. For hours, now, ever since Tuckworth had left, the old woman had fretted and fussed over the vicar's parting words. It was a grave matter, to have a dead man's soul turned against you, and Polly had failed to enter that fact into her mental ledger. She was always calculating what profit might fall her way from any enterprise and was a great one for finding gain where others saw only scruples. But this time, the lure of four pounds sterling had sparkled in her eyes, blinding her to the darker consequences of her perjury. She might lie against the living easily and keep free from worry, but to lie against the dead, that was a thing she attempted only at her peril. And Adam Black would be dead soon enough.

Now she would have to take precautions. Not that the work was beyond her powers. She had battled the fairy world often and harnessed its spirits to her will. But this was different, and it required subtle care. Polly needed a protector, a jailer, a strong familiar who might keep Adam where he belonged among the dead, not hovering between the spheres to persecute the living. Summoning such a spirit would require an especially potent incantation.

Finding the jar at last, Polly opened the lid to inhale the rich, almost heady scent of the root. Some knew it by one name and some another, but she had learned its lore as Spiritflox, for it had an aroma that carried beyond life. Satisfied for the moment, Polly turned her attention back to the bubbling pot over the fire. A simple thing, that, though it took time and a deal of attention. Throw in the proper herbs, let it simmer through a frosty night, mix it with bone meal and salt the next morning to make a cake, bake it and give it to someone you wish to get over, some fellow you have dealings with or a maiden you want to tumble. Soon her vital spirits flag, her sanguinary humors ebb as the phlegm rises in her veins. A chill settles over her heart, making her more compliant to suggestion, less firm in her resolve. Dread Cakes, Polly called them.

A hiss erupted behind her, and she turned a sharp eye to the corner where her mottled cat was standing, back arched, fur bristling as it faced the door. Polly reached into a cupboard by the fire and tossed a piece of meat at the creature, which instantly relaxed. Strange, she thought. Not near dawn yet, and sure to be black as the inside of a sack without. Still, folks keep their own hours, and hers weren't particularly regular if it came to that. She waited a moment and then called aloud, "Come in, if you've a mind to warm yourself this cold night!"

No one entered. She hesitated a moment longer, then called more loudly still, "Come in, I tell ya! I've no use for your bashful airs!" Only silence answered her cry.

Polly leered at the cat languidly chewing its treat. "Are you losin' your good senses, Wick?" she remarked. "Is it the pot for you soon? I'll not have you hangin' about 'less you earns your keep." The cat ignored this dire threat, however, and continued to gnaw at the strip of flesh between its paws.

Outside, the wind ruffled the tops of the trees but failed to descend with any force into the dell, only nudging the gathering mists into strange, unreal shapes that lost themselves amid the shadows. The glow from Polly's fire sneaked out the windows of her cottage and the cracks in the door and casements, but did not travel far before the darkness swallowed it. Beyond the fragile boundary of her gate, no ray could pierce the gloom, no eye discern what figures might be moving there. The sound of a sudden gust stirred the corpses of the leaves on the forest floor, though no breeze blew.

One shadow among the army of shadows detached itself from the darkness and eased its way farther down the path to Polly's door. It passed through the gate silently, its cautious tread making no more noise than the smoke issuing from above. It approached the window and looked with cold, colorless eyes into the cottage, at the old woman hunched over her pot. It paused, in no hurry, certain of its intent, confident of its cause. It merely watched as the minutes passed by, just one more shadow stopping by the way, one more idle spirit attending to the old witch at her conjurings.

Yet time was passing, and there was work to be done before dawn approached. A sidling step, a hand upon the latch, a moment longer to wait, and then the hinges screamed as the door flew open.

Polly spun about, a cry held on her lips. The cat cowered in its corner, protecting its meat. The fire flared in raging protest, yet all to no purpose. A figure cloaked in black swooped across the room and fell upon the witch. Strong, squat fingers reached out of the formlessness and grasped her throat, pressing the cry back down inside her. With brittle claws she tried to fend it off, this shape, this devil, tried to reach its face, its eyes, but with a madman's strength it shook her like a bundle of rags, squeezing tighter, tighter, so that she could not even let a final rasping breath escape to mark her death. Her hands ceased their frantic scraping of the air. Her lips stopped their silent screams. The blackness sank into her eyes.

He let her drop to the floor. Reaching into the deeper darkness of his cloak, he pulled out a sack and shook it open. It took some bit of time to work it over her limp form, but she was a wisp of a woman, and he was strong enough to shoulder the burden of her with little effort. He left, the fire still burning in the hearth, the smoke rising out of the chimney. He passed with his bundle out the door, back into the shadows, into the night.

The cat looked cautiously about the empty room, and then returned to its meat.

CHAPTER THE ELEVENTH
CHECKMATE

uckworth took the better part of two hours the next morning persuading Myles to come with him into the cathedral that night. The vicar's eyes were red and stinging, his head woolen, his mouth dry, but in the end he succeeded: one small success after a short history of failure. It had not been a certain thing, not by any means, and Tuckworth was forced to invoke Lord Granby's name (on specious authority) before the inspector would entertain the notion of a midnight vigil. Even then, Myles had seemed at times on the verge of another eruption, his patience taxed by what he termed "this damn foolish persistence in a lost cause." Such zealous confessions were common in notorious and noteworthy cases, he asserted, and might be discounted out of hand. Yet Tuckworth was able to inject just enough doubt into the man, to infect the inspector with his own querulous curiosity, so that he elicited at last a promise to meet at the vicarage no later then ten o'clock.

Droplets of moisture, not quite sleet yet sharper than rain, were falling when Tuckworth came out of the constabulary-house. Pulling up his collar, the vicar hung his head and walked back home. His mind was empty. He carried no thoughts about with him any longer, no plans or schemes. His work was almost finished, and nothing he might do now could help or hinder his cause further. He had only to bring two men together, Myles and the mysterious figure on the scaffold, and his labors for Adam Black would be accomplished. Or so he hoped. For the time being, he allowed the blessing of a torpid numbness to embrace him.

Arriving at the vicarage, he told Lucy briefly how matters stood, let Mrs. Cutler know he would not be having luncheon, and crawled into bed, where he stayed for the remainder of the day, sleeping the deathlike slumber of a child. And if, occasionally, his rest was accompanied by plaintive cries and haunting moans that set Mrs. Cutler wringing her hands and Lucy saying a silent prayer, and if his dreams were infested with shapeless figures swooping through the air, tortured inventions of the mind, phantoms of darkness and mad fear, what child's slumbers are not plagued by nightmarish fancies? Rest how he might, Tuckworth slept through all the hours of the day, and that was a benison of sorts.

Tuckworth arose after nightfall, his muscles aching and his head still cloudy, and descended to the parlor to discover Raphael in close conference with Lucy upon the settee. The sight pleased him in spite of his misgivings about the lad, an artist's life, after all, being no pattern for stability. He coughed once before entering the room, so as not to surprise the young couple.

"Father"—Lucy turned to him, a look of resolution upon her face—"Raphael is going to join you tonight."

"What?" Tuckworth exclaimed.

"I'm joining you and the inspector," Raphael said, rising.

The vicar shook his head. "Out of the question. I've had enough trouble getting Myles this far. I'll not jeopardize my progress by bringing the two of you together again."

"But that's precisely why I must be there, sir," Raphael insisted. "Can you really trust the man to report what he sees tonight? He's already manipulated and sequestered facts about this case. That dead woman in the garret, for one, and Old Polly's evidence. You must have a third pair of eyes present, someone to hold Myles to the truth."

Tuckworth paused. Of course, it was a very sane and logical precaution. Yet he wanted to keep this business as simple as possible, the fewer hands involved making for the greater chance of success. And he remembered the last time Myles and Raphael had met. He looked sidewise at the young man, who pulled himself up rather as a corporal on inspection.

"You promise me that you'll be silent, absolutely quiet. I don't want a word out of you that might cross Inspector Myles. Understood?" Raphael nodded so sharply that Tuckworth half expected a salute to follow. "All right. We'll see if the inspector agrees." That decided, the three went in to a late dinner and to await the final member of the night's party.

Myles was punctual, his knock at the door coinciding with the chimes of the clock on the wall. A terse, "Evening," was all his greeting as he stepped inside, a darkened lantern clutched in his fist, and looked in some surprise at the size of the company before him.

"If it's all the same to you, Myles," Tuckworth explained, "I'd like young Amaldi here to come with us."

"And why would you want that?" the inspector asked suspiciously.

Tuckworth thought over his answer, and then replied, "I'd like some corroboration for tonight's work. So that no disagreements can arise later." Myles appeared doubtful for a moment, but he acquiesced, though not without a look at Raphael that Tuckworth wished were more forgiving.

It had been one o'clock the night before when the vicar stumbled upon the man on the scaffolding. Tuckworth did not expect him before that hour again tonight, and the inspector had arrived early so as to avoid any chance discovery that might frighten away their quarry. They had almost three hours now to wait, and it was agreed that they should pass their time in the study. Tuckworth quickly ushered Myles into his sanctum, therefore, leaving Raphael behind to share a private word with Lucy.

"Raphael," she said, her voice strong and steady as she watched her father disappear behind the door, "do you think there's any real danger in this plan?"

"No, not much," he assured her. "There are three of us, after all. If this fellow attempts anything, we're more than enough to manage him, whoever he is."

"Look after Father still," she begged. "He slept so fitfully today, I know he's terribly afraid."

"Don't worry for him, Lucia. He's as safe by my side as you would be." Raphael spoke the words as tenderly as he could, looking upon her with eyes that searched for some sympathetic response, some fellow feeling, some clue as to what was passing in her heart. Her eyes met his, refusing to hide behind a coy modesty that did not become her so much as this proud stare. She looked at him, unflinching, determined, not willing to acknowledge the depth of his love, or her own profound affections, not entirely, not now. Yet her strength made her appear lovelier still.

"Raphael," she whispered, "take good care for yourself."

"Why look after myself, Lucia?" he implored her. "That I might return to hear you say you worried for my safety? That I might live to hear you utter a single word of genuine feeling for me?"

She had used to deflect these amorous advances with a laugh, but for some reason—she could not say what—her laughter gave way to a shy smile and a solitary tear. He caught her hand up suddenly, feverishly in his own and pressed it to his lips. A banging of pots from the kitchen startled them both, and Lucy withdrew her fingers, slowly. But she did not retire, and what was left to say between them passed in comparative silence.

On the other side of the study door, Myles appeared to relax as he entered that realm of masculine clutter, the musty shelves filled with random bric-a-brac, the overturned books like fallen leaves about the forest floor, balls of dust skittering along the wainscoting, glasses waiting to be washed with some more of the wine that had sullied them. He was not much startled when the bird hopped from its high perch atop a bookcase and fluttered onto Tuckworth's arm in its ungainly fashion. As neat and well-appointed as he kept his own offices, Myles found something about Tuckworth's slapdash system that appealed to him nonetheless, rather like a sinful liberty of his own too rarely indulged.

He gravitated to the single point of order in the room, the chessboard, and lifted one of the men in his fingers. "Handsome set. Do you play?"

"Not well," Tuckworth demurred. "I'm working on a little puzzle, to capture the black queen."

Without a word, Myles sat down on one side of the little table, placing the lantern on the floor beside him. Tuckworth took his accustomed place in the easy chair.

"Black or white?" the vicar asked.

"Black."

So the two began the long wait. They played, at first silently, soon scattering a few odd remarks between moves.

"McWhirter has been to visit my office, you know," Myles informed the vicar at one point. "He's aware of your efforts on the prisoner's behalf. He wants me to stifle you."

"McWhirter would like to stifle a great deal in this town. Check."

"What? I thought you were after my queen."

"Yes, but you can't take your eye off the chief objective, can you? Shall we start again?"

They played on. After a bit, Raphael entered and settled into a corner, picking up a book nearby and thumbing abstractedly through its pages.

Myles took a knight. "You know, Vicar, you really might have made a formidable detective. If it weren't for your religious bent."

"Yes, you've mentioned that. Rather high praise from you."

"Merely an observation. Check."

"I'm afraid you stepped into a trap. And there's your queen."

"Where'd that bloody bishop come from?" Myles looked in sullen disbelief at the board. "Let's switch sides."

It was evident that Tuckworth was the more skillful player, although Myles concocted aggressive strategies that at times disrupted the vicar's more studied, traditional style. Still, as often as the inspector prodded Tuckworth into some weakened position, Tuckworth would display a remarkable inventiveness, working out daring escapes that turned the fox into the hound. It was not an even match, but it was instructive, and each man profited from his game.

"Tell me, Myles," Tuckworth asked when they had started over for the fifth time, "why do you believe I would make a detective?"

Myles paused, bristled his mustache, moved a pawn, then sat back. "Your doggedness, for one thing. That and your intuition. But as I said, a parson's no detective."

"Why not?"

"It's nature," Myles asserted, warming unusually to his theme. "A religious man, now, he wants to have everything up front. Always got some answer or other ready at hand. But your detective, he's got to begin from ignorance, you see. Knows nothing. Thinks nothing. He only collects facts. Soon, the facts start to tell a story. More likely several stories. Now he's got to sift through it all. Figure out which tale fits the facts best, which one answers his purposes. But the facts are always changing, and there's no place to get comfortable in."

Tuckworth pushed his queen across the board, unbalancing his opponent's defenses. "Now, I would have thought our professions had a great deal in common," he hazarded.

"How's that?"

"Well, it's a question of meaning, really. People come to us, you and me, searching for a meaning that explains their experience of life. From the cleric they require something a touch more cosmic, perhaps, more everlasting, but the desire is the same. They're confused by what's going on around them, and they want to be reassured that all's well and will come right in the end."

"Yes, but if you'll pardon me, I give them facts. You give them fairy stories."

"We both give them stories, Inspector. You said so yourself. That's all meaning is, really. A story that fits, that makes us want to believe. Whether or not it's true, that's something else."

Myles looked up from the board briefly to glance at Tuckworth, a quick, searching gaze. "Is that what you call faith, then?"

"For want of a better word."

The inspector returned to the board. "I wouldn't have thought you'd want a better word. Check."

Tuckworth paused. Had he said too much? He was so accustomed to relaxing his armor in the privacy of the study, allowing his thoughts to run freely, that perhaps he had admitted more than he ought to have done. The bird hopped onto his shoulder and nibbled at his ear.

A new game, another problem to be solved. "Tell me, Myles, how does one become an inspector of police? There's a great deal of training, I suppose. Did you begin as a constable?"

"Bow Street likes to recruit from outside the established force."

"And where did they find you?"

Myles did not answer at once. He did not move, but kept his head down, his eyes upon the game before him. Finally he replied, "I was a cutpurse."

"What?" Tuckworth exclaimed, with more vehemence than tact, and Raphael looked up from his book. "A cutpurse?"

"Yes," Myles said, staring straight ahead now, seeming almost proud of his history. "I began in the streets. That's how most of our detectives begin. A wallet here, a watch there. Soon the constables get to know you, start to bring you in for information. Word gets to the detectives at Bow Street that you're a source. That's lucrative business, good training, but it don't last." Myles's words took on the clipped accents that escaped him at times, the sound of the London streets. "You get seen with the wrong chap once or twice and you make enemies. If you're good, I mean resourceful, Bow Street do more than take a notice of you. They bring you in."

"And if you're not resourceful?"

"Well," Myles replied, dropping his eyes to the game, "as I said, you make enemies."

Tuckworth let the conversation slide. "I believe I've almost got you mated," he observed, motioning toward the board.

The minutes slipped past, and eventually Tuckworth began to tire. His attention drifted from the game and he started to lose, not that he noted the fact much. His mind was occupied by other thoughts. At last he glanced at his watch, holding it away from his face that he might focus the hands. "It's time, I think."

Myles took his lantern from the floor, lit the wick and closed the shutter. They rose, the three men, nervous, expectant, each with his own reason for being there, his own measure of success in this adventure, and they moved as a group toward the door.

"Is this the only passage from the vicarage to the cathedral?" Myles asked.

"Yes."

"And you usually keep it bolted like this?"

"Well, no, actually I don't," Tuckworth confessed. "Only, after last night, I thought it best to be cautious." He reached out and unlocked the door with a sharp click, then paused. "It might be wise to refrain from saying anything once inside. If he's there at all, he's certain to expect only me."

Myles and Raphael nodded together. Tuckworth opened the door, and the vicar, the inspector and the artist stepped into the side chapel.

The morning's rain had cleared, the wind had washed the sky, and now the half-moon shone brightly through the colored glass of the windows. The party crept quietly to the very verge of the aisle, and Tuckworth turned and motioned for the others to wait there, out of sight from the nave. Holding a deep breath in his lungs, he walked out into the swirling, variegated air of the cathedral.

The light danced in its gay attire about Tuckworth, but as he looked up into the reaches of the scaffold, the shadows and colors made that hard webbing even more of a mystery, a senseless pattern of light and dark where everything seemed to be in motion, though all was still and silent as the grave. Tuckworth found the place where he had stood the night before, directly under the timbers, and looked up.

"Hello?" he whispered, only just breaking the reverential chill.

Nothing.

"Hello," he tried louder. "Are you there?" This time his voice echoed into the vault where the light could not reach, and a faint rustling of wings answered him.

A noise drifted down from above, hardly more certain than the fluttering of the birds. "Vicar," it said, and was silent.

Tuckworth felt his stomach tighten and twist at the sound, so soft, almost tender. "You see," he called loudly now, to encourage his companion overhead to speak up as well, "I've returned. I said I would be back, and here I am."

"Here you are."

Tuckworth rubbed his eyes, still without his spectacles, and squinted. For an instant he thought he detected some movement above, a shadow more substantial than the rest, not the shape of a man exactly, but a figure nonetheless, a concentration of darkness huddled amid the shimmering hues.

"Last night," Tuckworth ventured, "you said something about your calling. What was it you meant?"

A pause, like a catching of breath, and then a rush of hurried words. "Not mine! God's call to me! His will, not mine!"

"Yes, of course. You are only performing His will. But what is His will precisely?"

"He forces me to it! He speaks His will, and I obey."

"He speaks to you?"

"Yes."

"How? As we are speaking now?"

"As He spoke to the patriarchs and the prophets. As He spoke to the saints and the evangelists. He speaks to me as He speaks to the righteous in every age, though they heed not."

"And you are one of the righteous?"

"I am."

Tuckworth glanced away for a moment, a furtive look toward the others, waiting in the shadows, listening to all this. He reached a hand to his brow and realized he was awash with sweat.

"Why did God tell you to kill Will Shaperston?" he asked, but there was no immediate answer. "Did He tell you to kill Josiah Mallard?" Again, only silence, and for a moment Tuckworth feared that the man had vanished. "You mentioned 'the unrepentant' before. Who are they? Does God give you their names?"

"God knows them."

"Yes, yes," the vicar sighed, relieved that he had not frightened the man away. "But how do *you* know them, these unrepentant? Is there a sign? Might I learn to recognize them?"

"You?" The man sounded affronted, as though Tuckworth were being impertinent.

"I only mean, if I can know who they are, I might help them to repentance, that's all. Certainly that's a better solution."

"No!"

"But if I could only—"

"No!" the voice hissed from its perch on high, and the word resounded to the farthest corners of the cathedral, seeming to resonate among the bells in the tower.

Tuckworth turned the conversation aside at once, frightened by this sudden outburst. "A note," he called up, whispering, trying to calm the moment. "You promised me a note, that I might rescue Adam Black. Have you brought it?"

"A false witness shall not be unpunished," the voice barked harshly, "and he that speaketh lies shall not escape. Here is your note!" Tuckworth looked for a flutter of paper, a drifting page to sail down through the air. Instead, there was a creaking movement above, a deep-throated growl, and a shadow like a great bat plunged down through the colors of light, swooping, plummeting at Tuckworth, stooping upon him like a falcon at a sparrow. He fell to the ground, cried aloud in terror. A horrid snap and the figure stopped in midair, danced and twirled upon the void, hovering in the nothingness. A beam of light flashed through the darkness, Myles's lantern casting its blaze upon the thing. Then another, and another, three converging beams illuminating the horrid shape, the awful form of Polly Burdon, hanging by a rope about her neck, above their heads, stuck between heaven and hell.

The sound of hurrying feet broke across the wooden planks of the scaffolding. Myles's voice shattered the darkness. "Hopgood! Wily! Up there and get him!"

Two of the lantern beams now dipped down, and two men emerged from their hiding places inside the cathedral. The constables raced to the base of the scaffold and began to climb upward, while Myles searched overhead with his light.

"Sir! Are you all right?" Raphael reached the vicar's side just as Tuckworth was rising from the stone floor, his eyes riveted by the dreadful apparition still spinning slowly above him.

"I'm fine," he responded, though his voice trembled in his throat. "I'm fine. What's going on here?"

Raphael looked up at the constables still scaling the ladders, hurrying upward to where Myles's light swept the wooden framework vainly. "They must have been hiding in here all along. I told you the inspector is not to be trusted, sir."

The constables had come at last to the upper reaches of the scaffold, only to find it deserted. "There's naught here, Inspector," Hopgood shouted down.

"That's impossible! The man couldn't have flown away through the rafters!"

"The triforium," Tuckworth advised. "It's near enough. He might have climbed over into the triforium."

"Where's it lead?" Myles demanded.

"Everywhere. It runs the length of the nave."

"Damn!" the inspector muttered. "Hopgood, take one side, Wily, the other, and work your way back down here. I'll watch the front of the church. You, Amaldi, take the back. Hurry! He's still in here, and by God, I won't have him get away!"

The party split up, leaving Tuckworth alone in the cathedral, standing in the open, surrounded by pillars and piers, shadows and vibrant light. Now that his first shock was past, he felt strangely relaxed, almost peaceful. Of course, he thought, Myles had not left this whole business to chance. He had stationed Hopgood and Wily hours before, the two men keeping their silent watch in the cathedral while he had been playing chess with Tuckworth in the study. And that meant Myles had believed him, at some level he had credited Tuckworth's story all along and prepared for it. The vicar felt a pleasant vindication at this, in spite of his pounding heart and panting breaths. Myles had believed him after all.

A noise in the shadows drew Tuckworth's attention. "Raphael?" he asked. "Did you find anything?" There was no answer, not at once, and a cold place spread through Tuckworth's soul. "Raphael?" he repeated.

"You let them in." The voice was still soft, almost childlike.

Tuckworth's skin went cold and damp, his mouth dry. "I had to. Don't you see?"

"Why?" it begged, dismayed.

"You cannot go on," Tuckworth explained, more calmly than he felt. "This killing, it's got to stop."

"It's God's will!"

"God doesn't want this of you. You know it yourself. That's why doubt plagues you, because you know this isn't His way."

"Death is His way!" the voice snapped, though there was suffering in the sound, a pained plea for release. "I must work His will. Don't you see? I can't stop or I am damned."

"You *can* stop!" Tuckworth insisted. "You *must* stop!"

"No!"

"Vicar!" Myles called from a distance, a great distance away.

"Why won't you understand?" the voice pleaded, and Tuckworth saw a shadow step away from the darker shadows, move into the light and reveal itself, a man in a cloak. He squinted, unable to resolve the shape into anything more familiar than a form, a human form. It took a step closer to him.

Instantly another shadow leapt out of the darkness and rushed upon the cloaked figure. Raphael grappled the man about the waist, pushed him back into the shadows, pressed him against the stone face of a pillar, trying to pin him there, crying out, "Inspector! He's here!"

But the figure fought back, balled his fists together and brought them down upon Raphael's skull. Raphael collapsed to his knees and the figure struck again and again. The youth tried to hold on, but he was defenseless against this onslaught and was forced to back away. In an instant, the figure disappeared into the shadows once more, returning to the enshrouding darkness of night.

Myles came up at last, his lantern in one hand, a revolver in the other. "Where?" he barked. Raphael motioned from where he knelt on the floor, and Myles bolted off into the blackness, sweeping the beam of his light back and forth. But it was too late. There was nothing for him to find. The man had escaped into the streets of Bellminster.

Tuckworth stepped to Raphael's side and helped him up. "There, now, brave lad," he said soothingly, all his fears now focused on his young friend. "Come on. Let's get you back into the study and get that head looked to. You suffered quite a beating."

"I wish I might have given as good," Raphael moaned.

"Of course you do, of course." Hopgood and Wily came up now, and Tuckworth sent them on after the inspector as he helped Raphael along. The pair hobbled down the breadth of the nave, under the scaffolding again, through its shadow, beneath the lonely form of Polly Burdon. A cloud passed in front of the moon, and the colors about them were extinguished, snuffed like a candle blowing out. They were thrown into darkness, and Tuckworth caught his breath for a moment, fear holding a tightened grip at his throat.

"Sir?" Raphael asked, hearing the vicar gasp.

"Nothing, my boy. Come on. I can find my way in the dark well enough." And they moved on. Yet before they left, Tuckworth turned back and looked. He looked at the vastness behind and above him, at the wan lights of the lanterns casting about hungrily for answers, at the great expanse of evil that had taken over his cathedral, his home. A shiver ran through him like a mounting wave, and he turned back to assist Raphael.

CHAPTER THE TWELFTH
SHADOWED

What the hell do you mean, she wasn't hung?" McWhirter stormed. "The damn rope nearly pulled her head off! Snapped her neck like a dry twig!"

"I'm telling you, she was already dead, just like the others," Dr. Warrick answered, staying as calm as he might under this rude interrogation. "The marks about her throat are clearly the signs of strangulation."

"There!" McWhirter crowed. "She was hung!"

"She was strangled. The marks I refer to are the marks of a man's fingers about her throat. She was killed at least a day before this unhappy business."

"All right," Myles interjected, attempting to regain some control over this meeting. "We know near enough when she died. The vicar admits to having spoken with her at six o'clock the previous evening. And he met with the murderer about one the next morning."

McWhirter's whiskers flared contemptuously. "Fat load of good that does us! The old bitch might have died whenever she liked. What I want to know is how this fellow carried her up into the rafters of the cathedral without your two men seeing or hearing a damn thing."

Another meeting in the office of the mayor of Bellminster, and Tuckworth was once again stifling in the back of the airless room. The same cast of important people was assembled, with the notable addition of Myles and the merciful exception of most of McWhirter's entourage. The same tone of frantic desperation colored the discussion. The same sense of senseless activity pervaded the proceedings. Only the inspector tried to give direction to it all, and he was floundering against the tide of Bellminster politics.

"Mr. McWhirter's raised a strong point, Inspector," the mayor declared, seconded by Bick and reseconded by Bates. "How . . . how did your men fail to detect this villain?"

"These are your men, not mine," answered Myles.

"Sir," jumped Hopgood to his own defense, "the fellow must have climbed up through the triforium, same as he got out. We'd have spotted him any other way. And as to hearing him? Well, you'd be surprised how that scaffold creaks and moans there in the dark, all on its own."

It was just more of the same wrangling, Tuckworth thought. But let them wrangle. His role in this was finished, and he was only there to answer any final questions. The order for Adam's release had already been signed, and by that afternoon he would be back in the world, he and Mary returned to whatever life they might build for themselves. Tuckworth wondered what kind of life that could be.

"Mr. Tuckworth," the rector was calling to him, Reverend Mortimer trying to assert his own sensible influence over the prevailing confusion, "what can you tell us of this man?"

"Nothing more than I've already told the inspector," Tuckworth replied.

"But surely you have had closer relations with him than anyone else. Your observations of his manner, his appearance, his very mental processes, these must offer us some helpful insight."

McWhirter laughed. "Mental processes? The man's a lunatic!"

"Actually," Tuckworth said, "I'm not convinced of that."

"What?" the mayor gasped, though whether he was more shocked at Tuckworth's admission or the fact that he had openly contradicted McWhirter, it would be hard to say.

"Well," began Tuckworth, "certainly there's a degree of madness about the man, the talk of hearing God's voice and having a divine calling and all that. Still, I think we can agree that the fellow has displayed a remarkable ingenuity."

"Ingenuity?" scoffed Bick.

"Remarkable?" howled Bates.

"Diabolical, if you prefer, but still, he's been sharp enough to keep us on the run thus far. And there's something else about him, a kind of remorse."

"Do you mean he regrets these killings?" Mortimer asked.

"Yes, I believe he does. He sounds so confused, like a man who has lost the power to resist the evil within him. And he speaks of doubts, as though some part of him is as horrified by this as we are."

"To hear God's voice must be horrible," Mr. March sympathized.

"I suppose that's how it affects him, yes," Tuckworth considered. "But all this merely scratches the surface of the man, and I'm afraid we'll never arrive at the truth that lies beneath."

"To hell with that!" blasted McWhirter. "I don't give a goddamn for the truth, so long as we get the man!" And the meeting fell to pieces once again. Not that this mattered. Tuckworth knew Myles well enough to be sure that he would not be dictated to by a committee. This gathering was more for form's sake, a way to answer all the questions at one time and then get on with things. So when it finally broke apart, and they each scattered on their various ways, Tuckworth was not very surprised that the only firm resolution they left with was to carry on.

Outside again, in the freshness of the late morning air, Tuckworth stopped to enjoy the freedom he felt, released from these recent cares. He had set out to do a good turn for someone in need, and he allowed himself to marvel at his own success against such odds as fate had laid against him. It had been a trial, one that had wearied and worn away at him, yet it had also brought a renewed vitality to his step, a strength of purpose to his actions. He was not an inordinately proud or self-concerned man, but he could still entertain the notion that someone else might not have fared so well.

The day was bright and breezy. A parade of people already crowded along the pavement, and Tuckworth was reminded of that first day, when all this had begun. It was only a few days past, four or five, perhaps. Or six. He had trouble remembering precisely. So much activity piled onto such a brief span of life, with too little sleep along the way. Now, in the glow of the warming sun, with the sounds of a pleasant day resounding about him, he might imagine that the world was fine, that all was indeed well and comfortable.

Myles stepped up beside him, throwing a shadow across the ground at his feet. "Do you believe what that little fellow said?" he asked.

"Which little fellow is that?"

"The curate, March. Is this just a madman hearing God's voice like he says, or is there some underlying cause to this?"

Tuckworth considered the question for the briefest instant. "It's interesting you should mention voices, Inspector," he replied. "The killer spoke of God talking to the prophets and the patriarchs. They heard voices, too, you know, voices in the desert." Tuckworth sighed and rubbed his weary eyes. He must remember to get to the surgeon for a new pair of spectacles. "Really not much space between a madman and a messiah. Anyway, this is entirely your affair now. I'm happy to be beyond it all."

Myles looked at Tuckworth. "Are you so certain you're beyond it?"

"You clearly think otherwise. I've been followed along all morning by your men," and Tuckworth pointed to a tall, gangly person standing at a fruit stall, looking desperately as if he wanted to buy something. "That chap's been after me all day."

Myles could only shake his head and heave his own weary sigh. "Rustics," he muttered.

"Don't blame them, Myles. They're following your commands as well as they're able." Tuckworth started down the street, taking no direction in particular, only walking. Myles walked alongside him, and the tall man trailed behind at a distance.

"You're still a central part of this investigation," the inspector continued. "Perhaps you should be grateful that your movements are so plainly shadowed."

"For protection, you mean?"

"Yes, Vicar. For protection." Myles stared into the passing faces that surrounded them, peering, searching for something there. "This man is still about. And he's not through with you, I'm convinced of that."

Tuckworth stopped. Why did Myles's warning find an echo in his heart? The vicar wanted nothing so much as to be left alone now. Why must he still be dragged through this ugliness? Was this the price to be paid for his good deed? "Have you any new developments from last night?" he asked. "Anything that might lead you to this man?"

"No, nothing," Myles admitted. "Amaldi got closer to him than anyone, but he never got a glimpse of the man's face."

"I know. Without my spectacles, I fear I was helpless as well. He was little more than a shade to me. I'm sorry we're none of us much use to you, Inspector."

"It doesn't matter. These cases rarely come down to bits and pieces of evidence. It's usually some mistake the culprit makes, some growing arrogance in him that leads to a capture. We just have to bide our time."

"And wait for another murder?" Tuckworth asked, though sure of his answer.

The two walked on for a bit, until Myles went off to consult with Dr. Warrick. He admonished Tuckworth before he left, however, not to undervalue his shadowing protector. "These men are clumsy, but they serve," he said, though Tuckworth silently wished they might be made to serve elsewhere.

The vicar strolled along, not really alone. Indeed, even if he weren't being followed, it would be hard to say that Tuckworth enjoyed any solitude on the streets. Everyone he passed greeted him with a smile and a nod, a warm wave for the vicar of Bellminster. Tuckworth had always enjoyed a degree of celebrity, owing to his station in the town, if for no other reason. But now there was an added fascination about him that the wags and gossips found irresistible. For now he was the man who had braved the villain, lured the killer into the very heart of his home, shared words with the monster as easily as you might sit outside the pub and pass the day with your cronies. There was a new admiration in the faces that passed Tuckworth, and if he was not entirely easy with it, he still acknowledged every winking eye with a polite smile and, perhaps, just the touch of a proud air.

Yet Myles's warning continued to echo in Tuckworth's thoughts, and he soon found himself squinting intently into every friendly face, every welcoming smile, hunting for some spark of recognition, a knowing glance, the sullen expectancy of an assignation deferred. One of these, he wondered, one of these might be him. One of these faces so close, these hands so near, might find in me something more than they tell. And suddenly the bright day turned pale and cold to Tuckworth, his freedom transformed into a close and suffocating destiny. He turned about, and for a frightening second he could not locate the tall figure of his trailing shadow. The man appeared, however, an instant later, hiding from the light, making a great effort not to watch anything. Tuckworth was relieved, and disturbed that he was relieved. Had he still so much to fear, then?

He turned his steps at last for the vicarage, pausing only occasionally on his way so as not to lose his distant companion. Stepping through the front door and into the warmth of his own hearth, all signs of gloom were swept away from his brow.

"Hello, Vicar!" Adam called joyfully to him, and Mary Black leapt from her brother's side to throw her tiny child's frame about Tuckworth's neck, dampening his collar as before with her tears, weeping this time from the fullness of her gratitude.

"Bless you!" she cried in his arms, over and again. "Bless you, Vicar! Bless you!"

"Now, child," he murmured, astonished, embarrassed at this profusion of feeling. Then his gaze alighted on his daughter, Lucy, standing by the roaring fire, its ruddiness coloring her cheek, the dancing flames causing drops of moisture to glisten and sparkle in her eye, a look of sublime contentment glowing from her loving face, and Tuckworth felt his emotions well up inside of him, too.

They made a great party of their day together. Mrs. Cutler emerged from the pantry with a vast tray of cheese and biscuits, fruits and cakes, and they made a picnic of it all, there in front of the hearthstone. Lucy played upon the pianoforte and they sang children's songs, Adam's trembling bass sounding incongruous with the pure delight he took in the music. They had forfeits and games, stories and more songs. Mary and Adam were perfectly united in the simplicity of their pleasure at all this, and even Mrs. Cutler found herself showing how a proper jig ought to be danced. Yet Lucy felt something in her father, not a sadness at all, but a frantic hunger for happiness, a willfulness to his enjoyment, that made her only love him the more. Could they so readily forget the terrors of the night before, the awful dangers not more than a few hours past? Could they choose to ignore the future, and the questions that yet loomed in their paths? Yes, they could forget it all for the length of an afternoon, and be grateful for the blessing.

The afternoon faded into evening too soon, however. A knock on the door interrupted their revelries at last, and Mrs. Cutler ushered Reverend Mortimer into the parlor. After a few empty words to Adam and Mary, and a warmer greeting bestowed upon Lucy, the rector pulled Tuckworth aside.

"I was wondering if you might take me into the cathedral and show me the site of your adventures," he said, sounding as though he wanted something else entirely.

"Of course," Tuckworth answered, and the two men went out through the study and into that realm of evening light and magic, the setting sun adding its touch of radiance to the scene. Mortimer had no eye for this rare beauty, however. He had business to discuss.

"You have performed a magnificent act for those poor souls," he began. "An act of Christian charity, saving that poor wretched fellow's life."

Tuckworth recalled the merriment of watching Adam play and found it impossible to think of him as "wretched." But the vicar kept this observation to himself. "I'm sure I only did what you would have done yourself, Rector, had you the time."

Mortimer heard without listening, and nodded. "Yes, true charity, Vicar. Or should I call you 'Dean'? I hear Lord Granby is making the position new again."

"Yes," Tuckworth replied, looking up into the vault. "He mentioned the possibility."

"Congratulations. An honor well deserved for a faithful servant of the church. But, to return to this question of charity, now that you have effected the release of Adam Black from his peril, what plans did you have for the man?" Mortimer looked closely at Tuckworth as he asked this, and placed a heavy, paternal hand upon the elder man's shoulder.

"I hadn't really planned to do anything with him. He's his own man, and I'm afraid he and Mary must make their own life."

"Excellent," Mortimer exclaimed with a pat of his hand. "I was concerned that you might have more in mind for the fellow."

Tuckworth paused now, a slight note of indignation entering his tone. "I beg your pardon, what might I have had in mind?"

"Christian charity, after all, Tuckworth"—the rector chuckled—"it's for Christian souls, isn't it?"

"I don't follow you, Reverend Mortimer."

"I only mean that it might have proven awkward providing for a woman of that character out of the parish fund. I half suspected you had something like that in mind, you know. To take the couple of them up as wards of the cathedral, or some such business."

"No," Tuckworth responded thoughtfully. "No, I hadn't thought about taking them up as charity cases. I don't think they'd agree to it, actually." And he appeared to be struck by a sudden notion.

"Well, then this is all a deal of fuss for nothing," Mortimer concluded. "Now I must be off. Business of the parish. You understand what that means, of course, better than anyone."

"One thing before you go," Tuckworth ventured. "You say Lord Granby is preparing my appointment as dean."

"Yes, we're planning a little ceremony at the end of the year, when your retirement as vicar becomes official."

"I'm wondering," mused Tuckworth, "if it might be sped along. I don't need any ceremony. Can't we just agree that I'm dean of Bellminster and be done?"

Mortimer looked chagrined for a moment at this sudden and rather impetuous request. "I don't suppose there's any impediment to making it official sooner than was planned. All it really takes is a letter of appointment."

"From Lord Granby?"

"Yes, from His Lordship. Of course"—Mortimer coughed importantly—"Lord Granby has left all the formalities to me."

"Might you arrange things so I could have the letter this week, then? I know this sounds hurried, but all this excitement the past days, I've grown anxious to settle my life into a healthy routine again."

This explanation seemed reasonable enough to the reasonable Mortimer, and so it was decided that Tuckworth should have his letter handed to him in the next day's post. A formal handshake from the rector was the only ceremony he received, but it was enough for what he had in mind.

Seeing the rector out, Tuckworth returned to the vicarage—he would never be accustomed to thinking of it as the deanery—and settled into his armchair before the fire, with Adam and Mary and Lucy gathered together about him. He smiled at the picture they presented, and grinned at his own thoughts, for the vicar was up to mischief, and that always made him grin.

"Mary," he called to the young girl, "I have a question for you, and it's a very important question, so I want you to think it over carefully. What have you and Adam planned to do with yourselves, now that you have your freedom?"

"Do?" she pondered. "What's for us to do but go home?"

"Yes, but once you're home, how will you provide, with Mallard gone?"

A cloud descended on Mary Black. So much of her strength had been centered upon her immediate problems that she had yet to look into the future, and what she saw now clearly troubled her.

"I thought so," Tuckworth said. "Now, here's another important question for you to consider. How would you like to stay on here as sexton of the cathedral?"

The cloud did not lift at once, for Mary could not understand the offer. Lucy grasped it in an instant, however, and beamed her approval.

"Don't you see, Mary!" she exclaimed, taking the other girl's hand in her own. "You and Adam together! Your wits and his strength!"

"Sexton?" Mary repeated, the idea slowly becoming real to her.

"Adam," Tuckworth said, "would you like to live here with us, and help about the cathedral? You and Mary, I mean. Would that be agreeable to you?"

"Stay here?" the man whispered breathlessly, awed by the very notion of a house so fine and a life so pleasant.

"Well, not here, exactly. There are rooms for the sexton in the cathedral. You'd live next door. But it would mean hard work."

"In the cathedral," gasped Adam, and it was evident he had become lost in a dream of splendor so that the work meant nothing to him. He would work himself to death if he might live in the cathedral doing it.

It was decided, therefore. Adam and Mary Black were the new sexton of Bellminster Cathedral. Tuckworth had forgotten what it felt like to be involved in other people's lives this way. He looked on as the pair made magnificent plans for moving their few poor possessions, setting up a new life, a new hope for tomorrow, and he felt that this was right, this was the way life was meant to be lived. What difference did it make, the great truths of the heavens, if we might only make those few spirits happy who inhabit our tiny sphere?

Lucy joined in the planning enthusiastically. "I wish Raphael would get here," she exclaimed. "He'll be so happy for you."

"Where is Raphael?" Tuckworth asked.

"Painting. The light seems to be perfect for painting out-of-doors, he said, so he's gone into the Estwold. I do wish he'd return," and a look of fear fell across Lucy's face for an instant. They had each one managed to forget, for just a few hours, the dreadful things occurring around them, but now they all came back to Lucy as she looked out the window at the lowering dusk and the clouds looming in the distance.

"Don't worry for Raphael," Tuckworth assured her. "He's well up to handling himself." And he settled into his chair, pleased for once to spend an evening in the parlor, surrounded by noise and laughter.

At that moment, Raphael was surrounded by noise as well, the gathering noise of an oncoming storm. With the rashness of youth, he had set out with the first light of day. Raphael viewed his failure of the night before as a challenge, something wild and violent inside him answering to the beating he had received at the hands of this cloaked figure. That he might have saved the vicar's life, that he could have won some grain of respect from the inspector, these considerations carried no weight within him when compared to the bruise he carried at the base of his skull. And so he had come out to paint, to harness his anger on the canvas, hurling color at the taunting whiteness before him, the offending vacuity, the empty silence.

He had gone to the Estwold, because there alone could he find such subjects as might suit his temper. The tension of light and shade, the revolt of darkness against the luminous, these were the themes his soul played out in shape and color, form and hue. Red. Red answered to the violence of his mood, and red splashed across his palette. Magenta and crimson and scarlet and burgundy and the purity of honest, simple red. His brush he wielded like a blade, cutting the emptiness away, slashing at its very core. No sketches slowed this frenzied pace. Canvas after canvas he filled with his bemused madness. He knew they were worthless, too wild to be landscapes, too personal, too intense. They were not paintings at all, but mere expressions of his angry soul, assaults upon art.

At last, the very profusion of creativity wore him down, and Raphael slowed his hand, stilled his heart and opened his eye. The jagged stump of a great oak, at one time perhaps the ancient ruler of this wooded realm, squatted black and brooding before him. Now he took up his charcoal and, as the afternoon sun shifted to evening, he sketched quickly, fluidly. Then, taking up his paints again, he set to work in earnest. Shadows stretched and twisted, crawled and shifted across his field of vision, and so he made his palette shift as well, capturing every mood of the rotten wood, the mossy roots, the rich loam, as the daylight altered and redefined the stump at every moment. He lost his feel for time, for place. He was a part of the stump, expressing its being through his senseless hand.

Dusk settled over the woods and the noise of the storm approached. Now deep purples began to shoot like veins through his work. His brush traced an intricate vocabulary of despair and decay, fashioning meaning out of a meaningless reality, yet retaining that sense of chaos that resided at the heart of the whole.

It was dark now, as the noise gathered about him, too dark to see, and yet he continued for a time, flecking and dotting his canvas with the density of black, pure colorless black. He stopped at last, only because he could not go on. He could not even see what he had created, but his blood raced as though his life's work were held upon that canvas, and he squinted to make out anything of his painting.

Another pair of eyes looked on at Raphael. Cold, colorless eyes. They watched from the depths of the shadows as the painter packed his tools and wrapped his canvases in a large oilskin, protecting them from the threatening rain that had just begun to fall at last. They watched from the folds of a dark cloak, these eyes, as Raphael lifted his easel onto his back and set out, searching for the road, following the path of a trickling stream at the top of a steep ravine. A figure stepped out of the shadows and followed Raphael, followed closely, footsteps masked in the rush of the storm, gaining slowly, relentlessly, watching with cold, colorless eyes.

CHAPTER THE THIRTEENTH
A HEART MORE FAITHFUL

There is a sort of miracle that occurs among the denizens of that darker portion of the globe, those strange and alien creatures of the sea, whereby the basest and most primitive of that lot—whose abundance in vast oyster beds makes them regular victuals for the common board of men—produce in their turn the rarest of all nature's rare works. A single grain of sand slips, on underwater tides, between the fiercely shut halves of that bivalve's outer shell, lodges at its heart and there affects to irritate and rasp. In defense of which, the oyster transforms its greatest hurt into its most prized treasure, layering the offending stone into a precious and translucent marvel.

But sometimes it happens, and through what contrivance no man can say, that this miracle takes a sullen turn. That which might have been brilliant and lustrous, radiant beyond all measure, becomes dark and morbid. No less enticing, even more valuable, yet somehow sinister, the black pearl lies buried amid the bleakness of the ocean floor. What man who has seen it ever forgets that depth of malevolent allure, so forbidding, yet so impossible to put aside? It is the very product of anguish, the visible embodiment of suffering.

Such a pearl was hidden in Tuckworth's heart. Born of pain, grown now to a dreadful hardness, it hurt the less with time, yet fascinated more. Its ache had formed the object of his daily cares for months leading into years—until this business erupted to run his mental energies off their rutted paths and ease this dull hurt inside him. Through all the day just past, his thoughts had not once found that desperate spot in his soul. The joy of his success had been pulled like a curtain over that tormented place, leaving him free to feel the greatest pleasure at his triumph. And so, when Lucy darkened these bright moments with her concerns for Raphael's absence, Tuckworth at first ignored her worries. After he had shown Mary and Adam their new lodgings in the back of the cathedral, and arranged with them to move in the following evening, he had seen them happily off. When he then returned to the comfort of his own hearth, Lucy's relentless pleading left him feeling, for the first time that day, irritable.

"He's probably absorbed in his work," he snapped.

"But it's too dark for him to paint, and it's starting to rain."

"Then he's gone to his studio. You know how Raphael obsesses, Lucy. He undoubtedly found some subject that interests him and he's lost track of the time. He'll turn up tomorrow. I'm certain of it."

Still, his words did not allay her fears, though she, for her part, managed to dispel some part of his contentment. And when, next morning, Raphael did not turn up, despite having earlier forced a promise from Lucy to sit for him, and when she tried again to stir her father's slumbering doubts, this time some sympathetic anxiety within him woke to her appeal, and he determined to locate the young painter.

They started out together (for what power might Tuckworth exert to force his daughter to remain behind?), making their way first to Raphael's rooms in the Granby Arms. There they received what faulty intelligence might be gained when simple folk are asked about matters that concern them only slightly. The chambermaid was certain Raphael had left early the previous morning with his easel and canvases strapped to his back. The postboy thought he had seen him in the coachyard after midnight. A waiter insisted that "the Italian gent" had ordered dinner in his rooms at eight. And the bootblack guaranteed that the man had not been about all day or night.

A rapid inspection of Raphael's apartments, under the watchful eye of the innkeeper, made this last supposition appear only too likely. The rooms had not been inhabited in the past twenty-four hours at least.

"The Estwold," Lucy asserted when they were back on the street. "He's been wanting to capture some landscapes there, something for Ophelia. He set out yesterday forenoon and he looked terribly upset."

"But surely he wouldn't have camped there all night," exclaimed her father. "Why hasn't he returned home?"

Lucy's fear knew the answer instantly, and she failed to stifle a frightened gasp.

Tuckworth cut her off at once. "There's no cause for that, not yet. If he has been hurt—I say *if,* mind you—then we must stay calm. There's no reason to suppose the worst. I'm positive it's only an accident with a simple explanation."

Accident or not, Tuckworth knew that the next stop must be the constabulary-house. Not that this was anything with which to disturb Myles. Not every matter need be referred to his investigation, the vicar advised himself hopefully. Some things might yet be relegated to the commonplace. Their lives were not so inextricably mired in this wretched affair, were they, that every hardship must be made a party to it?

Were they? A trembling qualm rippled deep within Tuckworth's breast, a sense of having returned to the start of a mad gavotte. Were they ever to be free of this, or were they instead being sucked down in a relentless grasp, all revolving about this horror like battered hulks twisting around a whirling maelstrom? No! He denied it. Some quarter of his life, even this mystery concerning Raphael, serious though it might be, even this must break from the grip of that greater danger and return their lives to quiet normalcy. Yet Tuckworth's fears galloped ahead of him, beyond control.

"Quiet normalcy" was not an expression that might describe the constabulary-house at that moment. The entire building buzzed with the activity of a hive of warring bees. A host of anxious hearts had gathered to make report of their least suspicions. Names and reputations were tossed about, and more evil was done that day through the desire to do good than might have been accomplished by an entire band of soulless villains. Tuckworth kept Lucy close by him amid the hubbub as they found Chief Constable Hopgood. He, upon hearing the cause of their visit, looked as harried and distraught as any man might after a night spent chasing phantoms.

"It's not that I can't help you, Vicar," he explained. "It's a question of when, as you might say. These murders have the whole town at odds. We're looking for a round dozen of people right now, and that don't count your painter. Though all of them we look for turn up back at home safe as safe. On top of which, we're pursuing any number of mysterious characters what get reported to us like orders at a butcher's stall. And I've sent every available man out to keep the peace, which looks about to break at any minute with neighbor accusing neighbor and folks protecting themselves against any shadow what moves. Three times last night guns went off, Vicar, and it's a wonder no one was killed. I don't know who's more the lunatic, the fellow what's doing all this or them as he's doing it to." The best the chief constable could offer was to take down their information and promise a thorough search once he had the men. "But that'll be late afternoon at the soonest," he said, "or even tomorrow."

Tuckworth tried to check his fears, to remain calm. No need to add his panic to the whole, he considered. Yet the further he was kept from aid, the more hungrily he sought it. "Could I see Inspector Myles?" he asked Hopgood, loath to work his influence with the man, but unwilling to attempt less.

"Inspector's gone to London."

"London?"

"This morning, and wouldn't say when he'd be back. If you'll pardon me now. Good day, Vicar. You, too, miss."

Dejected, father and daughter turned their steps back to the vicarage. The sodden clouds rolled fat and pendulous over their heads, tumbling across the sky, looking to unburden themselves of their soggy load. The day struck cold to the very heart, and people tramped the streets like soldiers on a mud-weary march. Tuckworth put his arm about Lucy, and she settled into the comfort of his embrace. The pair moved as one amid the chill of the day, one purpose, one desire, a single intent thwarted, a lonely fear exposed. As they passed through the door of their home, Tuckworth hoped he might see Raphael's coat hanging on its accustomed peg, and he noticed Lucy dart a breathless glance about the parlor, longing to find him resting in his uneasy fashion upon the settee. But he was not there.

Mrs. Cutler entered screaming from the pantry, dusting the flour off her sallow cheek and wiping her hands on her apron. "Where in the name of all's holy have you two been, then? And what a sight you make of yourselves!"

"Have you heard from Raphael this morning?" Lucy begged, crossing the room and clutching the housekeeper's hands in her own.

"You're 'most froze to the bone!" Mrs. Cutler cried, ignoring the question for the moment and rubbing Lucy's fingers vigorously. "Come have a warm by the fire, child." Turning to the vicar, she added, "What on earth's got into yourself, running off so soon after daybreak on a cold, heartless day as this?"

"We've been hunting for Raphael."

A hard look came over Mrs. Cutler's face at this second mention of the painter's name. She huffed. "Got hisself in difficulties, has he?"

"We don't know that for certain," Tuckworth answered, looking anxiously at Lucy. "We believe he went off to the Estwold yesterday, but no one's seen him since."

"Father," Lucy pleaded from the fireside, "we must go out again at once and search for him there."

Tuckworth shook his head. "The woods are too vast. We'd better wait for Hopgood to send his men along. Be patient, my dear, be calm." He paused. Yes, they must remain calm. The town was engulfed in fear, and they must not contribute their widow's mite of worry. Besides, this was all probably nothing, as Hopgood had intimated, a wayward terror, a childish nightmare left over from the past days' adventures. Raphael would surely walk through their door at any moment. Best to be cautious. Best to be rational. But opposed to these sane thoughts, Tuckworth beheld the trembling tears in his daughter's eyes.

"Perhaps I'll just wander out there and see what's to be done."

"I'll come with you!"

"No, Lucy. You have to wait here for Hopgood's men. Send them along directly. I'll not stray far from the road, not in weather like this."

Mrs. Cutler heaved a disapproving sigh. "And I suppose there's not a soul about to help? All too lazy and full of their own troubles to lend a hand?"

Tuckworth shook his head as he pulled on his overcoat, but he said nothing. She was right. These murders had divided the town into ten thousand little islands, ten thousand separate concerns, each one threatened by the interests of the others. He could see it in the shapes that passed him as he walked through the streets: huddled forms, eyes cast down, hands drawn in, minds focused on their own lives, their own worries. It was the shape of fear, a community gripped, not in terror, but in uncertainty. For who would reach out a hand to help another, when it might be a killer's grasp they took?

He left Bellminster behind, moved mindlessly past the fields and pastures. The rain began to fall. Winds blowing from the town froze his thoughts within him. Indeed, he had no more thoughts to offer. He had spent himself already, called up his last dram of effort for Adam's sake and had supposed he was done with it all. Now here they were again, the doubts, the fears, the anxious pursuit. And all he had left to give was this, an old man wandering a solitary road on an impossible search. Tuckworth might have abandoned the entire business, had he not occasionally wondered, Where the devil is Raphael?

He came at last through rain and cold to the Estwold. It loomed above him, reaching out on his left and his right, dark, secret, impenetrable. And he felt, more sharply than he could understand, the absence of Myles. With the inspector at his side, directing matters, leading the investigation, Tuckworth had managed to keep himself aloof, disinterested, to allow the more grisly aspects of this affair to drift past him while he pursued the nobler work of exonerating Adam Black. Now Tuckworth feared some dire matter ahead, something near and horrible that he must confront without Myles, alone.

"Hey, there! You, Vicar!" A voice from behind called out to him, and Tuckworth turned around. Four men, laborers from the cathedral, came rumbling up in a cart. "We been following ahind of you all this long way," said the fellow with the reins. "We'd've caught up sooner, only you're a spry old chap. A'most runnin', you was," and he grinned with blackened, broken teeth.

"I'm sorry," Tuckworth replied, confused. "Did you need me for something?"

"It's you as needs us," said a surly man in the back of the cart. "So missus said. Out lookin' for poor chap lost in them woods."

"It's your lady what sent us after you," added a third, hopping down. "Fair give us a thrashing, she did."

"Mrs. Cutler?" asked Tuckworth, amazed.

"Aye, that's the one. Right regular amazon, that woman. Dragged us down from our work, and then bustled off to the pub to fetch them others." And with a jerk of his thumb, he drew Tuckworth's attention to the road he had just traveled. A small caravan of wagons was strung out from the town, a half dozen at least, each carrying four or five rough-looking fellows. It was a formidable party, a score of men and more, and Tuckworth marveled, both at Mrs. Cutler's industry and his own lack of faith in those he should have known so well and trusted.

There were many familiar faces among the crowd that finally assembled there, but no time to note them all. The work ahead of them, though easier now, was still uncertain. The man with the broken teeth took charge of their company, and after asking Tuckworth a few questions about Raphael's habits, and receiving no very satisfactory answers, he arrayed his forces across the path through the Estwold, a dozen men to each side spread out within clear sight of one another, perhaps ten or twenty paces between. Then off they moved like a great machine, calling and halloing, stirring the bushes and brambles about, driving the birds and hares ahead of them.

They muttered to one another, communicating in short bursts of speech, concise and businesslike. They hunted as men hunt who have the cunning to provide for their own, with eyes trained to see what Tuckworth missed, the mark of a passing stag, the sign of a nesting quail, all the dark and hidden life of the forest.

Tuckworth stayed in the middle of the line, directly on the path as it wound through the woods. "Don't you fret, Vicar," the broken-toothed man muttered from within the undergrowth at his side. "We'll find the lad if he's here. And if he ain't, we'll find his trail and follow him out." Tuckworth nodded, feeling chastised for the guilty doubts that had led him to wander off on this mission alone.

They swept along, slowly but relentlessly, scouring the forest floor for signs of Raphael's passing. One pair of eyes looked sharper than the rest, however. One man, positioned at the far end of the line, moved ahead with a surer step, a quicker pace, as though he knew the way he must follow and hurried to arrive there first. He panted in nervous fear, a hidden dread working through his veins, causing the sweat to bead across his brow. He scanned the woods with cold, colorless eyes, and moved ahead all the faster.

There was a creek bed, he recalled, engorged and rushing, at the bottom of a steep ravine. That was where he had lost him, the painter. That was where he must find him again, before the others. He must find him soon and finish the work he had been given to do, recover this unaccountable failure. In whatever danger he might place himself, whether he understood his calling or not, he must accomplish this act of atonement.

He had been on his way to the Estwold that morning, alone on the road, when he was caught up by this party of common sinners, forced to come along, to join these ungodly men in their search, that they might not notice his. He was fifty yards or more ahead now, hidden by the thick growth of trees and brush. It had gone so wrong, last night's labors, so dreadfully wrong. It should have been like that old woman and the sexton and the rest, a divine work that could not fail. How could it fail, how unless God wanted it to fail? Wasn't this the same as the others? And yet, those callings had come to him in a holy place, with the certainty of divine authority. This last came to him in his rooms, at his prayers, not in the cathedral at all. In truth, he was afraid to venture back into the cathedral.

Was his fear a sin, then? Was this the punishment for his lack of faith? Must his doubts be corrected? Was God driving him back to the cathedral, in spite of the danger, sending him back to the one place in all the world where heaven touched earth, where the clouds that fogged his mind were blown asunder and all was made clear to him? Questions, questions, questions! He raised his hands to his ears, trying to silence the doubts that flew at him from out of the recesses of his brain. When he took his hands away again, he could just hear the surging of the creek under the patter of raindrops.

He quickly came to the ravine, like a scar cut across the depths of the Estwold, a sharp descent some twenty feet down to the banks of a swollen stream. Where had they struggled? He looked up and down the top of the cut, trying to find the spot again. There, a few yards ahead, some bushes crushed and trampled. He hurried on, for the others were coming up quickly. Looking down from this spot, he saw a maze of brambles and driftwood that had been carried along by the growing flood until it came to this shallow place and stuck to the bank. This was where he had lost him. The painter had disappeared as into a void, fallen into the pit of hell, and the dark of the night and the roar of the stream had covered him, hidden him.

The man squinted, his colorless eyes scanning the shadowy depths below. His fingers nervously stroked the edge of the blade he carried under his coat, near his breast. Behind, he heard the searching party move toward the spot. There was no time. He dropped down into the ravine, hoping to hide and let the men pass, to give himself the breathing space to finish his work.

He waited, breathlessly, cowering in the brush, his legs in the rushing chill of the water, his hands gripping the muddy bank. He must have lain like this, he thought, the painter must have lain just here, like this, here in the mud and mire of his sin where he belonged. He moved his hand about, searching for a root to hold on to. Suddenly his hand brushed against something slick and silken, the smooth surface of wet skin. The knife was out in an instant, and he brought its edge across the spot, slashing again and again, hurriedly, madly. But it was not the painter. It was only the oilskin he had been carrying, covering his paintings.

"Eh?" a voice called down to him. "What's that? Found something there?"

He buried the knife back in his coat pocket. Soon others had assembled at the top of the ravine, and two men came scampering and sliding down. "We've got something!" one of them shouted up to the rest. "He's been here, all right!"

The man cursed his failure and this sinful crew that had thwarted his holy purpose, clambered up with the others and fell back once more to lose himself in the crowd.

The oilskin was brought up, along with the few canvases left within it, slashed and torn. Men were gathered about now, looking at these strange painted shapes in the dim light, when Tuckworth came up. "That's Raphael's!" he cried. But his joy was short-lived. They had the work, but not yet the man.

The fellow with broken teeth slipped down the bank and, after a few minutes, he shouted up to his companions. "He crawled off downstream! Towards town! And I think he's been hurt! Poor lad's pullin' hisself along somethin' awful!"

The hunt now became a chase, as they spread themselves out from the ravine with four men in the waters below. They moved more quickly, called louder, made better progress, for each man now felt the urgency of their work. Raphael had been hurt, grievously hurt. He must have been unable to climb out, and that meant he would be dragging himself along with the waters rising about him, freezing his blood in this cursed cold.

Tuckworth hurried ahead at the top of the ravine, calling Raphael's name, squinting to pierce the gloom of the forest and the shadows gathering in the stream below. And yet, for all their care, they might have wandered past Raphael, so hidden was he in a muddy hole covered by thorny shrubs halfway up the steep bank. One sharp-eyed fellow on the opposite side spotted a boot sticking out as the party moved by, and, with a triumphant shout, he called the rest of them to the spot.

Six strong, callused hands reached in and pulled Raphael out of his resting place as gently as they might take a baby from its crib. All the time he murmured and whimpered, wincing and reaching for his side. Some sort of stick, a shaft of polished wood, protruded from his ribs, and the men were careful not to worry the wound as Raphael struggled against the blackness that had descended over his brain. They lifted him up to the top of the bank and laid him down gingerly.

Tuckworth knelt beside him and washed away the dirt and mud from his scratched face. "My boy," he called softly. "Dear boy, you're going to be well. Can you answer me, Raphael? You're going to be well, son."

Raphael opened an eye and looked about, confused, unsure. Then his sight settled upon Tuckworth, and a calm came over him. "Sir," he murmured, and Tuckworth patted him delicately on the hand.

"That's right, lad. You'll be fine now. You're going to be fine." Yet he glanced at the blood on Raphael's torn shirt, the shaft stuck in his side, and he wondered if his words were to be trusted.

They took him to the vicarage, moving as quickly as they dared along the road, sending a group ahead to alert the town. Dr. Warrick and Hopgood were waiting for them when they arrived. So were a hundred others, curious and silently terrified. So was Lucy, happy and frightened, caught in a dreadful purgatory of confused emotion. She rushed to Raphael's side as the cart came up to the vicarage gate, and Tuckworth went to her, taking her in his fatherly embrace.

"He's not that badly hurt," he said, telling her both the best and the worst at once.

They carried Raphael upon an unhinged door into Tuckworth's study, where the doctor might work in peace. A tense quiet settled over and about the vicarage as they waited for Warrick to emerge. He came out shortly, only to acquire the services of four strong men, and then returned behind the study door. A slight commotion, a cry from Raphael, and soon the doctor came out again.

"He'll need rest," he told Tuckworth, "but I expect he'll be all right. It hadn't lodged very deeply, thank God." And Warrick held out the broken half of an arrow.

"Raphael was shot?" the vicar asked, taking the offending weapon with Raphael's blood still on it and turning it over in his hands.

"No, I don't think so. He was more likely stabbed."

"Stabbed? With an arrow?" The doctor nodded his head, and then set about to supervise proper accommodations for his patient. Naturally, Tuckworth gave up his room, that Raphael might have the best bed, and Lucy and Mrs. Cutler turned the vicarage upside down to transform it into a reasonable infirmary.

While all this activity was progressing, Hopgood pulled Tuckworth aside. "I hope, Vicar . . ." he begged clumsily, "I hope you'll be able to forgive me."

"Forgive you?" Tuckworth exclaimed. "Whatever for?"

"For not assisting you when you needed me."

"But my dear fellow," Tuckworth assured him, "there's no way you might have known about this. None of us could tell that our fears were justified."

"I should have done something, still," the chief constable grumbled, shaking his head. "Inspector Myles, he told me afore going off, 'You listen to the vicar if he comes to you, Hopgood.' He told me himself, only the whole town was in such a state—"

"Stop fretting over it," Tuckworth insisted, mollifying the man's guilt, laying a hand on the worried fellow's shoulder. "It's all past now, anyway. Let's just forget it." Yet the vicar could not forget the piercing pang of regret he felt himself, remorse at having doubted Lucy, his townsfolk, the danger they were all in, everything and everyone.

Later, when Raphael was comfortable and alert, though weak, Tuckworth and Hopgood were allowed to see him.

"Now, don't disturb the lad," Mrs. Cutler commanded as she bustled about. Her feelings toward the young painter had greatly improved, now that he was entrusted to her care, and she hovered over him like a ministering angel sent to save his soul.

"Raphael," Tuckworth asked, sitting by the bedside, "can you tell us what happened?"

"I'm afraid it's not much to tell, sir," he confessed, his voice a mere whisper. "I was returning later than I intended. The way was dark and I followed the stream out of the woods. What with the noise of the waters and the storm overhead, I didn't hear him come up behind me."

"Did you see him?" Hopgood jumped in.

Raphael shook his head slowly. "It was dark. And he came at me so quickly. He must have struck at me with some sort of club, sir, but he didn't think about my pack, the easel and the canvases. The blow should have laid me out proper, but I only stumbled to the ground. When he tried to come at me again, I fought him off as best I could. Until he thrust that stick into my side."

"It was an arrow, lad," Tuckworth corrected.

"An arrow?" Raphael muttered. His brow grew dark at this inexplicable news.

Mrs. Cutler swooped down upon her patient with a tumbler and forced a sip of water past his lips. "Now see how you've worried him, with your talk of arrows," she fussed.

"Just a bit more," Tuckworth promised. "What happened after you were stabbed, lad?"

"I fell back into the ravine. The mud and brambles broke my fall, and I hid there. I think he came down after me, but he mistook the spot. He must have. I heard him tearing through the brush some distance away. I lay still as a corpse, sir. I must have waited hours, thinking he would be coming at me again, but he didn't. When daylight finally broke and I was sure he'd gone, I tried to climb out. But it was no good. The wound in my side, and my weakness from the cold. I struggled along until I could go no farther."

"And a fine job you did, my boy," Tuckworth reassured him. But after the two men had retired, leaving Raphael to rest, Tuckworth had to admit to Hopgood that they had no more to go on than before. "It's encouraging to know that this monster has been thwarted, if only this once, but I'm afraid that's all the encouragement we can take from this."

"Well, Vicar," Hopgood said with a nod as Tuckworth showed him out, "we might not have had that much encouragement if it weren't for you."

Later that night in the privacy of his study, however, Tuckworth sat in silence, and he wept. He wept at the thought of how matters might have gone wrong, dreadfully wrong, if it weren't for Lucy and Mrs. Cutler. He wept at his fear and his mistaken desire to keep this terror at arm's length, to stay apart from it and alone. He wept that, in preserving his precious solitude, in failing to reach out to the community he professed to love, he might have cost Raphael his life. And he wept at the dull ache he had known so long as it returned to fill his heart with pain. He held his hands before his face, and the tears burned hot into his cheeks, scalding him with the shame he felt, the terrible shame.

The shame, yes, and the anger. Pulling his hands away, he found them balled into fists that were now wet with tears of hatred. He stared intently at the door leading into the cathedral. That was the way, the path he was now forced to take. Tuckworth realized it at last. He was a part of this, woven into the ghastly tapestry of these murders, and every effort he made to stay away from it all only made the danger that much more real, more present. The truth spread out across his soul like a black sun dawning, and his tears made the violence in his own heart grow and take deep root. Until now he had acted only to save the innocent, Adam and Raphael. That time was finished. Now he must look to discover this fiend, this monster, to discover and, if possible, stop him. For the danger was no longer out there. It was here, among them, hidden but near. He must be ready for it. Next time, he would be ready, ready to end this. And if he had to, he would be ready to destroy this devil any way available to him.

After all, Tuckworth thought, I have killed before. Mightn't it be a simple thing to kill again?

CHAPTER THE FOURTEENTH
THE KILLING SEASON

Night in Bellminster once more? No, the following day, but a day as dank and loathsome as any day had dawned. A dark, spiritless day of falling rain and caking ice crawling down the gutters and the storefronts, the homes and houses, coating all in a black porcelain glaze against which every door was closed, every soul cloistered. A day of sinister fears, of ten thousand worried minds, ten thousand trembling hearts beating faintly in the gloom. Life continued, faltering and fearful. Life always continues. The figures in the streets moved furtively, scuttling along the pavement. Frightened shadows scurried from doorway to doorway like vermin, cautious of their footing, testing each step to make certain it was sure, navigating the icy paths as though distrustful that the earth would hold them up. Or did something other than the ice leave their world unsettled and precarious, something in the murky dark itself, some deeper shadow, a lightless figure moving at their sides through the streets, prodding their fears, coaxing the terrors of childhood back into memory, back into life?

It was day in Bellminster, but a day beaten down by night, and the town was at the mercy of the dark and ice. The babe in its cradle whimpered pitifully, unheard by its mother, as the encroaching chill sank into its wordless dreams. The aged pensioner, alone at the close of a hard and fruitless life, shivered under a thin blanket before a dying fire. The poor family huddled together in the brick anonymity of their factory home, with not enough food, not enough fuel, and too much sweat demanded of them that they might survive their poverty and keep beggary at bay. A comfortless day that promised naught but comfortless days ahead. And foremost in every mind, in every thought, the mute question, What is out there? In the rain, in the dark, what is out there?

A cold, cheerless day. But might there not be a single spot in the town where a spirit was lifted above the darkness? Where the warmth of human kindness, the love of a human heart, might hold back this unnatural terror; was there such a place?

In the vicarage, a candle burned in Tuckworth's bedroom, turned now into a sickroom for Raphael's convalescence. Raphael rested at last after a feverish night. A few drops of laudanum and he slept, though fitfully. Lucy watched him from the doorway, in the candlelight. His eyes shut, his features animated by dreams, tossing and fighting against phantoms that would not cease their assault, he grumbled and groaned, though insensible to the world. Moving to the bedside, Lucy laid her cool fingers upon him, and Raphael at once lapsed into a more peaceful slumber. He moaned softly, taking unconscious comfort from her delicate touch, and the phantoms of his mind were swept away.

The girl peered down at him, and something strange passed through her. As by some mystical communication, she felt the need that was inside his heart, the longing that he suffered, struggled always to fulfill through his painting and his life. Lucy smoothed the wanton hair from his face so that it fell about the pillow like a halo. She stilled his need, and Raphael appeared, for the first time in her memory, at ease. Why did he seem always troubled? Now, as she stared down at his handsome features, his face unworried by cares and the abiding passion to create, his brow uncreased, his full lips relaxed and turned up slightly in a subtle smile, he looked a different man. And with that strange shock that occurs when one discovers something familiar, she realized how much she cared for the man she knew, yet how much she loved this new man she had only just noticed.

His eyelids flickered and opened, and Raphael looked about the room, confused but not afraid. Lucy saw that her hand still rested on his forehead. She did not remove it.

"Are you well?" she asked softly.

"Lucia," was all he could murmur, though with greater feeling than his strength might allow.

"Sleep now, Raphael," she cooed, stroking his brow. "Sleep and get better." And leaning over, she pressed her lips to his cheek.

She left him there to slumber. Yet she left a part of herself as well, a part that she had not expected to lose, but which she gave up freely.

Below, she was surprised to discover a visitor to the vicarage. Reverend Mortimer sat in the parlor, in the best chair, and he was handing over an envelope to her father.

"Lucy, my child." The rector grinned awkwardly, rising to his feet. "I was just making your father's appointment official. Allow me to present to you the new dean of Bellminster Cathedral." He proclaimed the news with great ceremony, as though his audience were the entire parish, and not just Tuckworth and his daughter.

"Dean of the cathedral! How wonderful!" Lucy beamed, crossing the room with her light, graceful step to give her father a congratulatory kiss.

"Y-yes, yes," stammered the vicar (how hard to call him "dean" after all this time), seemingly embarrassed by her joy. "Is our patient doing well?" he asked, as much from concern as to change the subject.

"He's sleeping very pleasantly now," she answered, a noticeable flush rising to her cheek.

"What patient might that be?" interposed Mortimer.

Lucy turned to the rector. "Didn't you hear, Jack? Of Raphael's encounter in the Estwold?"

"Yes, indeed I did." The rector assumed a sympathetic and compassionate attitude. "Horrific business. Brave young lad, of course, but foolhardy. I must look in on him. At times such as this, even the most recusant of souls can be turned to grace. He keeps rooms at the Granby Arms, does he not?"

"Mr. Amaldi is recuperating under our roof," Tuckworth informed him. "Dr. Warrick thought it best that he be attended regularly, and Lucy has been a proper nurse." The vicar approved of his daughter's fond interest in the young painter's recovery, and he smiled warmly at her.

Mortimer did not appear as pleased with this intelligence, however. "Am I to understand that Lucy is ministering to this gentleman alone?"

"I think Father overstates my role," Lucy laughed. "Mrs. Cutler is the true nurse. I'm only assisting her the best way I know." This hardly answered Mortimer's apprehensions, and he looked tellingly from the staircase Lucy had just descended to the candle in her hand to her still-crimson cheek.

A knock at the door interrupted their interview, and Mrs. Cutler appeared soon after to present the vicar with a note. "Lad left it," she announced curtly. "Wouldn't wait for an answer."

Tuckworth glanced over it quickly, and a worried look fell across his face.

"Father, what is it?"

"I'm sure it's nothing," he told her, failing to sound sure. "I need to step out for a few moments, that's all."

She said not a word, only looked at him severely, not believing him. Tuckworth handed over the note. It was useless to keep these matters from her any longer.

"Come to the pub at the Granby Arms. At once. Alone," it read, with no signature, no mark to reveal who gave this ominous command.

Her stern countenance changed to an anxious appeal. "You can't go!"

For the briefest instant, a cold, hard look came over her father, and she did not know him. The look passed quickly, however, and he laid a tender hand upon her. "There's no reason for alarm. The Arms is just the other side of the square. You can follow me from the upper windows most of the way."

"But the day is so dark, and we can't know who's waiting for you!"

"In a pub? I doubt it's anyone very suspect. I'll be surrounded by all sorts of people. Come, now, my girl. We've got to go on with life, haven't we?"

Lucy did not appear at first inclined to go on with life in the same carefree manner that was her custom, not if doing so meant threatening invitations from nameless, faceless correspondents. But in the end, she was forced to concede that the danger was slight, and the summons imperative.

Through this exchange, Mortimer had held himself aloof. Now that Tuckworth was determined to go, however, he stepped forward. "Allow me to watch over your little household in your absence, Vicar. Dean, I should say." He gave Lucy a meaningful look. "These are treacherous days we live in, and like the man in the parable who discovered a pearl of great price, we must guard what we hold dear."

Tuckworth thanked him. He had not been overly concerned for Lucy there in the safety of the vicarage, it was true. But it was preferable to be cautious, he reasoned. He had been too lax with his suspicions in the past. Perhaps they should always be a little afraid. He left, therefore, and Lucy and Mortimer watched him for a time through the parlor window, though the day was too dark and the rain too heavy to follow the vicar much beyond the gate.

"I feel certain your father is perfectly safe," Mortimer assured Lucy, seating himself once more in the best chair. "He goes with a companion at his side who will not abandon him. 'Though I walk through the Valley of the Shadow of Death, I will fear no evil, for Thou art with me.'"

Lucy was not relieved by these assurances, least of all by the mention of the shadow of death. Such sentiments, coming as they did from the comfort of a warm fireside, lacked the strength of reliable authority. She sat in her own chair, therefore, determined not to move until her father returned.

It took Mortimer some few seconds to start speaking of the true matter that had prompted him to stay. "Lucy," he began, after clearing his throat and arranging himself slightly forward in the chair. "Lucy, this business you tell me of, nursing a strange man in your home, under the very roof of the cathedral, it hardly seems the proper thing with which a young girl ought to be involved."

Lucy did not answer. Indeed, she was not much interested in Mortimer's opinion on this topic and hadn't noticed that he'd asked her anything requiring a response.

The rector cleared his throat again. "I say, it seems hardly proper."

"And what on earth is improper about it, Jack?" she snapped. "If you had seen Raphael when they brought him here yesterday, near death, with an arrow stuck in his side, you might not deny him a bit of compassion."

Mortimer smiled a suffering smile, an indulgent smile. "My purpose in speaking is not to deny Mr. Amaldi anything, not anything he deserves. But I am concerned for your good name, my child. It doesn't look right, a single girl like yourself nursing a fellow of that sort. Or any other fellow, if it comes to that."

"Mrs. Cutler is a single lady. I don't suppose you object to her looking after Raphael."

"Mrs. Cutler is an elderly widow lacking prospects, Lucy." A banging of dishes in the pantry seemed to emphasize this point. "You, on the other hand, are but a child in matters of this nature. A delightful child, I might add, yet a child nonetheless. And your name is as a delicate orchid that must be tended with the utmost care."

Lucy stared at the rector as if he were speaking some foreign tongue. "My name is a what, Jack?"

"A precious and a very delicate jewel," Mortimer tried, "that must not be sullied lest it lose its luster."

Lucy furrowed her brow, looking oddly like her father, and turned away. "Jack," she said as calmly as she was able, "do me the favor to please shut up."

The rector sat for the half of a minute in solemn silence. Then, as if collapsing, he gasped and sputtered, attempting to form words of astonishment and reproach, though managing no intelligible sound.

"I'm sorry, Jack," Lucy continued, "but right now I'm more worried about Father than I am your concerns for my precious orchid, or whatever it is you're babbling on about. If we decide to allow

Raphael the use of our home after his harrowing ordeal, and if I administer that ounce of Christian charity that it's my duty to provide, I should think you'd understand, of all people. And I don't see that it's any of your business anyway."

"There are limits, Lucy, even to Christian charity."

She sighed. "You'd really best be quiet. You're just sounding ridiculous."

The rector sat bolt upright as though he had been slapped. He glanced to left and right about the room, searching for someone to bear witness to this impossible affront. Then, not finding any immediate assistance and not having an appropriate rejoinder at hand, he sank back into the best chair and folded his arms across his thin chest, sulking.

What pity she could afford for him, Lucy now felt. Mortimer wasn't so bad as all that most of the time, she thought, only he could be so pompous. "Look, Jack, I'm sorry," she offered. "It's just our way here at the vicarage to try to help people. Raphael's no different than Adam Black and Mary, not really. We've let them all into our lives because it's the right thing to do."

Mortimer leaned forward again with the gravest interest at this. "And how have you let that woman into your lives?"

"Didn't Father tell you? Adam and Mary have been made sexton, the pair of them together. Isn't it ingenious?"

Mortimer's eyes widened in shock and dismay. "That—that woman?" he stammered. "That woman?"

"Yes, that woman," Lucy shot back, all patience gone at last. "And her brother, and a fine sexton the two of them will make, too."

The last veil of studied calm seemed to tear away from the rector's pastoral mien, and he erupted in a fit of offended fury. "It's insupportable, a woman of that reputation! Laboring in God's house! I'll not allow it!"

"You haven't much choice. Lord Granby has named Father dean of the cathedral. It's his decision to make now."

Mortimer was silenced at this sudden revelation. It all came clear to him at last. He had been duped, worked upon, maneuvered by the old man to a precipitate appointment so that a common whore might be made an officer of the church. He fumed and fretted, but he was powerless to change it. Lucy even felt sorry for him in a distant, benign sort of fashion.

Reverend Mortimer rose from the best chair, stiffly formal. "If you will forgive me," he announced, "I must be leaving."

Lucy saw him out with hardly a word shared between them, grateful to be rid of him in the end. In fact, though Mortimer had never done the least thing that might be considered forward, his recent attentions toward her struck Lucy suddenly as unctuous. She put such memories from her mind easily, however. She had other worries. Returning to the parlor, she sat at the window and stared out into the darkness, thinking of her father, and occasionally, or perhaps more than just occasionally, of Raphael.

Tuckworth, meanwhile, had stepped out of the last faint glow from the vicarage windows and moved through the steady fall of rain into the thick shadows of the Cathedral Square. From the houses about, dim candles burned and hearths cast a far-off glint against the glistening shimmer of the ice. Like stars fallen from the skies about the pavement of the town, strange flashes of translucence danced before and about him, but his mind refused to see the weird beauty of the scene, and his way was wrapped in darkness. He had wanted to appear brave to Lucy, to still her fears and ease her anxious cares. He had tried to sound confident and convincing, strong and sure, but his heart pounded violently in his chest now. He had spent all morning in his study in contemplation of their plight, suffering misgivings at Myles's absence, unwilling, like most of the rest of the town, to venture out and he wondered too late whether Lucy's caution might not have been the better wisdom.

A noise ahead stopped his progress. A dull crack interrupted the patter of the rain, as of something hard and solid snapping, and for an instant he steadied himself on the uncertain ice beneath his feet, almost expecting it to break apart into drifting floes. The square about him remained whole, however. The sound came again, accompanied by a muffled grunt. Tuckworth was unsure what to make of it, here in the middle of the square, so drear, so dark. No one should be about in this weather.

"Hello?" he whispered, too softly to be heard. He coughed and tried again. "Hello?"

"It'll be a grand fire, Vicar!" It was the cheery voice of Adam Black, hidden in the darkness.

"Good God! Adam, what are you doing out here?" Tuckworth stepped forward a few paces so that he could just see the figure of the new sexton working in front of what appeared to be some enormous machine.

"It's my fire, Vicar! For Guy Fawkes! I gets to make the bonfire myself, Mary says, a'cause of us bein' sexton and all!" The man was giddy with delight at the prospect, and despite the dark and the danger, Tuckworth could not suppress a smile at Adam's irrepressible joy. Of course, he remembered. Tomorrow was the fifth of November, Guy Fawkes Day, with its bonfires and antics, dancing and revels. And it was customary for the sexton to oversee the town's bonfire, there at the highest point in Bellminster, the open square before the cathedral.

"But should you be working in this wet, Adam?" Tuckworth wondered. "And shouldn't you want some help? It's almost black out."

The man paused from his labors. "Help?" he said, sounding a bit hurt. "But it's to be my fire." And Tuckworth could see from the massive structure of old boards and broken chairs, crates and brush rising before him, with an oilskin sheet over all to keep it dry, that this was indeed Adam's work alone.

"Of course it's your fire, my man," he said kindly. "And it's sure to be the finest bonfire we've seen in many years. Why, the flames should reach to the very tops of the towers." Adam's smile might have lit the fire prematurely, so bright and beaming it was. "Only don't stay out too late. There's time enough tomorrow for the last little flourishes."

Adam promised to finish soon and returned merrily to his work. Tuckworth walked on, skirting the pile. Yet, as he returned to the loneliness of the dark, he was almost surprised that anyone out in such gloom could feel so great a happiness, and his pulse beat a little less fiercely, his spirit felt a touch less troubled, owing to Adam's abounding joy.

As a ship sails out of the vastness of the tossing seas and approaches the comparative calm of safe harbor, so Tuckworth now entered the faint glow from the light of the Granby Arms. He passed into the silent coachyard, abandoned save for the postboy sleeping in the back of a convenient wagon, and stepped within the warmth of the public house. A steam filled the air as he crossed the threshold, the heady mist from a dozen hot rums which lined the great breadth of the bar. A dozen broad backs stood hunched over their dim mugs, burying a dozen hard faces in rude libation. At the tables, a few parties leaned close together, to whisper to one another, not from any sense of intimacy, but so as not to disturb the shrinelike atmosphere that had fallen over the place. For, in spite of the crowd and the nature of their custom, there was an awful stillness upon the Granby Arms that day. Each heart beat alone. Every mind worked to keep its thoughts secret and separate. What conversations passed among the members of this profane congregation were furtive and close, as though too loud an utterance, too strident a voice might draw the attention of the dark and a vengeful, dreadful fate.

Tuckworth took all of this in with a quick glance about the room. Then, in the farthest corner, in the deepest shadow, a motion caught his eye. He squinted through the pale light. A hand waved to him, calling him over. The vicar wove his way through the room toward his appointment, drawing some slight interest, though no one dared speak a warm greeting. His blood roared so as to deafen him, and he swayed drunkenly as he moved. He could not see until he was right upon the table itself, and then he had to peer hard into that shrunken hole.

"Hello, Vicar." It was Myles.

"Inspector!" Tuckworth gasped softly, unconsciously respecting the somber atmosphere of the place. "I thought you were away in London!"

"I want people to think I'm away." And he motioned for Tuckworth to take a seat opposite him.

"I don't understand."

"You will," Myles answered, his words carrying a dire portent. "First, tell me about the painter."

Tuckworth leaned over the table, immediately adopting the inspector's clandestine manner as his own. His nerves steadied as he related Raphael's adventure, every detail reported with the cool precision of a trained observer. Tuckworth had forgotten how natural it felt to him, this business of question and answer, the calm control of the investigator assembling facts into neat piles, sorting them through his mind, yet somehow detached from his work. How easily he fell back into it.

Myles displayed his usual bland interest in these facts, only absorbing them as a sponge takes in water, until Tuckworth mentioned the arrow.

"An arrow?" he muttered. "You're certain it was an arrow?"

"The half of one, actually. The rest broke off when Raphael fell into the ravine. Hopgood is in possession of it now, if you'd care to examine it."

The inspector sat in quiet thought for a moment, then allowed Tuckworth to complete his narrative. When the vicar was finished, Myles asked, "The boy is in your home at this moment?"

Tuckworth nodded and looked sharply at his companion. Myles seemed troubled, more profoundly troubled than he had yet appeared. His severe, supremely confident facade, though not crumbling, showed telltale cracks, and his dark eyes receded under a careworn brow as he pondered these new, yet too familiar details.

"All right, then," he said at last, almost to himself. "Let me tell you what we're about." Tuckworth hunched forward expectantly. "I'm through dealing with the local constabulary," Myles announced. "Provincial idiots! I've called some help into this matter, some special help from London."

"When will they arrive?"

"They're all about you now," Myles answered with a surreptitious sweep of his hand. "They've been coming in over the last three days, by coach and horseback and on foot, so as not to draw attention to themselves."

Tuckworth denied the urge to glance behind him. "And how do you plan to use these men?" he asked.

"We're going to spring a trap."

"That's why you've adopted such secrecy," Tuckworth said, nodding. "You need him to feel secure, at his ease."

"Precisely. Even my presence in town might alarm him. But if he believes I'm gone . . ."

The truth struck Tuckworth with the shock of a sudden blow. "He'll come to me."

Myles folded his hands upon the table and looked into Tuckworth's eyes. "You and the cathedral. That's where he feels safe."

"And I am the bait that brings him in."

"Not the bait," Myles tried to assure Tuckworth. "More like the key. I don't think you're in any danger. He feels a sort of respect for you. From what you tell me and from what I've heard myself, he's adopted you as his confessor."

Tuckworth could not deny it. Some diabolical bond had developed between himself and the murderer, why or from what cause he was frankly too disturbed to wonder. Yet it was there, the sole thread that might link them to the man, and to the end of this nightmare.

"What is it you need me to do?" he asked coldly.

"Nothing, for now. He'll get in touch with you," Myles instructed. "The painter, what room is he occupying in your home?"

"My own, the front upper window."

"Good. I want you to keep the curtains drawn in that room. When he contacts you, open them and leave them open."

Tuckworth agreed, and he noted within himself a strange calm. In his soul he might be afraid, yet his mind was steady, certain that this was the right way, the only way.

"One last thing I want you to be aware of," Myles warned. "To stop this man we might be forced to use violence. Perhaps in the cathedral itself." He paused.

Tuckworth understood at once. "Trust me, Inspector," he stated, in tones strong and harsh. "I am prepared to do whatever is necessary to finish this."

"Are you quite certain of that?"

Tuckworth considered. It was not a decision he made lightly, though it was one he felt deeply. He had thought on this matter all day. How far was he willing to go? Now that he was determined to see this through, how committed was he to the ultimate, inevitable end? "If it comes down to killing," he told Myles in a voice not his own, "if that's what will stop this, then that's how it must be."

"You'll assist me completely?"

"I will."

Myles sat back for the first time and appeared to relax. "Fine, then," he murmured.

Tuckworth prepared to leave, but before rising from the table, he asked, "By the way, what do you make of the arrow?"

The inspector only shook his head. "Shall I confess something to you, Vicar? I don't know. Arrows, beheadings, hangings, mutilation, and all after the fact, like links in a chain that won't come together. I've never encountered anything like this before."

"Never?" Tuckworth repeated. "I thought this sort of thing wasn't unfamiliar in London."

"Mass slayings, yes, we've had them," Myles admitted. "Madness and lunatics, but not like this. This man seems to be killing with a feverish lust. Always in the past there's been time from one murder to the next to plan, to consider, to uncover the reason behind it all. But this fellow leaves no time! It's like he's harvesting madly, hurrying before the killing season ends! And there's no method! He's as random as fate and as arbitrary as God!" The inspector stopped and collected himself. "Sorry, Vicar," he muttered.

Tuckworth looked on, shocked at this sudden despair that seemed to overwhelm Myles, this sense of futility and vain pursuit. "You don't expect him to kill again before we have the chance to move?" he asked.

Myles looked at the table in front of him. "I'm certain of it."

Tuckworth could feel the blackness of the day creep in beside them, to sit between the men, reach out at them with its cold, insinuating fingers, to close upon their hearts with its icy grip. And perhaps for the first time in Myles's presence, Tuckworth felt afraid.

But these were not the only men made fearful by the dark. Later, after night had settled on Bellminster, a solitary figure stood staring at the distant towers of the cathedral rising above the town,

piles of a denser black than even the night could construct. He
stared with his cold eyes, his colorless eyes, and he longed for the
comfort of the towers' shadow. He was afraid to go near them, afraid
to venture too close. Yet he was grateful, too. Yes, grateful that the
decision seemed to be taken from him. For how could he go there
now? Surely the cathedral was being watched. Maybe dozens of eyes
were keeping a vigil over its magnificence, awaiting his return, hungry for his blood.

Or maybe none were there at all. The inspector had left, hadn't
he? Had gone back to London, given up? Perhaps his way was clear
again. Yet why should he be forced to continue this work? Mightn't
he at last deny the calling? Hadn't Christ denied the cup of bitter-
ness in Gethsemane? Couldn't he do the same? He didn't want to
kill! It was God's will, not his own, that drove him to it. And what
certainty did he have that this calling came from God? Now that he
might be denied the cathedral, by the authorities and his own fear,
shouldn't he pause? Shouldn't he await a sign that was impossible
to question? Wasn't it right for him to doubt?

Yet there could be no doubt. For doubt itself was born of weakness, reared in sin. He must be strong, as Abraham was strong,
wielding the knife of God's commandment over Isaac, raising it to
heaven, ready to plunge it into the breast of his own son, his only
future. Until the angel came to hold back the lethal blow. And if now
no angel descended to stay *his* sacrifice, who, then, had the right to
question divine judgment? Wasn't *this* a greater calling even than
that rendered to Abraham? For the patriarch had been spared that
awful act of murder! Yet *these* killings must continue! They must!
They *must*!

He turned away from the towers, clutched his hands to his tem-
ples to still the pounding. There was work to be done, God's work.
And he must do it. He must return to the cathedral. But not now.
Later.

Night in Bellminster, and a solitary figure walked the streets,
down, down toward the bowels of the city, toward the river, toward
the factory.

CHAPTER THE FIFTEENTH
MIDNIGHT LABORS

The mill had ceased its rancorous clamor: the daily screaming and fuming of steam, the mechanical clank and drone of a hundred engines pounding frantically, a hundred looms weaving thoughtlessly. The mill's labors were done, and the laborers dispersed into the night. All had settled into quiescence at this modern temple, this factory that fed, and fed upon, its human parts.

Not quite all. A single light flared from an upper story window, last vestige of the day just dead. Its glow illuminated a half dozen faces. A half dozen dispirited minds hovered about the flame like moths. A half dozen pairs of eyes strained in the dim illumination, staring, not at the candle, but at the cloth being held scant inches in front of it.

"You see! You see!" roared McWhirter, holding the square of material at arm's length. "Too goddamn generous with the wool! That's the problem! The weave is too damn close! We might squeeze out an extra yard a bolt!"

"A yard, at least."

"At least that. Perhaps more."

"More, I'd say. Definitely more."

The voices competed with one another in agreement.

"Excuse me, sir." One lone fellow begged for attention from behind the others. "If we were to squeeze any more out of that wool, it'd hardly be thick enough to call cloth."

McWhirter's whiskers spread out from his face like the wings of a bird, and the five dutiful acolytes separated themselves from their apostate brother. The mill owner leaned forward across his desk, clutching the bit of fabric, crushing it in his red fist. "I don't give a monkey's goddamn arse what you call it," he seethed. "I'm not in the business of naming things! I want to make money!"

"Of course, sir. Yes, sir," the man sputtered abjectly, but it was clear his life was over. In just so quick an instant do the fates snip their spidery thread.

"If there are no further objections, then," McWhirter asserted forcibly, "I'll expect estimates from each of you this time tomorrow. I want those looms retooled to give out more cloth inside of a fortnight! Less wool and more cloth! That's what I want!"

A half dozen frightened souls trailed out of the office and into the night, leaving McWhirter alone.

"Damn fools and idiots," he insisted to himself. "Idiots and fools who'd run the whole place into the river if they had it to themselves for a single day! They couldn't shit on themselves without being told how." He chuckled quietly in the solitude of his office. "They couldn't even shit," he repeated, smiling. McWhirter was not a man for witticisms, his humor being of a blunt and literal nature, but he allowed as this was rather a merry quip, and he took pleasure in the image it brought to mind. "They couldn't even take a shit unless I told them how!" he said one last time, laughing out loud in a single, explosive blast.

The day had been long and extraordinarily tedious, and this unexpected levity passed as swiftly as the clouds racing across the sky outside his window, billowy black chargers blotting out the heavens with their endless parade, rattling icy pellets against the sooty panes. McWhirter swept up an armful of papers, thrust them into a dirty portfolio and stormed out to the coach waiting for him below.

He shot out of the building and leapt inside the carriage as quickly as his massive frame would allow, causing the leather springs to creak in complaint. The horses shuffled nervously, but the coach remained still. McWhirter pounded on the roof above him. "All right!

All right! Be off with you!" he commanded. The horses ignored him, however.

He pulled down the glass and looked ahead. There was no one holding the animals, no one in the yard at all. McWhirter screamed over the patter of the ice falling. "Coachman! Goddamn you, coachman!"

A cloaked figure emerged from the shadows and swept up into the box. A moment's hesitation, and the great coach rolled out of the millyard, past the gate, into the night.

McWhirter looked out through the streaked glass as this impressive conveyance maneuvered its way along the icy streets. An endless line of brick greeted him, and he thought how he had made this city. Six years past, only six years since he had found it: dirty, tired little cathedral town, forgotten by the world, wallowing in its own decay. Now look at it! Modern, strong, solid, built on a foundation of commerce!

These were the thoughts that always occurred to him as he rode alone at night through Bellminster. For he had it set in his mind that the city was his, and would be his, and nothing Granby might do could deny it to him. First, however, he needed the political power to match his commercial strength. And that meant putting his own man in Parliament, defying Granby, his cronies and the established prerogative. "Bunch of goddamn Tories! Bloody aristocrats!"

The coach rolled on its way, oblivious of the night and the weather, carrying its lone occupant along.

What man to put up for it? That had been the question he considered every night as he traveled home. That stuttering imbecile of a lord mayor? He'd kowtow to anything with a pocketbook attached, but he was still Granby's man. Someone from the factory? Idiots and fools! He had mulled over the matter, worked it about in the machinery of his brain, but only recently had he devised an answer that might satisfy. Bick, that was the man, the mayor's obsequious little toady, him or Bates. McWhirter could never remember which one was which, though it hardly mattered. Both were ambitious, stupid, and pliant, just the sort of man who was wanted. The only question now was how to approach Bick. Politics must be handled delicately, strategically. He sat back in the coach, closed his eyes, and considered. How best to do it? How best to? How?

Soon, the sound of his rumbling snores could just be detected over the fall of rain. The coach moved out of the city, beyond the brick and mortar that were McWhirter's legacy, out into the countryside, out toward the ancient blackness of the Estwold.

What was it that caused McWhirter suddenly to spring forward, awake? They were stopped. The gentle rolling of the coach had ceased, but something made him believe that they were not arrived where they should have been. Something distant about the sound of the rain. Some odd list to the carriage, as the coach's wheels dug into a muddy road, not the firm smoothness of his drive. Something there was, something strange and unfamiliar about the world, that his mind failed to comprehend in its sluggish escape from slumber.

He peered out the window. Nothing. Complete darkness. No lights of the manor. No lanterns carried by hurrying servants with umbrellas. Nothing but impenetrable black.

"Coachman!" he shouted, pounding on the roof of the carriage once more. "Goddamn it, where the hell are we? Is the road washed away?"

No answer.

He lowered the glass and stuck out his head. He could vaguely discern the shapes of trees and branches around and above him. Looking forward, he tried to make out the shape of the driver, but no one appeared to be sitting in the box.

"Coachman!" he shouted one last time. "Coach—"

His voice was choked off as a loop of wire descended from above, passed smoothly over his head, tightened about his throat. Panicking, McWhirter clutched with fat, rough fingers, but the noose buried itself in the rolls of his neck, tightening further, cutting into the flesh, cutting off the air.

McWhirter gurgled and gasped, struggling to draw breath. He wanted to look up, to see what was strangling him. But he could not move. He tried to pull away, back into the coach, to free himself from the deadly grip. But the noose only tightened, digging deeper, drawing him back toward death. Blood flowed over his collar and shirtfront, began to stream from his nose and mouth as he fought for air against the taut inevitability of the wire. His body convulsed in a final wrenching spasm, a last unconscious struggle for life, and his great bulk nearly toppled the coach, almost succeeded in over-throwing the morbid power at the other end of the wire, the mur-derous intent of a black, cloaked figure standing, leaning back, bracing himself against the battle raging below.

The mill owner slumped lifeless at last, his great whiskers going limp beside his blood-smeared face. The figure above gently lowered McWhirter's weight, dropping him delicately against the window frame of the coach. For a moment, the man stood tense and shaking, tested but not tired, trembling more from exhilaration than exhaus-tion. Leaping down, he looked at his victim, lifted his head and stared into the bulging eyes, the grotesque, distorted expression fill-ing him with a sense of disgust and dread. Yet he was relieved, too. This work was almost done.

From under his cloak he pulled a sack, a common sack. He stuffed McWhirter roughly into its folds, then pushed the dead thing back into the carriage and raised the window glass. Jumping back into the box, he drove forward to a wide place in the road, turned the coach about, and set off back the way he had come, back through the Estwold, to the plain, down into the town.

CHAPTER THE SIXTEENTH
GUY FAWKES DAY

Morning broke, dull and drear. Though the rain had stopped, a dry, chill wind blew through the trees of Bellminster, stinging flesh and numbing bone, fit accompaniment to Tuckworth's simmering temper. The vicar had lain fitfully in his study all night, nursing his anger upon the sofa dragged in for his slumber. He rarely slept well, however, so these rough accommodations made no difference. He emerged from his makeshift bedchamber only to be greeted by the sickening sweetness of blood upon the air. Mrs. Cutler was already fussing about in the kitchen, preparing the black pudding on which she prided herself, her traditional fare for Guy Fawkes Day. Tuckworth shivered, as much from the thought of those bloody sausages as from the cold, and wandered up the stairs to have a peek at Raphael. Before entering the sickroom, he steadied himself and put on as bright a face as he could manage, lest his foul mood bring contagion into the room. He opened the door and discovered his young friend sitting up in bed, being tended by Lucy.

"Feeling strong, are you?" he inquired.

"Passably fit, sir," Raphael replied, though his weak voice belied this opinion somewhat. "I was just telling Lucy how I'd like a bit of charcoal and my sketch pad while I'm stuck here."

"And I was telling him he might wish for a better appetite first," she scolded. "He hardly touched his breakfast at all."

"Well, that's sure to come back to him with rest," the vicar said.

"If he doesn't eat more than a few crumbs, he won't have strength enough to rest," she went on chiding him, though happily, and crossed over to the curtains to let the faint light of day into the shadowy room.

"Lucy! Wait!" shouted Tuckworth, raising a hand to stop her.

"What is it?" she started, frightened at this outburst.

He had told her nothing the night before of Myles's plan and their secret communication, only assuring her vaguely that all was well. "It's just the cold I'm concerned about," he answered, though not very convincingly. "The draft. Can't have Raphael risking a chill in his weakened state. Best to leave the curtains closed until . . . well, until I say we should open them."

Neither Lucy nor Raphael understood this sudden precaution, but neither felt right in questioning it, either. The girl only looked grimly at her father and stepped back from the window. After a few more awkward pleasantries, none of which eased the somber mood that had fallen upon all three, Tuckworth retired. He descended to the parlor, where he was confronted again by the odor of Mrs. Cutler's black pudding boiling in the pot. He poked his head into the kitchen and saw the housekeeper, stained in gore and ruddy with the heat from the fire, working merrily at her sausages.

"Are you going to be about that all day, Mrs. Cutler?" the vicar asked.

"Black pudding don't cook itself," she advised him. Then, wiping a smear of blood from her cheek, she said, "Message arrived for you before the sun was up."

"A message? From whom?"

"From him as sent it, I expect. No name given. It's lyin' out by the front door."

Tuckworth turned back into the entry hall, and there on a side table lay a crisp square of plain white paper, neatly folded and official-looking. He opened it quickly. From Hopgood, he saw, asking him to come by the constabulary-house at his soonest convenience. No sudden dread rose up in the pit of his stomach. His heart did not ice over as it might have done before. His mood left him immune to such shocks, and a dark shadow settled over his mind at the subtle implication of this bare missive. Wrapping himself warmly against the cold and informing Mrs. Cutler hastily of his purpose, Tuckworth left.

Though the sun was a stranger to the place, Bellminster still looked cheerier now in the diffuse light that seeped through the white-gray clouds overhead. The insane forebodings of the night were vanished with the darkness. Tuckworth could sense as much in the faces he saw and the voices he heard. Yet there remained an unspoken expectancy about the town, a sullen reticence, a reluctance to allow all the shadows to dissipate entirely, a concerted effort to retain just a trace of disaffection. For despite the comfort and safety the daylight seemed to extend, what security could it truly offer? What guarantee did any man of them have that the next face he saw, the next smile he greeted might not hide a murderer? Who knew but that this passing stranger or that old, dear neighbor might not harbor a sinister purpose, a deadly will? So Bellminster lurched through the morning, weary of fear, though unwilling to welcome an untried hope, and Tuckworth felt deep pangs that the town, his town, should have arrived at such a pass.

Against this pall, the colors of the approaching festival were nevertheless starting to shine through the bleak landscape. The children—be it ever the children—warmed to the frigid day like tongues of flame, flickering in their excitement and tripping about in anticipation of the coming revelry, with its dancing and forfeits, its firecrackers and its great bonfire. They darted out of lanes and alleys, pestering each shopkeeper and colliding with the passersby, destroying the peace of the streets utterly, rushing upon anyone and everyone with outstretched hands, screaming, "Penny for the Guy! A penny for the Guy!" Some had already begun to drag their straw dummies about, ready to throw them on the fire once darkness fell. Their laughs rang like chimes on the smoke-filled air, and their lightness and gaiety infected some few corners of Bellminster, pockets of boundless cheer that started to spread and grow as the day progressed. Guy Fawkes Day was a children's holiday, after all, when every man and woman might recall that spirit of abandon, the license of merriment that is the first, best birthright of childhood.

Tuckworth felt himself grow young in spirit as well, delighting in the antics of these boys and girls as the marauding Genius of Youth swept through Bellminster. By the time he stopped to see where he had come, the town seemed to be wearing its old face of joyous simplicity again, as if none of the past days' malevolence had been more than an unsettling dream.

Tuckworth looked about and realized that he had wandered into the neighborhood of the constabulary-house. With a bitter sigh, he turned the last corner and entered that grim reminder of a world far removed from childhood. The jolly infection could find no entry into that cruel, hard bastion, and when he stepped through the doors, the air within felt colder than the icy blast without.

"Vicar, glad I am to see you," Hopgood welcomed him, though with more care than joy in his voice. "Something's happened, and I'm at the end of my tether to deal with it."

"Another slaying?"

The chief constable appeared unable to answer for a moment. "I don't know," he blurted out at last. "I pray not, but it's terrible."

"What is it, then?" the vicar asked impatiently.

"It's McWhirter!"

"Dead?"

"We can't be sure," Hopgood cried, throwing up his hands in an impotent display. "We fear he might be. But we ain't certain one way or t'other." It was clear that, without Myles nearby to direct him, the man was overwhelmed by these morbid duties.

Tuckworth tried to calm him. "Just give me the facts, Hopgood, and I'm sure we can discover what's happened to Mr. McWhirter."

Hopgood nodded. "It's simple enough in the telling. McWhirter left the mill about midnight last night. We've got reliable proof of the time. Only he never came home."

"All right," the vicar said quietly. "And how did he travel?"

"His coach carried him off, the last anyone saw of the man."

"Did you question the coachman?"

"That's the worst of it!" exclaimed Hopgood. "We found the coach down an alley near the cathedral this morning. Only no coachman and no McWhirter! He's vanished like some black magic's got him!"

"Nonsense, man. Talk sensibly." Tuckworth thought for a moment. "I assume you've been over the coach thoroughly?"

"Bloodstains all about the door and inside," Hopgood answered, shaking his head and moaning.

"Have you searched the mill?"

"We went over the man's office. I was hoping we might find some evidence of an appointment, or maybe a journey. But there've been no coaches out this night past, and besides, what man would travel by public coach when he had his own to go by?"

"Quite right," the vicar agreed hastily. "And what of the coachman?"

"The coachman?"

"What exertions have you made to find the coachman?"

"Well . . ." Hopgood hesitated. "I mean, McWhirter has been our main concern, naturally."

"But one is likely to lead to the other," Tuckworth barked angrily. "And odds may be that, if this is murder, our man's overreached himself at last. If the coachman's alive, then he's sure to have some information. If not . . . well, the murderer's never killed two at one time before. It must have been risky for him. If he's liable to slip up, then he's likely to do it now."

"I hadn't thought of that," the chief constable admitted sheepishly, and he set out at once to redirect some part of his investigation toward discovering this second, lesser victim.

Tuckworth, meanwhile, felt these new developments thrill through his veins, not even pausing to consider whether such excitement was appropriate to the circumstances. Here was perhaps the opportunity they had waited for, and its sudden manifestation left him eager to carry on.

"I was wondering, Hopgood," he asked after the chief constable returned, "might I have a look at that arrow we drew from Raphael's side?"

Hopgood relayed this request to a tired-looking young officer standing idly by, who shot off and reappeared just as suddenly, carrying the arrow wrapped in a cloth. He handed it to Tuckworth, who uncovered it and held it in his hands, turning it over. There was nothing unusual about the weapon, with its dark shaft and steel point. He might wander out and purchase the same almost anywhere in town.

"There must be a connection among these murders, Hopgood. Something is escaping us. The beheading, the mutilation, the stones burying Jo Mallard's body. Some dark secret binds them all together, with each other and with this." He stared at the shaft of dark wood in his hands, but nothing presented itself to his imagination. "Well, continue your investigations, Hopgood," he said, handing the arrow back. "I'll stay in touch."

"Yes, sir," the chief constable responded with a smart salute, accepting the authority of Tuckworth without question, almost without thought.

Back amid the mounting excitement of the day, Tuckworth found everything sharper and clearer, a little more animated, a bit less dismal. It may be nothing, he thought as he walked aimlessly. Perhaps just another tragedy, but still, it might lead to the end. And the thought quickened his step. If we can only connect these murders, somehow bring them together, then we might understand why this is happening and finish it. There must be a reason, some cause we're overlooking. He stopped to glance in at a shop window, not really seeing, only pausing to breathe. Squinting, he caught the sight of himself reflected in the glass, and for a moment the vision startled him. He looked vital, almost young again, his eyes keen and bright, his brow unclouded by doubt, his manner intent and purposeful. Yet something else lay behind this newfound strength. The anger he had been nurturing stared out at him, confronting him, forcing him to face himself. Stark and dire, it made him seem a different man than he was.

And now McWhirter is dead, he thought, turning away, ignoring this apparition. Another murder, one victim more, or two, to be added to the list. Yet he could not make himself feel the loss. True, before he had been startled, almost repulsed by the complacency that was growing within him, the icy spot on his heart engendered by such unremitting violence. But no longer. It was all just a puzzle, a desperate puzzle that must be solved at all costs. He continued his meandering course through the streets.

He let the day slip by him, passed a solitary luncheon in a dusty inn, ventured at last to the surgeon's for new spectacles, tried on pair after pair, finding nothing that suited, each only making the world seem more distant and distorted than the last. He settled finally on a pair that pinched the corners of his nose and caused the world to loom menacingly about him. But what did he care? Always his mind lay somewhere else, some dark and hidden place to which he tried to bring the light of revelation, to no avail. What was he up to, this killer? How did he choose his victims? What spurred on his malevolent intent? And as the hours wore on and no connection occurred to Tuckworth to link these killings, his enthusiasm waned, his anger dulled. For hours on end he would line up the victims in his mind like pieces on a chessboard. The poor woman in the filthy garret, Josiah Mallard, Will Shaperston, Old Pol, Raphael, now McWhirter and perhaps his coachman. Seven attacks, maybe six deaths, all discovered in little more than a week. Rich and poor, old and young, men and women. Nothing seemed to fit together. The pieces made no pattern, no sense. What had the murderer called them all, there on the scaffold? The unrepentant. But aren't we all unrepentant? What man ever truly repents?

A child ran up to Tuckworth with a dirty palm held out. "Penny for the Guy?" she cried. Without thinking, Tuckworth reached into his pocket and dropped a shilling into the startled girl's hand. " 'Cor!" she gasped, eyes bulging at this unexpected fortune, and without pausing for thanks, she darted off. Tuckworth followed her with his eyes, not quite aware of what had transpired, when he realized where he had come in his musings. He was outside the Granby Arms.

With a start, he turned his steps rapidly away. His frustration had drawn him inadvertently to Myles, and he hurried off so as not to attract attention to the place. He wandered out into the Cathedral Square and was surprised to see that the day had worn almost completely away. A crowd was starting to assemble, and the shadow of the cathedral stretched itself out until it already engulfed Adam's bonfire. There the fellow was, working about the pile of sticks, worrying it, unable or unwilling to call it finished. A strange image for us all, Tuckworth thought, fretting out our lives only to see them consumed at last.

Tuckworth walked across the square to the steps of the cathedral and sat down to observe the crowd from a distance. People, mostly children, had begun to gather about, getting their straw dummies ready for the flames, awaiting nightfall and the public conflagration. Men and women stood about the open square, chatting in small groups here and there, tiny islands scattered across a paved sea. Some one or the other might break loose from her companions and drift off to an adjacent anchorage, or shift furtively about the outskirts of his chosen harbor, but all in all these celebrants were a solid, sedentary lot.

Sailing in, around and about this archipelago, however, was an armada of children. They raced and spun wildly, running to one another and dashing off again, grouping and regrouping, circling the sticks and lumber of the bonfire, the dry, cold refuse of the year, stacked high at the center of the square. They played their games with no respect for rules, no honor and no civility, obeying only that paramount dictate of childhood: They were having fun. Some were bullies and some were cowards, some boisterous and some silent, some clinging, some charging, some retreating, some dancing, some skipping, some fighting, but all and every one of them was celebrating. It was Guy Fawkes Day, a day of festival, and they understood its importance as only children could.

The picture seemed so typical of the life of Bellminster that Tuckworth once more marveled at this resilience of spirit, ever ready to embrace the usual, the comfortable. This holiday was a welcome relief from the tensions that had overswept the town, a celebration of the mundane. How quickly the people had accepted this terror among them. How readily shock gave way to horror, and horror to resignation, and now resignation had transformed to forgetfulness, the blindness of routine acting like the waters of Lethe to wash away the memory of their fear. And this eager ignorance surrounding him filled Tuckworth's soul with an even greater anger, that they should leave to him the task of ending this, Myles and Hopgood and all the rest. That all action was left to him to work, that he must be drawn deeper into it all. It enraged him. He had known such anger once before, and for a fleeting instant, the dark place in Tuckworth's heart stung with a flash of startled light.

No. No one was forcing him to take this role. Only, perhaps, fate or God. Shivering against the cold, he ceased such thoughts.

His attention was now drawn to one little savage band of urchins, off in a corner of the square, a boy rampaging over a gaggle of girls. They seemed involved in some kind of military contest, a cat-and-mouse game, one against the rest. The boy's attacks were not a direct assault. He was far too outnumbered for that. He would follow the girls, stalk along behind them as they moved, hiding among the grown-ups, behind a cart, under a shadow, until he noticed his moment, one stray lamb cut from the fold. Then he would descend and drag her away, chanting a childish rhyme as he did so. Despite all their screams, the girls seemed to participate willingly in the game, for once he had swept another victim off, she was forever banished from her companions. It was the sort of bloodthirsty play that children love best.

The game came closer to Tuckworth, and he could see the boy ready for another rush. From behind the cover of an old woman tottering past, the young Lothario leapt upon a girl to the shrieking delight of her callow sisters and began his victorious chant. This time, Tuckworth could hear the words clearly.

"Hanging or stones to break your bones! Lop off your head to make you dead! Plunge in an arrow to pierce to the marrow!" Tuckworth shuddered. The children had made a game of the killings.

He was not the only one to mark this macabre pastime. A figure shot past the vicar, someone darting out of the cathedral, swooping down on the lad like a vengeful spirit. "None of that, you little scoundrel!" Mr. March scolded, taking the young rogue by the ear and twisting until the poor wretch howled. "None of your blasphemous songs under the shadow of this blessed house."

The boy squealed his innocence, but the curate was implacable and dragged the would-be assassin away. I wish it were only that simple, Tuckworth begged silently.

The curate soon returned to the cathedral and walked up the steps to the vicar. "Mr. Tuckworth," he greeted, rather formally.

"You were a bit harsh on the young scamp, don't you think, March?"

Mr. March was breathing heavily, however, and it was clear that he was in no mood to be tolerant. "Such goings-on, at the very feet of the cathedral," he muttered.

"It's only Guy Fawkes," sighed Tuckworth irritably. "We should allow the people their bit of amusement, especially now."

But the curate only shook his head woefully. "Especially now they might think of their souls and less of their revels."

How often had Tuckworth heard sympathies less generous than this from the curate and felt pity for the man's intransigence? How many times had he tried to ease that unrelenting creed, to stir some compassion in that too-ardent heart? Yet not today.

"March," Tuckworth muttered, his temper coming undone at last, "can you not allow them some hours of entertainment?"

"What?" the curate gasped, shocked at the vicar's too-apparent anger.

"Is it so beyond your character to understand what these people have suffered, what they suffer every day?"

"Suffering is a gift from God, Vicar."

"What complete rubbish you talk," Tuckworth seethed, vaguely aware of, though unable to stop the hurtful tirade escaping from him. "Suffering is just suffering, can't you see that? Pain is pain, no more! And you're too righteous to allow them even an ounce of repose from it all, from that incessant hurt of living!"

"I am only considering the state of their souls," Mr. March answered in confused defense.

"Oh, their souls, their souls!" Tuckworth scoffed with a wave of his hand, as though their souls were nothing but wind. "What of their lives now? What of their fears and their nightmares?"

"If you refer to these incidents of the past days—"

"But it's more than that," Tuckworth went on, ignoring the curate, looking out over the expanse of faces below him. "It's not just the killings. Every day is a trial to these people. Days of pain and hardship, loneliness and loss. The fear of death and the fear of going on with life. And what can we offer them in answer to their fears? No comfort. No healing. Just words."

Like a sudden tempest that spills itself out and moves on, Tuckworth's anger vanished, having spent itself against the hapless curate. Mr. March looked in disbelief at the vicar, unable to make a sound.

Tuckworth seemed lost for a moment, as though he did not know where he was. Then he turned to apologize to the poor curate. Before he could speak, however, a voice called from the square below, and Tuckworth looked to see Chief Constable Hopgood come bustling up the cathedral steps. When the vicar turned back again, Mr. March had gone.

"We've been searching all over for you, Vicar," Hopgood managed to say between wheezing gasps. "We found the coachman!"

"Dead?"

Hopgood nodded. "Throat sliced through and left buried in a pile of refuse at the mill. The murderer must have taken his place."

Tuckworth considered, his passions of the past minute forgotten in the problem before him. "He would have driven McWhirter to some lonely spot, away from town, and killed him."

"You don't believe there's half a chance of McWhirter's bein' held somewhere?"

The vicar shook his head. "Of course, we might hope, but the murderer's never shown the least mercy, and there's no reason to assume he'd start with McWhirter."

"But if he's dead, where's the corpse?"

Tuckworth turned around to face the cathedral. "Hopgood," he said slowly, "you stay out here."

"D'you suppose he's in there?" the chief constable whispered, pointing to the cathedral doors.

"I don't know. I don't believe so. But the place holds some special meaning in all this, something over and above itself. The murderer keeps returning here, as though he's drawn by a vision. I want to see what he's seen." Tuckworth climbed the remaining steps, leaving the town and townspeople behind him, and entered the sparkling twilight of Bellminster Cathedral.

The light of the day's last rays played their magic on the interior, making the forest of piers and columns appear a forest indeed, an autumnal glade of color and shimmering life. He wandered for a time amid this magic woods, himself painted with translucent hues, made a part of the mystical scenery. He held his hand up in front of his eyes, that he might watch his fingers dance among the brilliant shades. Suddenly, with a final burst of color, the light was extinguished about him. The sun had set, draping the cathedral in darkness.

Not all the cathedral embraced the night as yet, however. Tuckworth looked up to see the farthest regions of the vault still alive with color, the setting sun slanting upward to fill that dark realm with light. He moved to the scaffold and began to climb the series of ladders reaching upward. This was the journey he knew he must take, up, up into *his* space, invading *his* world, that dreadful purgatory floating between heaven and earth that the murderer had claimed for his own. As Tuckworth rose higher above the cathedral floor, he heard cries arise from without. The bonfire, he thought. They must be lighting the fire, starting the celebration in earnest now.

As the people pursued their revels outside, he continued his climb, higher and higher still. He glanced down. At times before, he had peered like this into the nave, upon the heads of the faithful from the solid safety of the triforium, but never had he felt so like one of the cathedral birds, flying straight up, like a spirit rising to celestial glory.

At last, he reached the place where the murderer had been. It was a work area for the laborers, a place for masons and sculptors to hammer away at their chisels, sending flakes of stone down upon the world below. Tuckworth stood on a level with the triforium, and it was clear that the scaffold might more easily be entered that way than by the long, arduous ladders that snaked through the timbers. Tuckworth prowled backward and forward along the planks of the platform, trying to feel his way into the mind of the man. Why did he come here? he wondered. Looking up, he saw that there were still levels to be scaled, platforms nearer heaven than this one. Why did the fellow stop here?

He looked about, and his eyes fell upon other eyes, stone eyes. Statues lined the walls of the cathedral at this height, saints guarding the sanctity of the cathedral. Tuckworth felt a quick tingle within as he looked at their blank faces, their frozen faces. He did not feel alone in this place. The line of figures reaching down both sides of the aisle gave a sense of companionship, provided a blessed community here, so high above the real world of men, and Tuckworth caught a glimpse of the murderer's soul. Here was the reason the murderer was called to this spot: to commune with these holy guardians, these saints.

What did they tell him? The man had said his calling was from God. Yet he seemed troubled by this call, as though the weight of it were a burden that would crush him. Did he derive an insane strength from these, his fellows? In the final flaring moments of light before the sun dipped away for the night, Tuckworth stared more closely at the statues surrounding him. What was it about them, St. Peter with his keys, St. Denis holding his head in his hands? What did they offer this man, St. Stephen Martyr, St. Sebastian? Were they accomplices to these crimes? He turned about again, and his eyes fell upon a sight that caused his legs to tremble with excitement.

There, peering at him, staring at him, stood St. Agatha, that pitiful martyr, aglow with beatific serenity, her hands holding a plate, a plate upon which she displayed the signature of her martyrdom, her severed breasts.

Martyrs! They were all martyrs! Tuckworth's head swam as he called up the list. Beheading, St. Denis! Stones, Stephen Martyr! Arrows, Sebastian! Agatha, the horrid mutilation! They were all martyrs of the church!

He raced down the ladders, falling and tripping most of the way. His panting breaths echoed about the cathedral as he rushed through the doors and back out into the night. There, before him, the bonfire was just beginning to blaze and the square was filled with merry revelers. Hopgood! He had to find Hopgood! In his exuberance he collided with several people as he hunted about in the infernal light from the fire, its glow sending all into a nether realm that was neither night nor day.

At last he saw the chief constable standing at the edge of the crowd, talking to one of his subordinates, keeping an eye on the festivities. "Hopgood!" he cried, rushing up to the startled man. "They're martyrs! Every victim has been transformed into a martyr! That's what he's about!"

Hopgood looked confused. "How d'you mean, 'martyrs'?"

"The arrow, that's how St. Sebastian was martyred! St. Stephen was stoned! St. Denis was beheaded! St. Agatha was mutilated just the way that poor woman was! He's made them all martyrs!"

"And hanging?"

"Yes, yes! Hanging, too!"

Hopgood considered this for a bare moment. "So, what's he like to have done with McWhirter?"

Tuckworth paused. Martyrdom, he thought. How else were saints martyred? A roar from the square interrupted him, and he looked up at the flames rising higher now, illuminating the facade of the cathedral with its diabolical light. "Dear God!" he cried, and bolted off toward the center of the crowd, toward the inferno.

Adam Black was dancing about the pile, reaching in with a torch here and there to ignite the pile of dry sticks and timbers. Tuckworth ran up to him and took the torch from his hands, casting it down. Adam stared in dismay, and then terror, as the vicar turned and dove into the bonfire, working his way into its dark heart. The onlookers were suddenly silenced, stunned and horrified at this show of madness. Only Adam moved, leaping into the pile himself, after the vicar.

Hopgood came up and cleared a space away from the fire. Moments passed, a few short moments that might have lasted all eternity. Then, with a crash, Adam burst out of the pile, scattering smoldering, burning timbers before him, carrying a sack over his shoulder. Tuckworth emerged behind him, and the two men stumbled coughing and gasping into the square, amid the people.

Adam dropped his burden and sank to his knees. Tuckworth knelt beside him. Hopgood ran up to them, and the crowd closed in. Still coughing, Tuckworth opened the sack to reveal its fiendish contents.

McWhirter, his eyes bulging and his face encrusted with blood, stared up into the crowd, the very devil himself called forth from the depths of hell.

BOOK III

CHAPTER THE SEVENTEENTH
SABBATH PRAYERS

Tuckworth entered the pub and sat down in the same darkened corner where he had met Myles before. No one noted his presence there. No one rose or left the room, yet it was only a matter of some few moments before Myles slid across the table from him, a stern, disapproving look upon his face.

"You shouldn't be here."

"McWhirter is dead."

"I know. And the coachman."

"Do you know that I've found out his method? I know why he's been staging these displays, killing people after they're already dead." Myles leaned forward, unable to disguise his interest. "He's been making martyrs of them. Will Shaperston was beheaded. That's St. Denis. But no, the woman came first. She was St. Agatha."

"Mutilated?"

"Yes, in the same fashion."

"And the stones covering Mallard?"

"Stephen Martyr. St. Sebastian for the arrow. And hanging and fire are plain enough, the gallows and the stake. But for Raphael, we would have six corpses for six martyrs. The fiend's been drawing his inspiration from the statues in the cathedral."

"But there's a seventh."

"The coachman, I know."

Myles folded his hands before him on the table. "It means he's getting desperate. He's altered his pattern, killing someone just to make the killing easier."

"But if he's desperate, doesn't that make him more dangerous?" Tuckworth asked.

"Yes, and more liable to slip up." Myles was excited now, his eyes flashing with energy and expectation.

"What should we do?"

"Nothing changes. We stick to the plan, only be ready. He's likely to contact you soon."

Tuckworth hesitated for an instant before speaking what was on his mind. "Isn't there something we can do to reach him, to avert another catastrophe? We understand his method now. Mightn't we take more aggressive action?"

Myles shook his head. "We still can't guess where he'll strike next. No, we have to wait."

"We wait," Tuckworth muttered in frustration. "We bide our time and wait upon his demented pleasure. And if he kills again?"

"Then he kills again!" Myles snarled through clenched teeth, his fists grinding into the tabletop. "Waiting's all we've got!"

"It's not good enough, Myles!" Tuckworth shouted, matching the inspector's barely contained fury with his own. "Not anymore! Men and women are dying, and we sit by and watch!"

Tuckworth's anger startled the inspector, who composed himself quickly. "Forgive me, Vicar," he said. "I forget how difficult this must be for you."

"How difficult do you think it was for that poor coachman?" Tuckworth spat out. "We all of us appear so eager to forget about him. But what of his life? His family? Was he unrepentant, too, or merely inconvenient?"

Myles lowered his eyes to the table. "What would you have me tell you, Vicar?" he answered hotly. "That the world is hard and cruel? That men die while others look on? Who needs a murderer to tell him that? I've got no answers for you, Vicar. Only this I know," and he glanced up again, staring intently into Tuckworth's eyes. "If we can't count on your patience, on your calm resolve to see this through, then all may be lost."

Tuckworth seethed. For a spare instant his anger flared, but it was the last heat of a dying flame, for he accepted the truth of Myles's words. He merely nodded his acquiescence and was silent.

"Very well, then. We understand one another," Myles stated. "I must be going now. Don't return here. It might undo everything." And without a further word, he was gone.

Tuckworth wandered out into the night. Some few people were still straggling about the square, although McWhirter's discovery had ended the festival, and the bonfire now smoldered uselessly before the cathedral. As he walked slowly back to the vicarage, Tuckworth attempted to smother his emotions, to sink them in deliberation, to think the problem through. Surely we know more about him than we did, he reasoned. His affinity toward martyrdom, toward the saints, certainly that tells us something of his mind. Then why can't we get any closer to him? He stopped to stare into the jewel-like embers of the fire, shimmering among the ashes. It can't all be arbitrary. We've found some method, at least, some reason for these brutal displays. And he selects his victims for a reason, as well. Doesn't he? There must be a meaning behind it all. But there his thoughts were halted. Meaning? The word mocked him. Yes, meaning amid madness, that's what he was after. Wasn't that what he was always after?

Shuffling feet came up hesitantly behind Tuckworth and stopped beside him. "It were a beautiful fire, Vicar," Adam said flatly, sadly.

Tuckworth nodded, still gazing into the remains of that hellish blaze as it grew colder in the night air. "It was that, Adam. It was a beautiful fire." They stood side by side, neither speaking, each respecting the other's sorrow. After a time, Tuckworth took the sexton's arm and led him away.

The next day was Sunday, and a vast throng of the faithful crowded and pushed their way into the cathedral, blocking aisles and clogging the side chapels, squeezing tightly into pews and benches and corners. Men and women and children pressed in, shoulder against shoulder and breast to back. Irreverent young daredevils sat and hung from the scaffold as Mr. March tried frantically to dislodge them from that precarious roost. But every effort he made was only vain posturing. Indeed, should the Second Coming have occurred at just that unpropitious moment, the curate would have experienced no slight difficulty in making a way among the saved for the Son of Man to pass. It seemed that every soul in Bellminster was gathered at that moment under the broad vault of the cathedral. Such universal piety was uncommon, but what in these times could not be called uncommon?

The only person thoroughly pleased with this great show of religious fervor was the rector. Mortimer was in the vestry, at a priedieu, quietly meditating over the text of his sermon, one that he had expressly chosen for this rather unique occasion. As the rector knelt, head bowed, eyes cast down, the very image of pious devotion, Tuckworth peered into the room and coughed politely.

After a second of godly silence, Mortimer rose, crossed over to Tuckworth and, taking him by the arm, ushered the older gentleman formally into the room. "I sent for you, Mr. Tuckworth, on a serious matter," he announced with unwonted reserve, even for him. "I am afraid that I have a rather unfortunate question to put to you."

Tuckworth sighed to himself. "And what might that question be, Rector?"

"It concerns your appointment as dean of this cathedral. I believe, though I hope I am mistaken, that you have already filled the office of sexton."

Tuckworth coughed again. "Yes, that's so."

"And to whom did you award this august position?"

"You know perfectly well, Mortimer. I gave it jointly to Adam Black and his sister, Mary."

Mortimer waited for a further elucidation of this remarkable statement, but none appeared to be forthcoming. "May I inquire why you would perform such an unaccountable and, I might add, such an unwise act?"

"Because nobody else seemed half so well suited for the job."

"I see. And what of that woman's sinful history?"

"It is precisely that, Mr. Mortimer: history."

The rector released Tuckworth's arm and stood in front of him.

"Then I am afraid it is my unpleasant task to request that your letter of appointment as dean be returned to me. I have no intention of allowing a man capable of such opprobrious judgment to continue in a position of authority in my parish."

Tuckworth considered for the half of a half of a moment. "No, I don't think I'll return the letter. Good day." And before Mortimer could utter the least gasp of disbelief at this rebellion, Tuckworth turned and walked out. After spending a lifetime navigating the waters of parochial politics, he knew there was nothing the rector could do about the matter. The letter that Lord Granby had written contained language of such a remarkable and glowing nature, such paroxysms of praise, that Mortimer would look a fool trying to rescind the appointment now. Besides, Tuckworth didn't care what Mortimer thought of him, or of Mary Black. He cared for nothing at all, nothing except the business at hand, the business that occupied his every thought and every act.

Turning the corner of a side passage leading from the vestry, Tuckworth collided into the hurrying figure of the curate. "March! Good heavens, forgive me. I didn't hear you coming."

Mr. March only nodded curtly and prepared to pass on. "Just a moment," Tuckworth said, reaching out to take the man by the arm. March rather easily pulled himself free, however. "Yesterday, we exchanged some words," the vicar offered. "That is, I said some things that were entirely unwarranted. I apologize."

The curate stood before the vicar looking stiff and embarrassed. "No need," the man mumbled awkwardly, and with that he was off.

Tuckworth looked at March's back as he disappeared quietly down the hall. He regretted, sincerely regretted, that he should have vented his frustrations upon that simple man. True, the fellow's unforgiving attitude was damnably irritating, excused only by his perpetual confusion. Still, it was a shame, that's all.

Tuckworth went on his way, to wander through the halls and corridors and staircases of the cathedral, that secret city that even this Sunday throng left deserted, alone with his thoughts and his mood. The anger he had nurtured and tended this day past was upon him still, but grown into something calmer, quieter, though more terrible for all that. It burned in his heart with a cold, blue flame, and fed upon his soul with a gnawing hunger. To end this, that was his will. To find the fiend and destroy him, this was the vicar's wish. Yet there was in this hateful vision a blind spot. That place within him, where he never dared go, ached with a throbbing pain, a merciless suffering that he tried to ignore, to cast aside. Yet it would not be denied; it forced its way into his consciousness. No matter, though. He would not waste a thought on this private hurt. He determined to focus his energies here, only here on this other, outward danger.

Tuckworth found himself at last along the triforium, high above the crowded floor of the cathedral. None of the men watching from the scaffold had thought to climb over the stone partition to this more comfortable perch, and so he had its full length to himself. He peered over and saw that the service was already well progressed, and Mortimer was preparing to deliver his sermon.

The rector strode to the pulpit in the flowing black and white of his vestments, ascended the steps that led up to that platform raised high above the heads of common men, that minutely carved capsule of sanctity, and paused.

" 'In prosperity the destroyer shall come upon him!' " His voice echoed off the stone piers and pillars, and he paused again. "This is the word of God to you this morning! 'In prosperity the destroyer shall come upon him!' Do you heed its message? Do you take it into your hearts and learn its precept? For I tell you, the destroyer walks among you this very day! The devil is in Bellminster, and all the works of man cannot dislodge him!"

The statement lingered in the heavy air, quivering above the heads of the congregation like a hawk ready to stoop upon its prey.

"Do you feel his presence there, beside you? He sits and sees, watches and waits. He is a patient devil, and your time is as nothing to him! But when he acts, then is he a swift and terrible avenger! What can you, poor men that you be, what can you do to hold off this fiend, to put behind you this devil? Where is your solace? Where your sword of protection? Does it lie with men? No. Men have no power over the soul, and this devil pursues your soul as a hungry wolf attacks the fold! Then shall you find protection in your homes? But walls cannot keep him out! Brick and mortar do not stop him! Locks and bolts give him no pause! Where, then, is your protection?

"Heed the words of the text. 'In prosperity,' we read, 'the destroyer shall come upon him.' And are you not now a prosperous people? Is not Bellminster a prosperous town? Yet what have you wrought by your prosperity? Has it brought you closer to Him Who would protect you? Or has it bred vanity in your hearts, the vain security of fools in the night, who raise houses upon sand with walls of mud, that when the gale howls and the torrent pours, your walls shall crumble about you! Such houses are but paper billets against the devil's army!

"Shall you, therefore, be protected by your good works and reputation? Reputation? Your reputation is but words, tainted breath blown against the wind of destruction! And the good works upon which you place your pride may be likened to the sweat of laboring ants, that work and toil their days away, never heeding the beasts that pass in the field and will wipe out their works in the movement of a hoof, the instant of a treading step. For whom do you work? For what is your reputation amassed?"

Mortimer stopped and passed his glance across the throng, stoking the heat of their faith.

"Your prosperity is a blessing, a sign of His good grace, and not to be cast aside. But how many of you have held up your prosperity as a shield against the devil, and felt your lives protected against his onslaught by your gold, and turned away from the Lord? Who gave you your gold? Who proffers the blessings of His creation upon you? Who makes of your days a pleasure, and of your nights a soothing balm? You have forgotten His favor and His glory, and made of yourselves worshipers of the Golden Calf!

"Our text is given to us from the Book of Job. Job, who was prosperous as you are prosperous! Job, who had all good things given to him by God as you have all good things from God! Job, who was a virtuous and upright man! Yet can you say the same of yourselves? Which of you is virtuous? Which is upright? And still was Job thrown upon the dung heap! Tormented with boils and running sores and pestilence! Still did he lose his home, his wealth, his children, his all! Shall you ask more from God, you who are less than Job? Shall you be spared, who are less deserving, less virtuous?

"Look about you! Look at these walls, not walls of mud but walls of stone! Walls set to withstand the devil's blows! Walls that are strong, not with the strength of gold, but with the strength of righteousness! Here, here is where your protection lies! But how have you prepared your place in this house, His house Who saved you, His house Who saves you now? Do you use your gold to repay your incomparable debt, or to furnish your life with frivolities to wile away these days on earth? And when the devil calls, shall you be able to hide from him amid your frills and finery? Or shall you make your haven here? Yet how shall you gain your admittance, you who have neglected the house of God till now?"

Tuckworth stared down upon the rector and shook his head at such thinly veiled extortion.

"And so the devil walks among you! Your lives pass in fear and trepidation! Your days a punishment! Your nights a curse! This devil is a reminder! A reminder that your lives are ever forfeit to Him Who gave you life! Your prosperity is as smoke and fog to Him Who gave you riches everlasting! The devil walks among you, for the devil is of your own making, a judgment upon you all, a terrible and dreadful chastisement! It is upon you that the judgment has fallen, and upon you it shall lie, until you turn from your pride and vanity, turn back to Him Who is your solace and protection! Forswear your pride! Forswear your vanity! And the devil shall have no power over you! Or cling to your worldly cares, and be a generation accursed!"

Mortimer descended the pulpit and continued with the service while Tuckworth kept company with his own brooding thoughts. He paced about the cathedral, slowly working his way higher into its inner realm, up through hidden stairways and forgotten passages, until he finally arrived at the uppermost reaches of its towering height, beneath the very roof with its wooden beams and timbers supporting the lead tiles which covered all. Here, at the highest point man could soar in Bellminster or anywhere else in the countryside for a hundred miles around, Tuckworth sat. He sat in the half-light that seeped down through holes in the tiles, gaps created by the laborers, that their work might progress without the need of lantern or candle, for the wood of the roof, ancient and desiccated, crumbling in places to the touch, would have borne the fire too well. Tuckworth looked across the space before him, at the winch tied to a large pallet, that it might be lowered through a hole in the vault. Men labored here, replacing the old with new wood. It was the way of things in the world.

Tuckworth sat, and he thought over and again the same thoughts that had plagued his dreams and tormented his waking hours. What need to play the same moves on the same chessboard? What purpose was there in rote recitation? He could arrive at no firm conclusions, no picture of the man he pursued. He only sat, and sat some more, and after he was done sitting, he rose and crept back down the labyrinth, down the entire long way into the world of men. He would walk the streets of Bellminster, he thought, to work off his anxious energy.

He emerged from the cathedral into a milling crowd of bodies. The Sunday service was finished, but the congregation had only reassembled in the Cathedral Square, gossiping and worrying, whispering over every detail of the night before and the many nights before that, searching, as Tuckworth was searching, for answers.

The first person he met was Hopgood, accompanied by Dr. Warrick. "The doctor has finished his examination of McWhirter," the chief constable said, pressing close to the vicar.

"Anything unusual, Doctor?" Tuckworth asked laconically.

"The man was strangled," the doctor admitted, aware that his role in this affair had lost all significance. "I hear you've come up with a theory behind all of this?" Warrick inquired. "You've hit upon the man's method?"

Tuckworth shook his head. "I'm sure Hopgood can explain it to you, Doctor." And he strolled off. His theory seemed to have little practical value. It brought them no nearer a resolution, and he had no interest in repeating it.

He turned his way around, to head back to the vicarage, for this crowd would not let him be. Indeed, he had retreated only a few steps before he was stopped again, this time by an aged citizen of the town.

"What is't you make of it all, then, Vicar?"

"Make of all what, Parr?" he asked, irritated.

"Them words of that young minister, that it's all come a judgment on us. What makes you o' that?"

Tuckworth looked into the old man's eyes, and he saw the fear that was there, and the hunger for reassurance. "I wouldn't want to contradict the rector."

"But can it be so?" another voice, a woman's tense voice, asked from somewhere within the mass of bodies. "Can this be all our own doing? Are we so sinful as that?"

"Every man is responsible for his own sins," Tuckworth said, trying to calm them as the crowd moved in about him, accosting him. "And I'm certain God has known far worse sins than those He'll find among us here."

"Then why is He doing this to us?" someone demanded, and several tongues echoed the question.

"But God isn't doing this to us, don't you see? It's a man, a person, that's all." The vicar tried to move on.

" 'Tis the devil, rector preached."

Tuckworth paused. There was no avoiding it, he realized. They wanted someone to help them, to wipe away the fear from last night, the frightful vision of McWhirter casting his lifeless stare upon them all. "It's not the devil. It's only a man, a very wicked man."

"But why would he do this?" a young girl wondered querulously.

Tuckworth shook his head. "I don't know. I can't understand it, either. But this I'm certain of," and he raised his voice now, so that many could hear him. "We only have one protection. That's each other. Right now, gathered together like this, we are all safe from any evil that this man might do. But if we split apart, if we let him fracture Bellminster, then he can prey upon us at his whim. We are each other's security, do you all see that? Our community is our safety. Please, never forget, never allow yourselves to forget for one instant that we must pull together. This man, this fiend, whatever he may be, is nothing against so many who stand up as neighbors stand and watch out for our fellows. He is powerless against such a brotherhood of friends."

A confiding murmur rippled across the square, a feeling of comfort and certainty as each person heard Tuckworth's impromptu sermon. It was the first he had preached in a very great while. Then, looking down at the ground, feeling slightly embarrassed to have spoken so forthrightly, the vicar moved through the close crowd.

As he moved, he placed his hands in the pockets of his overcoat to warm them from the chill. His fist brushed against a slip of paper. Curious, he took it out and looked at it.

It was a scrap torn from some larger sheet, and it contained a single word: "Tonight."

Tuckworth's breath froze, and he stared as if to burn the message to cinders with his eyes. He spun around, his glance hunting through the crowd, searching for a face that sought out his own, but no eyes rose to meet him. Who had been near enough? Who could have done it? It might have been anyone, he considered. In this damn crowd it might have been anyone!

As quickly as he could, he made his way to the vicarage. Entering, he did not stop even to remove his coat, but bounded up the steps two at a time, raced down the hall, burst into Raphael's room. The painter was sitting up, sketching on the inside cover of a book Lucy had given him to read.

"Mr. Tuckworth, sir!" Raphael called, seeing the mad look on the vicar's face. But Tuckworth ignored him. He only strode to the window and pulled aside the curtains, almost tearing them down in his excitement.

"It's time you had some light in here," he said. "Leave these open. Leave them open all night." And with that, he turned and strode out of the room, passing Lucy in the hallway, and marched down the stairs, disappearing into his study.

CHAPTER THE EIGHTEENTH
THE TRAP IS SPRUNG

The bird hopped from bookcase to table, from table to lamp, from lamp to chair, making a frantic turn about the room, before alighting at last on Tuckworth's shoulder. He only pushed it away so that it fluttered with its mangled wing and spun to the ground, where it continued the odd circuit that had become its endless pattern.

The day had passed slowly, the sun hanging somewhere beyond the closed door of the study, high behind the clouds, inching its way across the invisible sky. Outside, in the hallway, sat a tray of meat and bread, warm ale and cold potatoes, which Mrs. Cutler had laid out. But Tuckworth did not even open the door to send it away. He communicated with no one, kept all the wide world at a distance, that he might better prepare for this meeting.

His anger had cooled in the hours since he had received the message. It had grown hard and cold, no longer a flame but a diamond sitting in the pit of his soul, frozen to a cruel and lifeless thing, brilliant but empty of all feeling, all meaning. It existed only for itself, with no thought given over to vengeance or justice, only hatred of a pure and merciless kind. Such a force of his will did Tuckworth expend to keep this anger present that he was almost exhausted when the hour came to act, his heart numb and his mind a blank.

And now the bird made its final round about the room, and now the chimes in the distant clock of the town rang the first hour of another morning, and the vicar rose to keep his appointment. Taking up the candle that had been his only light the whole dreary day and was now burned down to a stub, he moved mechanically toward the door. For a brief instant he paused, only to realize that he knew nothing of Myles's plan, how it was to be enacted or by what agency the inspector would know the time to strike. It hardly mattered. The vicar was prepared to risk anything, everything to keep the murderer there, at bay upon the scaffold, trapped like a beast in a cage.

The cathedral gaped before him like the mouth of a dark pit. Tuckworth stepped into that holy place and began to walk out from the chapel into the nave, to the scaffold rising before him in the dark.

"Vicar."

The voice came, not from above, but from beside him. The man was there, in the chapel with him, near him.

"Is it you?" Tuckworth asked.

"The candle. Extinguish it."

Tuckworth blew it out with a dry puff of breath. "What is it you want from me?"

A moment of silence followed. "Stop with me here a moment." In the darkness, the vicar could make out nothing for a time, not even shadows. Slowly, he began to notice subtle shades of gray at the corners of his sight. Then he saw the figure, closer than he had imagined, a dark shape wrapped in blackness.

"The hour is late," Tuckworth said, hoping to move the fellow along in his purpose. "Did you summon me here to kill me?"

"No!" The man sounded hurt by this harsh accusation.

"Then what is it you want?"

"I want?" the fellow repeated. "I want only to talk."

"Talk," Tuckworth replied. "I'll listen."

Yet silence followed. The two stood there, almost as if they were embarrassed at last to have been brought to this point, a pair of naive lovers awkwardly waiting out the time. Tuckworth could feel the suffering of this heart that beat so near his own, the pain and confusion wracking this wretched soul, and in spite of himself, he began to warm toward so pathetic an apparition.

"Why do you do it?"

"God commands me."

"Rubbish! Murder and bloodshed and death? God doesn't want that."

"He demands our lives! He wants our repentance!"

"And do these people repent before you kill them? Do they truly atone for their sins in their final agony?"

"Don't they?" the man replied, daring Tuckworth to belie the certainty of such bloody absolution.

Tuckworth hesitated. Did he know this voice? It was a whisper, barely audible, as difficult to identify as a wafting breeze. Yet had he heard it before? "So your work is to exact penance from your victims?"

"My work is to do God's will."

"Then why am I here? Why call to me?"

The figure took a lunging step forward, and Tuckworth instinctively leapt back. "Am I wrong to doubt?" the voice pleaded.

The vicar peered at the man before him. Who was this? Was it someone he knew? Might he not have talked to this man some other time, in the light of day? "Who are you?" he mumbled half aloud.

"No!" And the man vanished back into the black surrounding them.

"Wait!" Tuckworth called. "I'm sorry. I only spoke my thoughts!" There was no answer. "You asked me about your doubts. Why do you doubt?"

The sound emerged so close to his ear that it startled him. "God tells me to carry on, but it's so hard . . . so hard."

"If it's so hard, why don't you stop?"

"I cannot question God's calling!"

"Are you so convinced that your calling comes from God?"

"I feel His power at work in me!"

"But how can you know these doubts, the ones telling you to stop, how can you be certain that *they* don't come from God? How can we ever be sure what the right message is?"

A long emptiness engulfed Tuckworth so that he feared the man had slipped away once more, into the night. Then he heard a whisper. "I must obey Him."

"But how can you know His will?"

"I know because I kill! Would God allow this to continue if it were not His plan? Would He let innocent blood flow in His name?"

"The coachman was innocent."

"No man is innocent!"

"Then would you kill us all?" Tuckworth demanded. "Would you kill me?"

It was the vicar's last attempt to keep his hatred honed and alive, but the subtle madness of this man melted away the last ice of his anger, an anger that had hardly been real to start with, just a furious pose that might carry Tuckworth to this moment. All that remained was pity, pity for so misguided a zealot, this poor, insane man, whose reason was reduced to phantom voices. Having come at last to face the monster, the vicar wanted nothing but to help him. Tuckworth thought of the lives that had been destroyed in this mad affair, and counted now this one among the rest.

"Look within yourself," he advised calmly. "Peer into your heart and say honestly, Does God want this to go on? Does He ask you to murder again? Aren't six lives enough?"

"Six lives?" the man answered coldly. "Six? I've killed dozens."

The word crept into Tuckworth's mind like a sickness, his brow growing clammy with sweat and his mouth going dry as though filled with dust. "Dozens?"

"Here six. More at other times, in other places. Many more."

"How long?" the vicar gasped.

"Years."

As the two men stood motionless, a glow sprang up unnoticed behind them, spreading from one pier to the next, passing like a spirit through the massed array of columns, until at last its light broke upon them. The dark figure standing before Tuckworth turned, startled, and cried out, covering his face behind the cloak he wore.

"Vicar?" Adam called. "Are you all right?"

As if his voice had been the cue for some unreal drama to commence, cries erupted from every corner of the vast cathedral at once, echoing and reechoing until it seemed as though an army were assaulting the temple.

"Stand by your posts!" Myles could be heard shouting above the others. "Get your lights on that scaffold! Vicar! We've men at all the doors!"

"Myles! He's with me in the chapel!" Tuckworth called. For an instant all hung suspended. Then Tuckworth spoke to the man. "Your work is finished. Every avenue is barred to you."

The figure turned upon the vicar, confused, his arms outstretched in dismay, Adam's candle behind him casting his face into a deeper darkness. Then, his hands dropped to his sides, a hardness gripped his spare shadow, and he spat out a single, venomous word. "Judas!" He spun violently about and darted past, back through the one path left unguarded, the one path forgotten, back into the vicarage.

Without thinking, Tuckworth raced after him into the study, only vaguely hearing as the inspector called out behind, trying to find his way in that labyrinth of stone. All was black in the study. The faint glow of Adam's candle from the chapel behind outlined the doorway, but cast no light into that darkened chamber. Tuckworth listened. He heard the panting breaths of the murderer on the far side of the room.

"There's nowhere for you to turn," he said, trying to keep a strong and steady voice through his fear.

"You betrayed me!" the man hissed, and Tuckworth heard him stumble about the room, upsetting chairs and tables, trying to find a door, a window, any way out.

"It's no use."

"You betrayed God! You devil! You Judas!"

Someone called from beyond, within the vicarage. "Father? What's happening?"

The murderer pounced in the direction of Lucy's voice and found the door.

"Lucy!" her father shouted. "Your candle! Snuff it out!" As the door flew open, Tuckworth could see a momentary flicker of light, and then darkness again. "Make no sound!" he called to her, running after the murderer again in this halting game of hide and seek. He burst out of the study and tumbled over the forgotten tray of food that the killer had somehow avoided. Tuckworth fell to the floor. Raising his head, he looked into the blackness of the parlor. But that room was not dark, not entirely. A feeble light, not even starlight, but the pale luminescence of the clouds overhead, filtered in through the windows. Tuckworth saw for an instant a great black shape whirling in a demented dance some space before him. Then there was a crash and a shattering of glass, and the sound of footsteps disappearing into the distance.

At last, Myles came up behind Tuckworth with his lantern. The murderer had hurled a small chair through a window and made his escape. Lucy stood at the foot of the stairs, the smoke still rising from her extinguished candle, her eyes wide, her skin pale, with a glint of moisture upon her cheek. Tuckworth went to her side, and she buried her fear in his arms.

Soon the entire house was astir. Myles sent some few of his deputies off after the man, but there was no hope of catching him on such a dark and windswept night. Others he put to the task of examining every inch of ground where the villain might have stood, searching vainly for anything, the least clue. Tuckworth took Lucy upstairs, where he met Mrs. Cutler coming down and heard Raphael's voice calling for anyone to tell him what was about. Tuckworth gave his daughter over to the housekeeper, instructing them both to calm Raphael.

"Father," Lucy pleaded, turning to him before they parted. "Promise me you won't be a part of this anymore. Promise me."

"I hope I'm finished with it," was all he could truthfully answer.

Returning to the parlor, he found Myles fuming in outrage at this disastrous failure. "Was no one assigned to guard that goddamn door?" he demanded, pointing to the study. But none of his men seemed willing to reply.

"Myles," Tuckworth called to him.

"Vicar!" The inspector practically leapt upon Tuckworth. "What did you see? Can you describe the man?"

Tuckworth shook his head. "I never saw him, not his face. The dark and my eyesight. These new spectacles only seem to make it worse," he apologized, though he knew how foolish he sounded.

"You saw nothing?"

"I heard his voice. It might have sounded familiar to me."

"Yes?" urged Myles eagerly. "You can identify him, then?"

It was the hardest thing Tuckworth had yet to do, telling the inspector that he could not. "Not with any certainty. It just struck me as something I'd heard before, but I can't recall where."

This was the end, then. Their plans, their hopes to finish this, all gone up in a single clumsy moment. Tuckworth could no longer be angry. It was more terrible, it's true, infinitely more awful, finally knowing the truth of this man's history, that he had begun this nightmare before ever he arrived in Bellminster and would likely continue it somewhere else. But the vicar could not feel hatred toward that pitifully mad soul.

He told Myles all that he had learned, that the man had murdered many more people, in many different places. He could offer no opinion as to why the fellow killed, what was his secret cause. He doubted, in fact, that the man had one. "It's just what you suspected, Myles," Tuckworth reported. "He's as arbitrary as God."

After a time, the official work being completed, the inspector ordered his men to leave. "I'm sorry, Reverend Tuckworth," Myles muttered, the last to go. "I wish it had ended otherwise."

"What do we do now?" Tuckworth wondered.

"I don't know." As fatal as that answer sounded, it did not surprise Tuckworth in the least. He didn't know what to do, either.

The vicar saw Myles out before fastening the shutters over the broken window and retiring into the study. He felt calm, almost relaxed, though he couldn't think why. Perhaps this really is over, he considered. Maybe he'll just go away now and leave us all alone. But what of the next town he visits, the next city he preys upon, he thought. What of the lives that still lie in his path?

"Vicar?"

He heard the woman's voice, almost a soft coo, from beyond the still-open door that led to the cathedral. He walked over and peered into the chapel. There stood Adam Black, in much the same place he had been when he stepped into the middle of things, with his candle still glowing in his hand. And there stood Mary beside him, cradling him forlornly in her arms.

"Vicar," Mary called again. "I come up at all the noise and ruckus and found him like this."

"Adam, what are you still doing there?" Tuckworth asked.

"I'm sorry if I done something wrong, Vicar," the fellow moaned woefully, glancing at his sister.

Tuckworth went to them both and ushered them into the study. "Good heavens, have you supposed this was all your doing?"

Adam nodded silently, looking up at the vicar through his bushy eyebrows.

"No, Adam," and Tuckworth enjoyed his first mild chuckle in many days. "You've not done a thing to find fault with. You were only doing your duty as sexton."

"But he seemed so angry, sir."

"Who? Myles? He always seems that way."

"No, sir. The fellow you was talking with. Mr. March, sir, the curate."

CHAPTER THE NINETEENTH

THE DARK HEART

ess than an hour later, and Tuckworth sat with Adam in the inspector's office at the constabulary-house.

"Once more now, lad," Myles was saying from behind the new-made clutter of his desk. "You heard the voices echoing in the cathedral, so you lit the candle to come out and investigate."

Adam looked confused, and he clearly longed to be anywhere else but back within that brick-walled prison. Tuckworth patted him gently on the arm and nodded, however, so that the fellow took some courage. "Yes, sir," Adam mumbled.

"And what did you see when you came upon the vicar?"

"He was a-talkin' with Mr. March, sir. The curate, sir."

"And how was the curate dressed, again?"

"In a big black cloak, sir. And he wanted to cover his face like, I remember that now. Only I saw him afore he saw me."

Tuckworth nodded again, approvingly. "You're doing fine, Adam. Fine." The sexton gave a wan smile at this and looked back to the inspector with a determined and resolute stare.

"Yes, well, he's fine enough," Myles said, and Tuckworth noted the lack of conviction in this utterance. "If you'd just step outside for a few minutes, Black. I'd like to have some words with the vicar."

The thought of being separated from Tuckworth recalled to Adam all his fears of that place, but Tuckworth led him out and sat him on a nearby bench, reassuring him calmly that he was free to leave on his own anytime he felt like it. Adam appeared nervous (of course he did), but he trusted the vicar and said he would wait.

Returning to Myles, Tuckworth instantly began to plan. "March lodges not far from the cathedral, in the home of a widow, the upstairs rooms. If he's returned there it should be a simple matter to corner him. He can't leap out of a window there."

"Patience, Vicar," Myles said, a troubled look on his face. "There are other matters to discuss first."

"Other matters?" Tuckworth replied incredulously. "What other matters?"

"We need more than a name, Vicar. We need a case."

"But the man was sighted! Adam saw him as clearly as I see you now!"

"Yes, Adam Black," Myles grumbled, and Tuckworth saw the obstacle before them at once.

"My God."

"The man's evidence would be worthless in court. If the killer were just some vagabond, we might be able to rush a conviction through. But the curate? He'll have a wily barrister, no doubt. Your sexton wouldn't manage a minute before someone like that."

"Mightn't there be proof in the man's lodgings? Couldn't we find something there to implicate him in all this?"

"We might, Vicar. But there's another way. A surer way."

Myles hesitated so that Tuckworth had to prompt him along anxiously. "What's that way, then?"

"You said yourself that his voice was familiar to you. Do you believe now that the voice was March's?"

"Yes, yes, I suppose it was March's voice."

Myles hammered his desk. "There can be no 'supposes' in this, Vicar! Are you convinced that the simpleton has correctly identified the killer? Was March the man you spoke with tonight?"

Tuckworth thought hard on this. To accept what Adam had seen, not merely to accept Adam's certainty, but to be certain himself that it was true, this was more difficult than he had imagined. Could he state, without pause or doubt, that March was the right man?

"Yes, Inspector," he said at last. "Yes, it was March I spoke with. It was his voice."

Myles nodded. "Good. Your word will naturally carry more weight than the sexton's." The inspector began to straighten his desk, placing scattered papers in piles, and Tuckworth knew he was plotting something. "Now tell me this," continued Myles. "Can you state positively that you saw March tonight?"

"I saw a dark figure and heard March's voice."

"No, Vicar. That's not what I asked. That's not enough. I want to know, can you take your oath in a court of law that *you* saw March's face this night?"

Tuckworth was still confused at this. "If I can identify the man's voice—"

"That won't be sufficient. It won't be certain."

"But I didn't see March's face, Inspector."

Myles only looked hard at Tuckworth, and for a long time the two men were silent. Slowly, Tuckworth realized what the inspector was asking him to do.

"You want me to lie?"

"I want to end this, Vicar. You want to end it. Here's the way, the sure way."

"By perjuring myself?"

"You told me you're certain March is the man. You wanted to plan his capture just now, to send him away to the gallows. Good. We'll do that, as soon as I'm convinced that we have a case that can't be broken. Now, what are you willing to do to be quit of these killings?"

What was he willing to do? Tuckworth had no idea. When at last it came down to this, to subterfuge and deceit, could he make himself the arbiter of fate? Was he sure enough of himself, of Adam, to take this irrevocable step?

Myles interrupted these thoughts. "Tell me something of March, Vicar. When did he first come to Bellminster?"

"He arrived shortly after Mortimer did, as I recall. I'd never had use for a curate myself, but the rector required an assistant."

"In what parishes had he served before? Where had he been and where did he come from?"

"I'm not certain, though Mortimer would doubtless know."

"References, I suppose?"

"The usual letters. Mortimer would have insisted."

"But how closely would those letters have been examined?"

Tuckworth didn't know. "It's not usual to suspect a fellow clergyman of lying," he said with special emphasis.

The inspector nodded his head gravely. "Do you see how much time would be wasted building a likely case against the man? We would take weeks just uncovering his history. And how much longer to connect him to those other murders you say he's confessed to? And how many more might he commit in the meantime?"

Still Tuckworth had no clear answer within himself. Was he so surely convinced of March's guilt? Was Adam's word enough for him to send a man to his death?

Myles sat back in his chair. "I know it's not an easy decision for you to make, a man of your position," he began formally, stiffly. "Let me confess something to you that might help your decision. I have lied to you."

Tuckworth looked sharply at the inspector.

"I told you once that I came to my profession from the streets, that I was a common cutpurse. A cutthroat would be more accurate a description," Myles confided, and he waited for Tuckworth to express his shock at this revelation. The vicar remained self-possessed, however. "I say I was a cutthroat," Myles went on in his clipped London accent. "The first time was the hardest. I did it to protect myself, or so I imagined later. Poor chap put up a foolish struggle to keep hold of his purse. Started to call out. It was dark. I had the knife on me. Just for cutting purse strings, you understand. Only this time, I used it to silence the man." Myles paused once more, and he seemed to loathe something about this confession, something in him that reviled the memory of this act. "I killed the man, and I hated what I'd done for the doing of it. There was still that much in me that was right. But I was young, too. I was fourteen, and I soon grew out of my qualms. I was never reckless with the knife. That draws attention. But I kept it always handy, ready for use."

Tuckworth continued to stare at the inspector, a deep, emotionless stare.

"Bow Street knew of my history when they brought me on, though they never had any evidence that might prove embarrassing. It was something unspoken. They knew I could handle myself, the whole way if need be. That's all that mattered to them." Myles coughed nervously. He had hoped to arouse some response from Tuckworth with this confession, something he might use to convince the man to go along, but the vicar remained quiet and implacable. "And so when it came time for me to kill again, to kill in the law's behalf, I did it without thinking. I killed a man as he tried to escape me. He ran and I fired. His guilt was demonstrated later, beyond question, but I didn't know that at the time. I only knew I had a duty to perform, and I did it. All that ever matters is to stop the killing, Vicar," he said finally. "That's all we've got to do. Do you see? Just finish it any way we can."

Tuckworth looked away at last. He rested his elbows on his knees and folded his hands in front of him, glaring down at the buttons of his shoes. "You think I'm rather a simple old man, don't you, Inspector?"

Myles sighed. "I think you've been protected here in Bellminster, tucked away from cruelty until now. Life can be harder in London than you'd ever fathom, Vicar."

"Life can be hard here, too, Inspector," Tuckworth muttered. He did not know why he spoke, what it was about the inspector's confession that called forth this anguish inside him. He only knew that, for the first time in many months, in years, he looked into the dark hole in his heart and drew out what he found there, drew it into the light.

"Let me tell you about my life here, Myles. I'm sure it's as nothing compared to your years living off the streets of London, horrific existence for any child. But life here, it's not always the pastoral retreat you seem to want to make of it. I moved here, I can't even recall how long ago now, with my wife, my Eleanor. She was my all to me. We moved into the vicarage with no ambitions, no hopes for any better world. We liked Bellminster. It wasn't a perfect town, but it was a pleasant one. We were content with it, and with the life we had here. Our days, I suppose, were just as idyllic as you'd imagine them to be. After Lucy came along, it was easy to think of ourselves as blessed.

"Several years ago, my Eleanor fell ill. The doctors said it was the cancer, inside her, eating at her bones. I'm sure you've seen men die, Inspector. On the gallows, even at your own hands, or so you tell me. But that death's quick. It's sudden, and the suddenness takes most of the horror away. To die slowly is to suffer. To watch someone die that way, to see her devoured alive, every day writhing in new agonies, every night wreathed in despair, each breath a hot knife plunged deep into the marrow, to see someone die like that, and to love her, is more than any god could wish on any man. It is a godless way to die.

"At first we turned to prayer, my Eleanor and I. Lucy we sent off to relatives, that she needn't see her mother so. But I stayed on to nurse my love, my dear one. I saw her shrivel before my eyes, her body dissolve and decay, saw the life sucked from her, until there was nothing left lying in the bed but her pain, her awful, un-natural pain. She begged God, how often she begged Him to let her die, to stop her suffering. But she only suffered the more.

"The doctors gave her drugs. Bottles and bottles of drugs. Pills and elixirs and powders. They each of them worked for a time, but then the time ran out and the cancer progressed. And as the disease ate away at her, the drugs proved impotent. The only thing lasting was the pain, the pain that would not abate, that merely grew.

"One night I came to her, and I saw her resting in fitful slumber, if you can call that slumber which never ceases to feel. She tossed about, a film of perspiration covering her flesh, fearful moans rat-tling from her sunken frame. I knelt by her, hoping my prayer might ease her into a restful sleep. But no sooner had I joined my palms and folded my hands than her eyes shot open and she looked into mine. Her look filled me with her fear, her anguish, and her one, single desire, a solitary wish that I, that I alone could fulfill for her! Mine was the only love she knew at the end! Mine was the only faith she called upon! God was not there to comfort her! I was!" Tuckworth paused, gasping for air. A moment, and he subdued his heart, calmed his breath and went on to the end. "I took the pillow from beneath her head. I placed one final kiss upon her lips."

He stopped. His clasped hands were shaking, bathed in tears. His sobs flooded the hurt within him. Myles could only sit back, feeling stupid and useless. After a long while, Tuckworth composed himself. His tears did not dry, but they ran out, leaving the searing pain behind. He wiped his face with his shirtsleeves, keeping his head bowed, ashamed and shocked to have displayed such emotion.

"Forgive me, Myles," he begged. "I never thought I'd tell anyone. No one knows. No one must ever know." He hesitated and gave a worried glance at the inspector, who only nodded. "Not for my sake, you understand. But Lucy could not bear the truth. I just wanted you to know that I am not unfamiliar with death. I can do what needs to be done."

Myles leaned forward again. "Excuse me, Vicar, but will you give evidence against March?"

Tuckworth stood. "Give me time to think, Inspector. I'll let you know tomorrow." He pulled out his watch. " 'Today,' I should say. Later this morning."

Myles might have mentioned that time was too precious for them now. But he did not feel right pressuring the vicar. Tuckworth turned to go, and Myles stood, extending his hand. "Good night to you, sir. My thanks for your brave service."

Tuckworth looked uncomfortable for a moment, but he took the hand firmly. "We'll talk in the morning," he assured the inspector. Yet morning was a long way off, Myles knew, and he had a plan of his own to try before the sun dawned.

Tuckworth collected Adam, still waiting dutifully, and left the constabulary-house behind. "I'm going for a walk, Adam," he told the sexton after they stepped outside into the frigid night air.

"At this hour, Vicar?"

"There are some important matters I have to think over, and someone I must talk to. You go home, and should anyone ask after me, tell them I'm fine."

But Adam could see plainly that the vicar was not fine. He was far from fine. As Tuckworth wandered off into the night, therefore, with a light snow beginning to fall and swirl about him, another figure could be seen wandering a distance behind, trailing along as faithfully as a dog to guard his way.

CHAPTER THE TWENTIETH
DEAD OF NIGHT

Tuckworth stood before the house, waiting for some sign that his knocking had been heard. He glanced up and down the deserted street, anxious lest his importunate appeal arouse some other slumbering soul. A minute passed in silence, and he pounded again upon the richly appointed door. He had walked a great distance that night to arrive in the most fashionable district of Bellminster, far from the Old Town, and as he traveled the snow had begun to fall more heavily, muffling the wide world about in wisps of cotton and cloud.

Finally, a light appeared beyond the cut glass of the fan-shaped window above him. A clattering of locks ensued before the door creaked open slightly and a squinting face poked out.

"What d'you want?" the old woman asked crossly.

"I must see the rector."

"Get on with you," she enjoined him. "Calling on Rector at this hour? Be off!"

Tuckworth had no chance to answer before Mortimer's voice could be heard overhead, the rector leaning out a window to see what was the commotion. "Let him in, Mrs. Calloway," he ordered. "I'll be down presently."

With an annoyed grunt, the old woman opened the door just enough to allow Tuckworth to squeeze through. She led him to a darkened library and lit a gas lamp with her candle before tottering off once more. Tuckworth waited impatiently, standing the whole while until the rector appeared in a thick dressing gown of a lush, weighty material. Mortimer had clearly spent some time arranging himself to his most authoritative effect.

"Good morning, Mortimer," Tuckworth began.

"I am surprised, Reverend Tuckworth. This is most unusual. Still, I hope that it foretells a change of heart on your part."

"Change of heart?"

"I assume you have reconsidered your rashness of yesterday and have arrived to relinquish your appointment, although, I confess, you might have waited until a more civil hour."

Tuckworth shook his head. "I've come on other business, I'm afraid. I want some information on March."

"Mr. March?" the rector repeated, astonished.

"I need to know his history, as much as you've got. Any letters of reference or past appointments."

"This is highly irregular, Mr. Tuckworth."

"Yes. Well, the times are highly irregular. I assume you keep a file of such materials. In that desk, perhaps?"

The rector sat down in a nearby armchair. "Might I inquire why you need this information? Am I entitled to that much consideration?"

Tuckworth sighed. He knew this would not be easy. "I'm following up on some inquiries Inspector Myles made to me," he answered.

"Then the inspector can come himself and make his inquiries to me, with Mr. March present."

Tuckworth sat down across from the rector. "Of course," he said, "if you'd rather see a half dozen constables descending on the place, beating on your door inside of an hour, if that suits you better, then by all means we can send for the inspector at once."

Mortimer furrowed his brow at the picture these threats aroused in his weak imagination. Then, with a grudging and spiteful look, he rose and unlocked the desk. "I am greatly disappointed in your behavior, Tuckworth," he scolded as he bent over and rifled through the papers within. "Your involvement in this intrigue has reflected rather badly upon you, sir, and I fear for the example you are setting the town, and your daughter."

"What of my daughter?" demanded Tuckworth.

"She appears to have developed a headstrong attitude, sir, one that I believe she has gathered from you."

"Well," the vicar conceded, "I'll grant you, she is headstrong."

Straightening himself, Mortimer turned back around with the papers. "These are all the correspondence I received concerning Mr. March." And he handed them over.

Rising, Tuckworth took the pages and spread them out on a table beneath the light of the gas lamp. "March came here from Manchester?" he observed.

"From St. Dunstan's Abbey, a small congregation in a rather seedy district."

The letters appeared at first glance to be unexceptional. Tuckworth looked at the signatures, names of local citizens, no doubt, men of standing in the neighborhood. They all of them praised March as a diligent, industrious fellow, a simple parson eking out a meager living in a poor parish. Something about them seemed odd, however, something Tuckworth could not place at first. Not the wording or the style or the content. Nothing so evident as that. Then he saw it.

"These are all written in the same hand!" he exclaimed.

"What?" And Mortimer looked over the vicar's shoulder at the letters.

"The same hand wrote all of these!" He picked up the pages to study them more closely. "Look at the name 'March.' The hand-writing is identical!"

"I . . . I never noticed," Mortimer admitted. "I suppose these are fair copies."

"Copies? Why would he want copies of these?"

"Perhaps the original letters were destroyed in the fire, and March wrote these out from memory."

Tuckworth laid the papers down and turned to confront the rector. "Fire?" he asked, barely containing his fears. "What fire?"

"St. Dunstan's. It burned to the ground. Horrible business. That's why March was looking for a new position."

"How many died?"

"Well, yes, since you mention it, several poor souls passed away in the blaze. I can't remember offhand how many they were exactly. It seems some of the congregation were trapped inside. I say, are you well?"

Tuckworth passed a hand over his sweating brow. "Before St. Dunstan's," he went on. "Where was March before then?"

Mortimer picked up the papers and shuffled through them. "Somewhere up north, I believe. Everything appears somewhat hazy before that. But if all his records were destroyed in the fire, I don't see why that's so unusual."

"No," Tuckworth agreed grimly. "It would seem to be perfectly usual. Good morning, Rector." And without another word, he stalked off into the night.

A voice in the darkness. The evidence of a man barely more than a child. A fire that raged over a year ago in a distant city. Were these enough to condemn March? Tuckworth went over the same facts again and again as he trudged back to the vicarage. What if they were all just coincidence, the damning vagaries of haphazard fate? Could he take it upon himself to lie? And in the lie, to cause a man's death? And with what surety? Only a few disjointed bits of circumstance? For that's what it came to in the end. Could he kill March? On the strength of what he knew, of what he suspected, could he kill March?

The snow pelted down fiercely now, and Tuckworth had a long, long walk ahead of him before dawn.

The snow pelted down on Myles, as well. It covered his shoulders and outlined his slender figure from the depths of the shadow in which he stood, watching the house. He had taken some time to decide exactly how he wished to accomplish his task. He had needed information foremost, but he was reluctant to seek assistance. The fewer eyes involved in this business, the better. He had managed to discover the curate's residence simply enough. March's was just another name on a list of parish employees he would want to question at some later date. He had a more difficult time collecting the items he would require without attracting attention. The lockpick was his own, but the shuttered lantern had to be stolen from the constabulary-house. And the sack, procuring that had been touch and go. Still, he got it all right in the end, and now he stood before the address, looking at the smart little house along the quiet lane near the cathedral.

There was no moonlight, only the diffuse glow from the snow, and he had no trouble creeping through the shadows. Not that there was much likelihood he would be observed at this early hour. The towers of Bellminster Cathedral were the only witnesses to this nocturnal intrusion. He knew that the widow kept the downstairs rooms to herself, letting out the upper floor to March. Myles approached alongside the house and found a secluded entry at the back. With the deft motion of a practiced hand, he picked the lock and pushed the door silently open.

The house within was dark. He stepped out of the weather and warily closed the door behind him. Then, gently raising the shutter of the lantern, he sent out a thin shaft of light to pierce the blackness. He had entered by the kitchen, little more than a quaint and homely hearth, and as he had hoped, he found a back stairway leading to March's rooms. With a stealth born of dire experience, Myles made his way up, careful to tread near the wall so his footsteps shouldn't cause the floor to creak, his one pinpoint of light preceding him all the way.

He came to a closed door at the top of the staircase. Trying the doorknob, the inspector was relieved to feel the door swing open soundlessly at his touch. He was standing at the end of a short hallway, with a door to each side of him. At the far end, a room spread out. Myles cautiously approached one of the doors, which stood slightly ajar on his right hand, and put his head through the opening. He proceeded just far enough to detect the foot of a bed. Withdrawing slowly, he turned his attention to the other door. It was closed, and he reached out and turned the knob. A loud crack broke through the silence as the latch released, and for a moment he stood immobile, listening with an intensity that brought beads of sweat to his temples. No other sound ensued. Myles released the breath he had unconsciously held and opened the door. Beyond was a sort of sitting room, a polite little space with nothing but a table, a chair, a lamp and a modest desk. At the other side of the room, a curtain was pulled across a tiny alcove. Here was what he had been searching for.

Crossing the room quickly, he jerked the curtain aside. Yes, a small cupboard, with just a few shelves piled with boxes. Myles reached into his coat and brought forth the bloodstained sack, the one that had held McWhirter's gaping corpse, the one Tuckworth and the imbecile sexton had brought from under the bonfire. Myles had arranged for it to be taken from the scene by one of his mysterious London associates. It had never been entered in the official register of evidence at constabulary-house. It might have been used for any of the killings, or even for some as yet undiscovered violence. He had secreted it away in his office, to use as he deemed fit.

He used it now. He shoved it to the back of the cupboard, buried it behind a stack of boxes, hid it away, out of sight, so that it might be found later by an intrepid young officer of the force. It might even help make the fellow's career, finding such a prime piece of evidence as this, and Myles grinned at the thought. Satisfied with his work, he turned to leave.

March stood in the doorway. "Inspector?" he called in his soft, gentle voice. "What are you doing?"

Myles put his hand into his pocket. "March, I place you under arrest in the king's name, on suspicion of murder."

"Murder!" the man squeaked.

Myles pulled out a revolver. "You'll accompany me to the constabulary-house," he commanded.

March's eyes darted from Myles to the pistol and back again. "I'm afraid I don't understand."

"If you are innocent, you have nothing to fear."

"But what were you doing in here? What did you place among those shelves?"

Myles cursed his wretched luck. Still, it might be got over, with a bit of brass. Whose word would a judge likely believe, after all?

"I'm here to arrest you, March. That's all you need concern yourself with. Now step out into the passage." March retreated before the muzzle of the revolver, while Myles kept the light pointed in the man's eyes.

"This is so confusing," the curate fussed gently. "Might I at least get a proper overcoat? It's frightfully cold out."

"Where is it?"

"I keep one hanging in the front room," March stated, pointing down the hall.

"Go on, then," Myles said gruffly.

March walked ahead. The hallway opened up into a tidy parlor, a neatly appointed nest with a few pictures on the walls, a pair of simple chairs before the lace-curtained window, a table and a stove. March reached into a closet and pulled out a threadbare coat, barely enough to protect him on such an icy night.

"You're dressed," Myles observed as the curate swung the coat over his slight frame. "What have you been up to at this hour?"

"I always rise early. I was meditating over my scripture."

Myles nodded. "Back down the hall, then."

"The front stairway will be quicker," March advised. "And it's less likely to disturb Mrs. Walters." The man opened the door that led downstairs and passed through, with Myles close behind him.

They came out in another parlor, larger and more elaborately decorated than the one above. The two men stepped into the middle of the room and made toward the front door down a hallway when, with a sharp gasp, March stopped abruptly and pointed into the room. "Mrs. Walters!" he whispered.

Myles turned the light upon the figure of a woman sitting comfortably in a rocking chair before a cold and cheerless fireplace. She was dressed in a simple black frock, and her head lolled over to one side, resting upon her shoulder as though she were asleep. She might have proven a picture of serene repose, were it not for the dark stains streaking down her face from empty sockets. In a dish upon her lap, two orbs sat, staring into nothing.

Myles fell backward, taking a step away from this nightmare. He turned the light back upon March. But the man was gone. The inspector dashed into the hallway, finding it empty. With a curse under his breath, he paused and listened. No door had opened. The man must still be somewhere in the house. The quiet seemed to roar about Myles's ears. Then he heard a faint creak from the back stairway.

Spinning about, he ran up the front stairs, hoping to snare March as he came out into the upper passage. But when he got there, the curate was nowhere. Myles gripped the pistol fiercely in his fingers and turned about the room, spreading the sharp point of light about the walls, trying to catch some sign of the man. The shutters of the lantern were too close, the light too scant. He reached down to open the shutters fully and flood the room with light. And that was why he never saw the dark shape flying at him from behind, from out of the void of the front staircase.

March pounced on the inspector, got his arm about Myles's throat. Myles dropped the lantern, casting the struggle into a pitch of blackness. The inspector reached up and tried to wrench March's arm away, but the curate's strength was too great. Shocked at his own helplessness in the man's hands, the inspector tried to turn the revolver about, tried vainly to aim it behind him. It fired, but the bullet only lodged harmlessly in the wall. March took his hand and cupped it over the inspector's mouth and chin. Myles placed one final, muffled curse upon himself. Then, with a quick twist to left and right, March snapped his neck.

Myles went lifeless. His body sagged in the arms of the curate, who held him up almost effortlessly. March muttered a dire imprecation against the man. He had always been meddling, always yapping at March's heels like a terrier, ever since they found that drunken sexton in the woods. This inspector had even turned the vicar against him, against God! The vicar! Tuckworth must be made to pay the price of his betrayal! He must suffer! And not a momentary pain, but a lingering and daily suffering, that he might live his days in torment, remembering what he owed his God, and how he had failed. He must be made to lose all, all that he cherished, all that he cared for.

Dropping the corpse to the ground, March picked up the revolver and stuffed it into the pocket of his overcoat. Then he walked down the hall, into the small sitting room. He emerged after a moment, carrying the bloodstained sack.

An hour later, and Lucy sat nervously in the parlor of the vicarage in her usual chair, waiting for her father to return. She could not have slept had she wanted to, distraught as she was since the murderer had escaped, passing so near her. She always wanted to be brave, for her father's sake if for no other reason, but that moment in the darkness had proved more terrifying than she could live with at present. It had frankly undone her, and she wanted now to see her father, to talk him out of pursuing this deadly, dangerous game. It wasn't his responsibility, to unearth such wickedness, to pit himself against such evil. Let the authorities manage their job and let quiet people alone!

Yet some part of her, a tiny spark deep within, was proud of his courage, proud that he had braved so much, attempted so much to protect them all. And that same part was ashamed now at her own selfish fears.

A sound disturbed her thoughts, a knocking, as of someone trying to be let in. It seemed to be coming from the study. But her father could not be there, could he? Unless he had entered earlier from the cathedral. Lucy took up her candle, rose and crossed the room to the study door.

"Father," she called quietly, in respect to the lateness of the hour. "Father, are you returned? Is everything well?"

She received no answer but the same incessant knocking. Anxiously, Lucy placed a hand upon the knob and opened the door.

The room was empty. No sign of her father was visible to her quick eye. Only the bird hopped about nervously upon the back of a chair. She reached up and took the creature upon her fist. "What's troubling you, bird?" she inquired, hoping against hope that it might have an answer.

She heard the knocking again. Looking over, she saw the open door leading into the cathedral. That's where it was coming from, this sound. Keeping the bird with her, she stepped through into the chapel. A faint glow emanated from the nave, although she could not make out the source of this light as it shone off the hard stone of the columns. With a wary step, Lucy moved into that maze, weaving her way to the scaffold until she was near enough to see something.

There was a figure dressed in black, a man hunched over on the ground, hammering at something, nailing boards of wood together by the light of a lantern. The man raised up for a moment to mop the sweat from his brow, and Lucy breathed a welcome sigh. It was only the curate.

"Mr. March, what are you working on so late?" she asked, approaching the man from behind.

He spun about and now she could see the work he was at. He had constructed a wooden framework, and he was busy nailing the inspector's body to it.

Lucy dropped her candle and the bird fluttered to the ground.

March stood and faced her, a look of sublime rapture spreading over his face. "Thank You, Lord," he prayed. "Thank You for giving me these means to work Your will."

CHAPTER THE TWENTY-FIRST
IT IS FINISHED

as it dawn yet? Or had night finally vanquished the sun? Clouds were packed across the sky, and wet flakes crowded the air so thickly that it seemed no room was left in the world for light. Tuckworth glanced at his watch as he stepped into the darkened vicarage and brushed the piling snow from off his shoulders. Lucy was usually stirring by now, he considered. A clatter from the pantry let him know that Mrs. Cutler was awake, so he put his head in at the kitchen door and asked after his daughter.

"Is it a wonder the poor dear might want a bit of slumber after such a scare as she took last night?" the woman whispered, as though Lucy were sleeping in the same room.

"No, I suppose not," Tuckworth whispered in return, the gloom and shadows of the house making the time seem closer to midnight than to morning. "I'll be resting in the study for a bit, Mrs. Cutler, but you may wake me for breakfast." And the vicar backed out of the kitchen. He felt now, as he wandered in the darkness to his study, that he might sleep at last, truly sleep for hours. But he did not have hours. He must be about again soon, to tell Myles of his decision, and see what might be done to put an end to this affair.

He paused. The study door was open. Had he left it ajar after the excitement of last night? He couldn't remember. He might have done so, though it would have been hardly like him. Tuckworth crossed the threshold of the room, and his foot came down upon something soft and giving. He pulled back, startled, but could not make out in the blackness what it was. Going into the kitchen for a candle, he returned and shed its light upon the object.

It appeared to be some sort of bag at first. He knelt down to pick it up and dropped it at once. It was the bird. Its breast had been crushed and its neck twisted. Tuckworth turned his face to the parlor, uncertain for a moment, and looked at the empty chair where Lucy was used to wait for him. Instantly every fear he knew rushed upon his heart. Lucy! He ran up the staircase crying her name, hoping to rouse her, to wake her from sleep. "Lucy! Lucy!"

He came to her door and threw it open. The bed lay deserted, unused. He turned to find Raphael standing in the hallway, leaning against the wall, his eyes wide and worried. "What's happened, sir?" he demanded.

"He's been here! He's been in the house! Where's Lucy?" And Tuckworth raced down the stairs again. He ran past Mrs. Cutler, through the study, into the cathedral. "Lucy!" he called over and over in the echoing gloom, dreading the sight he feared must be, the terrible vision waiting to put a finish to his life. Tuckworth came upon the scaffold suddenly, and his heart burst within him in a wrenching gasp of shock and surprise.

Not Lucy, but Myles. The inspector hung before him, suspended head downward above the floor, nailed to a rough cross of planks in the humble fashion of St. Peter. Blood still dripped from his wounds, a pool of gore slowly forming beneath him. The scene was made more unearthly still by a strange glow, a beatific light that streamed from above, and snow that seemed to fall from the vault of the cathedral, weightless flakes drifting down, floating on currents of air. Tuckworth looked up and found no sunlight entering by the upper windows of the cathedral. Instead, he saw tongues of flame licking the highest reaches of the scaffold, whitened ash falling from the burning timbers. And outlined through the fire, a pair of figures.

Raphael came up beside Tuckworth and cried in dismay, "My God, it's March with Lucy!" Cupping his hands, he called upward, "Lucy! Stay close to March! We'll get you down!"

But March cried to them from above, "It's the day of calamity, Vicar! The day of repentance! You Judas, I'll make a Job of you!"

"Job," Tuckworth murmured, unsure what March meant. And then he understood, at once in a terrible flash he understood March's plan. "He wants to kill her!"

"March? Kill Lucy?"

"It's him, Raphael! He wants to destroy me by killing all I love!" One instant of revelation, and then without another word Raphael dashed to the foot of the scaffold. "No," Tuckworth commanded, stopping the young man's rashness. "You can't climb through the fire. You'll burn alive trying. Follow me."

Together, the pair began the long journey through the heart of the cathedral, with no light to guide their path, up through the stone stairways and cold, barren passages. Tuckworth knew his way without sight, knew it by touch, by instinct found the path they must follow. Raphael labored behind him, listening as the vicar's breath showed the way ahead. But with each step the pain in Raphael's side grew hotter, the stiffness greater, so that his lungs heaved and his heart pounded fiercely. And with each step, Tuckworth felt older and weaker, his years telling upon him with dreadful certainty as he raced a course that led them higher, higher, higher still into the frigid air of heaven.

They burst out at last above the ceiling of the cathedral, among the rafters and the beams, the crumbling timbers where workmen had been busy replacing the rotting wood. The fire had begun to invade this ancient space, this roosting place for birds, and soon this realm would be engulfed in flame. Tuckworth peered through the smoke swelling up from below, yet he could see nothing.

"Where are they?" Raphael wheezed.

Tuckworth shook his head in doubt. "We're here, March!" he called. "Let Lucy go and come to me now!"

A voice shouted from out of the sooty air. "This way, Judas! Your path lies through the fires of hell!"

Then another voice came to them both. "Father!" cried Lucy, somewhere ahead of them, somewhere in the smoke.

Tuckworth ducked low, trying to keep his lungs from filling with the noxious air, the stifling heat, and Raphael followed close behind. It was impossible to tell where they were going or what lay ahead. Flames began to leap and dance about them, and in one spot the floor beside them gave way, exposing a drop through fire and smoke to a distant death. Tuckworth stumbled to his hands and knees, and the floor felt hot on his palms. Then he saw, through the darkness, a light shape emerge, the outline of a doorway. He made toward it, and came out into the freezing wind of a black morning, on the roof of Bellminster Cathedral. He lay for an instant, gulping in the stinging air, until Raphael rolled out beside him, coughing and clutching his side. A stain of blood was growing under his shirt.

"My boy," Tuckworth said softly.

"I'm fine." And as if to prove himself, Raphael stood and looked about.

They had come out at the base of the roof, the steep pitch of the lead tiles rising beside them, reaching upward toward the towering height of the steeple. A short railing ornamented with iron spikes was all that separated them from the void. Walking calmly down this elevated path before them was March, pushing Lucy along ahead of him.

"March!" Raphael called. "We're coming for you!"

"Come along, then!" the man shouted.

Tuckworth was on his feet at once, and the two men made their way after March and Lucy, pressing as close as they could to the cathedral rooftop. There was not much farther March could travel, and it was clear that they would have him trapped unless he found some way down. Yet, when the curate reached the final extent of the path, so that nothing lay before him but the swirling air, he stopped and turned himself about to confront his pursuers.

"Come along, both of you," he invited them, the wind whipping the black cloak about his figure and tossing his gray hair, flecking it with snow. "Come to your judgment."

"Father!" Lucy cried. "Don't!"

They stopped, some dozen yards apart, and all three men looked at one another. Tuckworth could see Lucy clearly now, behind

March on the path, her hands bound with cords, a look of cold ferocity in her eyes.

"March," Tuckworth said, calmly, easily. "March, you can't kill her. She's innocent of any wrongdoing."

"No one is innocent!"

"But what is her sin?"

"God will judge her sins!"

"And what of me? I'm the one you want to hurt. I'm the one you should kill."

"Father, no!" Lucy pleaded.

But Tuckworth ignored her. "Pass your accursed judgment on me, March. I'm the true sinner."

March chuckled gently. "Don't fear for that, Judas. God will judge you at His leisure, every morning for years to come."

Raphael stepped forward. "Why don't you kill me first, then?" he taunted recklessly. "Have done killing women and old men! You failed to kill me once, you know! I'm still here waiting for you!"

"No, Raphael!" Lucy pleaded, but it was too late. Raphael had not seen the revolver in March's hand. March raised it suddenly and fired. Raphael gripped his elbow, spun and fell to the path. Tuckworth jumped to his aid, bent over the boy. He was alive. The wound was serious, but it didn't appear deadly. Tuckworth rose and turned.

"Why, March?" he cried. "Why?"

"God has shown His will to me!"

"God has told you to stop, only you won't listen! God pleads with you, He begs you to quit this!"

"No!" March screamed, bringing his hands to his ears.

So he did not hear Lucy run at him from behind, colliding with him, trying desperately to send him over the side of the cathedral. He stumbled, and in breaking his fall he dropped the pistol. It skittered across the icy path before sailing off into the air, down into the emptiness. Righting himself, March turned and struck the girl, sending her sprawling backward, blood streaming from her lip.

Tuckworth lunged upon the man. With all his might he rushed at March, grappling him from behind. But March was strong, strong beyond reason, strong with the strength of madness. He pushed

Tuckworth away effortlessly as a man disciplines a child, shoved him down to the path at his feet. Tuckworth stood again and swung, only sweeping his fist through the air. March slapped Tuckworth's hands aside and grasped him by the throat, shaking him until the vicar ceased to struggle, only stared into March's cold, colorless eyes.

"I am going to kill her now, squeeze the life from her here, above all you care for, all you love. And you shall watch," he whispered. "Then you will live on, like Job, live upon the dunghill of your sin. Fire is devouring your cathedral, God's home that you defiled with your betrayal. It will be reconsecrated to His glory, and you will find no place there. Your presence will no longer corrupt it. You will live alone, forgotten, and every morning God will see your sin and you will suffer."

March dropped Tuckworth, and the vicar sank to his knees exhausted, spent. Turning, March took a step toward Lucy's unconscious figure. With his final strength, Tuckworth lurched forward on his knees, his arms encircling the curate's legs. March stumbled to the edge of the path, but the railing caught his fall. Rising, he shook Tuckworth off and moved toward Lucy once more.

A shape flew out of the shadows behind the vicar and launched itself upon the curate. Tuckworth looked up. It was Adam Black. Adam took March about the waist in his massive arms and lifted him bodily up. March flailed about, unable to get a hold upon his assailant, unable to use that strength with which he had subdued so many. Tuckworth watched as Adam held the curate suspended for an instant. March looked up, appealing to the silent, passing clouds. Then Adam tossed him out into the air. March's scream faded, faded as he fell away, down toward the earth, down at last to be silenced forever on the steps of the cathedral.

Tuckworth's way was clear now. He rose and rushed to Lucy's side. "Dearest girl," he called gently. "Lucy, can you open your eyes?" He took her chin in his hands and delicately shook her, trying to rouse some response.

Her eyelids fluttered. "Father?" She grasped him about the neck sobbing, her tears flowing, relieved to see him alive. He let her weep for only a moment, and then he lifted her to her feet. "We still have much to do before we're safe," he informed her. "Adam!" he called, turning about. "Can you carry Raphael?"

Without a word, the sexton went to Raphael and raised him carefully in his arms. Lucy gasped when she saw him, the blood on his shirt and the lifeless fall of his limbs. She ran to him, and Tuckworth called out behind her, "Be careful, girl! He's been shot, though I suspect he'll be all right once we get him off this roof!"

The fire was spreading beneath their feet now. In places above them, the tiles began to break away, and flames leapt into the black sky. Tuckworth got them together quickly and they retreated along the path, back the way they had come. But when they reached the door, smoke was billowing out of it thick and deadly.

Tuckworth turned to Lucy. "Are you brave, girl?" he asked. She nodded, and raised her skirt to cover her mouth and nose. He turned to Adam. "Stay as low as you can, and keep close to me. Lucy, hold on to Adam's shirttail." Then the party entered the inferno.

But it was no good. They could not make their way back to the doorway on the far side. Every rafter was ablaze and the heat scorched them where they stood. Tuckworth looked about, frantic for some means to descend from this trap. The scaffold, he thought, but when he made his way to it and looked down, he saw that it had burned almost completely away. He turned, and then he found it, the only way down, their only hope.

The windlass and the pallet used to lower rotting timbers. It might carry them to safety. Tuckworth pointed it out to Adam and Lucy, and they all made their way to it. Tuckworth took Lucy's hand and tried to get her to step upon the platform, but she hesitated. He looked at her and saw that she understood. "There's only room for two," she said.

"We'll squeeze three on," he assured her. "You, and Adam can carry Raphael. I'll lower myself down after."

"How?" she cried. "How can you lower yourself down? Someone must work the winch!"

"Lucy!" Tuckworth shouted. "There's no time! You go down with Adam and Raphael! Now, Lucy! Now!"

She stepped onto the pallet, followed by Adam cradling Raphael in his arms. But Lucy never lost sight of her father. She looked on him, as if it were for the last time in all the world. Tuckworth stood at the handle of the winch and slowly began to lower the three of them to the cathedral floor.

"Father!" Lucy called up as she descended. "Father! I love you!" Their eyes locked one final second upon each other, and then the rising smoke obscured the platform with its precious cargo. Tuckworth worked as quickly as he dared amid the surging tide of fire, the intricate webbing of blocks, tackles and pulleys multiplying his strength yet robbing him of speed as the machinery worked slowly to its end. He turned faster, faster yet, but the rope before his eyes only inched its way down into the void. The time seemed long, dreadfully long that the winch turned and the pallet dropped to safety. At last, however, the rope went slack and Tuckworth knew they were at the bottom.

He wiped away his tears and stood looking into the empty space below him, the heat rushing upward to fan his weary face. Sections of the floor began to fall away under the assault of the flames, but he didn't move. He felt calm. Very calm. He looked up, through a hole in the roof, hoping to see stars. But the clouds and smoke hid the heavens. For how long did his eyes try to pierce that thick veil for but a glimpse of eternity? Suddenly the floor beneath him shook. He stumbled and dropped to his knees, though he continued to look upward. Another shiver, and a section of the floor close at hand fell away into nothing. Tuckworth looked down, down into the smoke and flame of the inferno, waiting for the inevitable end to his adventure, waiting for this final chapter to close.

His eyes smarted amid the soot and ash that flew into his face, and for a moment Tuckworth thought he saw the smoke swirl madly about. He rubbed his eyes, blinked and let the water of his tears cleanse them. He looked below again. A shadow appeared amid the haze rising from beneath. Was it a demon coming to possess him, like Mephistopheles, to carry him off to hell? He rubbed his eyes again and squinted into the smoke. The figure grew in the air until

THE DEVIL IN BELLMINSTER

at last it rose out of the black vapor, climbing hand over hand up the rope that led from the winch to the floor.

It was Adam, of course. He hoisted himself up the final few feet of space and plopped down on the floor next to Tuckworth. "Hello, Vicar," he said sheepishly.

"Adam," Tuckworth said, coughing through the smoke.

"It weren't my fault, Vicar," the man explained in a sudden rush of words. "Miss Lucy, she told me to come back for you. I'd have done what you said and took them all out, but she told me they might find their own way, and she told me to come up and bring you down. She made me, Vicar."

Tuckworth waved off the explanation and hurriedly got to his feet again. As it turned out, he was not quite ready to die yet.

Adam grabbed the rope between his meaty fists, and Tuckworth clasped his arms about the sexton's neck. Then they launched themselves into the void. They flew through the poisonous air, the knobby calluses of Adam's hands protecting him as he almost slid down the rope. Tuckworth, dangling like some apish babe in the jungle, tried to warn his carrier to slow their descent, but he could not find the breath in that noxious atmosphere, and so he only held tighter to Adam's broad shoulders.

The wearying work of the day had taken its toll upon his strength, however, and he felt his fingers slip. With an effort he pulled himself back up, yet he knew it was impossible to hold out much longer. The smoke still obscured everything, and there was no way for him to peer down and see the floor beneath. Flaming refuse now began to fall about them, left and right. Adam was huffing and straining, the exertion finally telling upon him as well.

Tuckworth's fingers slipped again, and suddenly he was hanging on by Adam's collar. "Vicar!" Adam gasped, choking against the shirtfront.

Another voice rose up to them in midair. "Father!" Lucy was below somewhere, but how far?

Adam made a gurgling sound, and Tuckworth heard the sickening rip of fabric as the shirt gave way and he plummeted through space. He landed, some dozen feet below, and crumpled to the floor. Lucy was on him in an instant, raising him up in her embrace, clutching him to her with the strength of a hope fulfilled. Beside her lay Raphael, still feeble but conscious. Adam dropped down beside them.

"Sorry, Vicar."

Tuckworth would have laughed, had not the breath been taken out of him by his fall, and had the fervency of Lucy's embrace not smothered him, and had not they all just then heard the creaking of the scaffolding as it tottered overhead.

They moved at once, Adam lifting Raphael, Lucy clinging to her father, Tuckworth leading the way. They had not gone far when a crash and a sudden eruption of flame burst out behind them. Then, another instant, and they were through the doors of the cathedral, in the cold, stinging air of a frosty autumn morning in Bellminster.

CHAPTER THE LAST
THE CHURCHYARD

The heavy stone slab dropped into place with a wet thud, and the birds that had gathered about the somber party in the churchyard rose up, fluttering through the empty windows of the cathedral, through the open nave into the cloud-filled sky. Raphael wrapped his healthy arm about Lucy, and she melted into the comfort of his embrace as the snow continued to fall. Tuckworth steadied the headstone, settled it into the sodden earth, then stepped back to look at it.

"That's well," he uttered flatly.

After a moment, Lucy stepped forward and laid a bough of holly, green and shining, upon the stone. The name carved deep into the slab shone out sharp and clear against the frost that still covered the world: Paul Randolph Myles.

The vicar turned to Granby, who was looking, not at the grave, but up into the emptiness of the cathedral. "Are we certain there's no family to tell of his death?" Tuckworth asked.

"No one at all," Granby answered, not moving his eyes from the hard stone above. "They tell me at Bow Street that he hadn't a family in the world." Then, turning his gaze around to Tuckworth, he added, "Hopgood tells me there are any number of deaths being lodged against March, or whoever he was. 'March' seems to be only one name he took over his lifetime. Appears he'd been going about killing people for longer than anyone knows. Unheard-of thing."

Tuckworth recalled something Myles had told him once, of the madness that can set upon men in the closeness of the city, and he hoped that such acts might remain unheard-of. He hoped for it deeply.

"Still," Granby continued, "there's no crime in being taken in by the scoundrel, though that's not saving Mortimer some embarrassment. He's already handed in his resignation to the archbishop."

"Oh, dear," Tuckworth gasped. "I hope His Lordship won't honor it," although from the looks of the faces standing about, the vicar was the only one to harbor this wish.

Granby chuckled. "Don't fret yourself, Tuckworth," he said. "We'll talk the silly prig into staying. After all, we can't be turning our dean back into a vicar."

"Dean?" repeated Tuckworth. "Dean of what? A hole in the sky?"

But Granby seemed not to have heard Tuckworth's objection. "Look at those walls," he boasted instead, pointing out the stone framework that was all that remained of Bellminster Cathedral. "Roof and ornaments we can replace, but walls like that were made for the ages, eh? Made for the ages." And he looked slyly down at Tuckworth. "It'll take a good deal of money, mind, and all your time and efforts into raising it."

"What?" Tuckworth gasped for a second time. "You don't mean we're going to rebuild?"

"And why not? This Gothic stuff is going up everywhere these days, only we've got the real thing here, and no sense in wasting those walls. You just ask your artist friend there if he's seen anything like those walls." But Raphael was at that moment engaged in a conversation of his own with Lucy, and was not to be disturbed on any account.

"But the cost!" Tuckworth exclaimed.

"That's why you can't be bothered with old duties, a vicar's duties. Did you think being named dean would be all tea cakes and crumpets? I'm surprised at you, Tuckworth, I truly am, shying away from a bit of hard work." Lord Granby made a tetchy sound with his tongue and looked mockingly stern.

Tuckworth might have objected that he was an old man and that this was young work. He might have complained that Mortimer would be a fitter man for the job, or that a new cathedral would be a waste of expense in a world with so much human suffering to ease. He might have said a great deal had not Mrs. Cutler come scuttling up at that moment.

"I've had the supper waiting this quarter hour since," she chided the company, "and I'll not be blamed if it's cold leavings you be eating this night."

And so they all trooped into the vicarage (or the deanery, as Mrs. Cutler insisted on calling it with a haughty sniff), which had been saved from the flames by the stout protection of the north wall. They made a merry party, in spite of the somber cause for their gathering, and they were all the merrier after Tuckworth sent Lucy off to fetch Adam and Mary, that they all might share the meal.

Later that night, back in the churchyard, under the icy ring of a fairy moon, and with his daughter clinging to his side, the new dean of Bellminster Cathedral laid an autumn wreath at the grave site of his wife. As they stood there in the moonlight, arms about each other to brace against the chill, they could hear the birds fluttering about the remains of the cathedral, stone walls with no roof. It was night in Bellminster, and down below, in the town, the wind whipped furiously its stinging blast, but beneath those stout, sturdy walls, it only moved the snow about in easy drifts.